CRY FROM THE GRAVE

BY

CAROLYN MAHONY

DEDICATION

To my family and friends for their encouragement over the many years I've been scribbling, and to my long-suffering husband, who has been incredibly patient when all things domestic have been totally abandoned in the pursuit of a good scene!

ACKNOWLEDGEMENTS

A huge thank you to my Ladies of Posara Writing Group for their fantastic support. We've come a long way, ladies, since first we met in Italy over four years ago.

A special thanks to Debbie Flint, Isabelle Goddard, Emily Harvale and Anne Hudson for their invaluable assistance at different stages of the creative and publishing process!

PROLOGUE

The bright sunlight glistening through the leafy avenue gave promise of a beautiful day, but even though the warmth brushed her skin, Hannah Walker shivered as she walked up the path to her front door. She remembered the first time she'd walked up this path with Ben, full of excitement at the prospect of moving in with him. Was it really only seven months ago?

She opened the front door and pushed the pram over the threshold, her eyes skimming the pristine, luxuriously furnished flat conversion. It did nothing for her now; but then, why should it? She'd had no input into the décor. Ben had chosen it all. Her glance fell on the telephone sitting on the hall table. One phone call - that was all it would take...

Hardly aware of what she was doing, she started to walk towards it.

'Is that you Hannah?'

She stopped in her tracks.

'Leave her out in the garden, the fresh air will do her good,' Ben said, coming into the hall and eyeing her steadily. 'Then you and I can make-up before I leave for my appointment.'

Was he serious? Hannah lifted her hand unconsciously to where clever makeup hid the bruise on her cheek. She wasn't about to antagonise him further.

'It's okay,' she said, avoiding his gaze as she parked the pram in the hallway. 'She's due a feed soon.'

'I said put her outside - she'll be fine in the back. You and I need to talk and I don't want her interrupting things.'

He was testing her, showing her who was boss, and after their argument earlier she knew better than to aggravate him further. She despised herself as she backed wordlessly out of the flat and did as he said.

You're a coward, Hannah Walker, why don't you stand up to him?

She parked the pram beneath the apple tree and leaned in to kiss Sophie on the cheek, breathing in the soft warmth of peachy skin, the familiar sweet baby scent that never failed to soothe her.

'You have a nice little snooze out here,' she murmured, smiling at the droopy blue eyes, battling to stay open. 'Mummy will come and get you very soon.'

She retraced her steps slowly. She didn't want to make up. He'd gone too far this time.

Inside the flat, Ben was standing by the lounge window staring at Sophie through the glass. He turned as Hannah came in and walked towards her. Without saying a word, he lifted his hand to her cheek and traced the bruise lightly with his thumb. 'I'm sorry for this, babe,' he said finally, his expressive blue eyes contrite. 'I didn't mean to hurt you, but I've got a lot on my plate right now, and you did push me.'

She kept her own face expressionless as she tried to ease out of his hold, but his hands dropped to her shoulders, drawing her resisting body tighter into his arms. 'Let's go and make up,' he whispered, nuzzling her neck. 'It's all this lack of sex, it's getting to me.'

He began to edge her clumsily into the hall. She could feel his arousal and shrank from it.

'The doctor said I should give things time to heal,' she said quickly, 'I don't feel ready yet.'

'You'll be fine. Come on, I'll be careful.'

His grip tightened as he backed her into the bedroom and her panic rose.

'No, Ben, I don't want to.'

She managed to shove him off, something snapping as she faced him. 'I can't just forget what you did, even if you can. There was no excuse for it.'

'So, what…?' His expression was ugly. 'You're going to punish me now by withholding sex? Is that what this is all about Hannah? Well, like hell you will …'

Afterwards, she kept her eyes closed, imagining herself a million miles away. She wouldn't look at him. Wouldn't give him the satisfaction of knowing he'd hurt her.

'You're about as responsive as a bloody marble statue,' he grumbled, throwing off the bed sheets and getting up. 'I'd get more enjoyment from a blow-up doll.'

She didn't answer.

'Don't ignore me, Hannah.'

She opened her eyes. 'It hurts me,' she said coldly. 'You know what the doctor said …'

'Oh, spare me all that six weeks bullshit. Dave and Laura were back in business after a fortnight. You just don't want me touching you. Admit it. Well don't blame me if I do what your father did and start looking around!'

He picked up his clothes and stalked off to the bathroom, leaving Hannah staring bleakly after him.

After a while, she rose and went into the lounge to check on Sophie through the window. She looked so peaceful and innocent sleeping there in her pram. It soothed Hannah's heart just looking at her.

She moved back into the bedroom and sat on the bed, waiting for Ben to finish in the shower. Across the room the mirror on the dresser wasn't kind to her. She stared hard at her reflection, comparing it to the smiling photo on the wall. She looked a mess. Her blond hair hung lankly around her shoulders and she had huge dark circles under her eyes. The slim figure she'd always taken for granted had been replaced by lumps and bumps that still hadn't diminished since giving birth. No wonder Ben had gone off her.

But there was more to it than that, she knew. Losing a bit of weight and glamming herself up wasn't going to make any difference. He was jealous of Sophie, resentful of the way she'd disrupted their life and come between them. It was becoming so obvious.

When he'd hit her that morning his anger had seemed to burst from nowhere, his hand lashing out before she'd even known what was happening.

'Don't defy me, Hannah. It's about time you realised who's running the show here ... who's paying for the food on our table. I don't give a toss that she's only three weeks old. I need you at this client's dinner tonight - and my needs come first. Always. Is that clear?'

He'd hit her before but this was the first time he'd done it when he was sober. It was a shocking awakening - stripping away the pathetic excuses she'd previously clung to that he didn't know what he was doing until she couldn't deny the unpalatable truth any longer. She, who'd been so condemning of her own mother's weakness in taking her father back, was no better a judge of character herself.

Tears filled her eyes and she rubbed at them fiercely. She was so tired; she didn't have the energy to cope with all this now.

But you need to cope with it, Hannah. You need to think of Sophie.

She looked up as Ben strode back into the room.

'So, I'll meet you at Green Park tube at seven-thirty,' he said, reaching for his tie and executing a perfect knot in the mirror.

Hannah's eyes met his reflection stormily. 'I don't know who you expect me to get to baby-sit at such short notice. Your mum's made it obvious that she's not interested and I haven't seen any of my friends in ages. I can't just randomly phone someone up and expect them to...'

'I'm not interested in how you do it. Just do it. Phone an agency if you have to.'

He picked up his jacket and eyed her coldly. 'You'd better be there or I'll be seriously pissed off, I'm warning you. I'll see you later.'

And he was gone, swinging away without a backward glance. The kitchen door slammed as he went out into the back garden, and she felt a slight easing of the tension in her stomach. Across the hall and through the lounge window she could see him stopping to bend over the pram. Not a single hair on his gleaming blond head was out of place - his lean face, still tanned from his recent business trip to Cannes, was eye-catchingly perfect. He looked every inch what he was – the suave, up and coming City stockbroker.

She looked at him in his impeccably cut Armani suit and realised how easily she'd been duped; how cleverly his outward perfection concealed the imperfections that lay beneath.

'That's fantastic Han,' he'd said when she'd broken down in shock and told him she was pregnant. 'No more talk about gap-years with your friends after uni now, eh? You'll be too busy bringing up our child. You'd better move in with me so I can make sure you're looked after properly.'

But being looked after properly had somehow turned into, 'where I can control you', and as his job had got more sociable, so his drinking had increased, until she realised she'd become trapped in a nightmare of her own making.

But not anymore, she resolved, jumping up from the bed and turning away from the sight of him in the garden. This time he really had gone too far - and it wasn't just about her any more.

She crossed to the wardrobe, hauled out her jeans and a tee-shirt and headed for the bathroom. Her heart raced at the enormity of what she was about to do. It wouldn't be easy. She hadn't seen her mother since her father's death five months ago and their parting had been bitter. But she'd understand – wouldn't she?

She hesitated, her glance falling on the phone again. Should she call her mother? Explain?

She rejected the idea. Easier to do it face to face. However upset her mother was. She wouldn't throw her back out on the street.

Ten minutes later she was dressed and headed for the

garden. A quick look around confirmed that Ben's car had gone. Now she'd made up her mind, she just wanted to be gone. She'd feed Sophie, then leave, and by the time Ben got back that evening, there'd be nothing he could do about it.

Slipping the brake off the pram she leaned in.

'Come on poppet, time to...'

She broke off, staring blankly at the little dent in the mattress where her daughter should have been. Her heart jolted.

'Sophie?'

She jerked her head up and looked around. The sunny garden with its flowering spring bulbs looked pretty as a picture but there was no sign of her daughter anywhere. And the peaceful silence felt suddenly hostile.

'Sophie!'

Panic gripped her. She felt disorientated, remembering with a rush of relief seeing Ben leaning over the pram, before realising in the next breath that he had a meeting in London and would never have taken Sophie with him.

Where was she? Her mind was muddled. Had she already taken her in?

Think...

But it seemed the more she tried to remember, the more jumbled up her thoughts became.

She started to run back towards the flat.

No, no, - the road.

She changed direction, her feet flying over the short tufts of grass, her breath coming in suffocating gasps as she raced out through the back gate onto the pavement.

The long, leafy street was deserted.

'Sophie...'

The scent of baby lotion clawed at her senses, squeezing her heart.

'Are you all right, Hannah?'

It was her neighbour's voice, coming from a million miles away.

6

Hannah spun round. 'Sophie's gone. She's gone.'

'What do you mean…?'

But already Hannah was swinging away, choking on the sobs as she raced down the path into the quiet, deserted flat. She knew it was pointless, knew she hadn't brought her in, but still she checked every room, flinging open each door before rushing back out into the sunshine to check the pram one final time.

And it was only as her blurred vision locked on the little indentation in the mattress – the only proof her daughter had ever been there – that she finally she gave vent to the scream lodged in her throat, the shrill sound echoing through the quiet neighbourhood as the full horror of what had happened washed over her.

Someone had taken her baby...

CHAPTER ONE

Six Years Later

Adam Campbell viewed the petulant expression on his wife's face across the breakfast table and knew it wasn't a good sign.

'I thought I might make a start on the new barbeque today,' he said, in an attempt at conversation. 'I know it's not the best time of year to be doing it but it would be nice to have it ready for spring.'

'If you think so.'

'Do you want to come and see what I'm thinking about doing?'

'Not particularly. I'm sure you'll do a thorough job. You always do.'

The look she gave him was accompanied by a brittle smile that left Adam unsure as to whether her words were meant as a compliment or an accusation. The latter, he suspected, but chose not to rise to the bait. That would be asking for trouble.

He rose from the table and started to clear away the breakfast dishes.

'Leave that, I'll do it.'

'It's fine...'

'I said, leave it. I'm not an invalid you know, despite the fact you treat me like one.'

'Natasha...'

She flashed him a look, her dark eyes round and accusing. 'What? It's true. You know it is.'

'I don't treat you like an invalid. I just try to make things easier for you.'

'And is that why you're still in the spare room? To make things *easier* for me?'

Adam's expression tightened. He could feel himself getting sucked into an argument, despite himself. 'You know why I moved into the spare room.'

'Yes, I do.'

She pushed back her own chair and whipped the breakfast plates out of his hands. 'And I've said I'm sorry. I don't know what more I can do. When are you going to realise that no marriage is perfect? Just because your parents had the bloody marriage made in heaven. I'm fed up hearing about it. You've got a family, a nice home and a secure job. What more do you want?'

Which was the crux of the matter he realised, staring after her as she spun away from him and headed for the dishwasher. What more did he want? Was it really too much to expect that there might be more to life than the endless bickering they seemed to do these days? He tried to remember a time when it hadn't been like that – when they'd laughed together, had fun. He was shocked to discover that the memory just wasn't there.

A wave of depression submerged him. Not for the first time he felt completely disconnected from his wife, and not for the first time, the realisation filled him with consuming guilt. He needed to get out of there before their conversation led to him saying something he really regretted. Like telling her the painful truth – that he didn't know how he felt about her any more.

Christ, where did he go with that?

The urge to escape became compulsive. Leaving the room, he went in search of his thick Barbour jacket and boots, and a few minutes later he was stomping up the garden with fork and spade in hand.

After two hours of backbreaking work he stood back and surveyed the results with satisfaction. Turning up tufts of green grass and hard clods of earth might not be everyone's idea of how to spend a freezing cold February morning, but it had certainly helped vent some of his frustration. He thrust his spade into the ground and blew some warmth into his hands, rubbing them together as he appraised his handiwork. He frowned as he took in the full impact of his digging. He'd got carried away. He shouldn't have dug as close to the trees as that.

He sighed and began to fill some of the soil in.

'Adam…?'

Her voice was all sweetness and light now, he noticed. As if their row had never been. It amazed him how she did that.

'I'm up here near the Orchard.'

He leant on his spade, looking around as he waited. It would be an attractive setting when it was finished. Once the hard-core base for the barbecue was done, he'd build a pergola and cover it with climbing plants so that it provided natural shade for the table and chairs.

He did a double take, his eyes locking on a small domed object protruding through the soil he'd exposed. What the–?

At first, he couldn't grasp what he was seeing as he bent down and carefully started to prise the mud away. But then, as he realised what it was he was touching, he recoiled. *'Jesus.'*

He jumped up just as Natasha reached him, the frown on her brow indicating her improved temper had been a thing of brief duration.

'What are you doing up here? I thought you were building the barbecue near the patio? It's way too far from the house here.'

He stepped quickly in front of the hole, blocking her view. 'Don't come any closer, Tash. Go back to the house.'

'Why?'

'Just do as I say. I'll explain in a minute.'

She looked at him impatiently, ignoring his efforts to deter her as she peered curiously around his body to see what he was concealing. She froze at the sight of the tiny skull and scattered bones he'd exposed.

'My God. What's that?'

'It's nothing.'

'Adam, it's a skull.'

10

Her eyes were locked in horror on the remains he'd unearthed, and acting swiftly, he covered them over before chucking the spade down on the ground and leading her firmly away.

'Come back to the house, we can talk about it there.'

The warmth of their lounge was a welcome contrast to the bitter cold horror of what they'd just witnessed and Adam shut the patio doors behind them, watching Natasha carefully as she sank shakily into a chair. She'd been better recently, they didn't need this.

She looked up at him her cheeks pale, her fingers plucking agitatedly in her lap. 'I know what I saw, Adam. That was horrible. What do you think it's doing there?'

'I don't know. It could be some sort of ancient relic or something I suppose, but ...' he took a breath, knowing he had no choice now that she'd also seen the findings. 'We should probably call the police.'

The suggestion didn't go down well, as he'd known it wouldn't, Natasha's eyes taking on a haunted look.

'But if we do that they'll be traipsing everywhere, all over our beautiful home and garden. It'll knock me back, the way I'm feeling at the moment, you know it will.'

She began to breathe hard and he could tell the tears weren't far away. He stared at her helplessly. 'Look, it'll be fine, don't get upset. I'll ring Mum and see if she can hang onto Katie for the rest of the weekend, until it's all sorted.'

'It was so tiny,' Natasha whispered, her eyes filled with the horror of what she'd seen. 'I can't bear the thought that it was a ...'

'Hey, come on, don't think about it.' Adam's tone was soothing as he felt himself slipping into the familiar role of carer. 'It's probably just some ancient relic as I say. Why don't you lay down for a bit and take one of your sedatives? You'll feel better if you rest.'

Natasha rose unsteadily from her chair. 'I think I will. I had a terrible night last night. Not that you'd know anything about that of course in your comfy spare room.'

'Let's not go there again, Tash …'

'Like we never go there you mean?'

She glared at him accusingly. He was the first to look away.

'Do you want some water to take up with you?'

'No.' Her response was sullen. 'Just make sure to wake me after a couple of hours or I'll have trouble sleeping again tonight.'

He waited until she'd gone before moving over to the cabinet and yanking the stopper off the brandy. His expression was brooding as he poured himself a drink. He was an idiot. He should have been quicker off the mark concealing those bones. It would have bought him some time at least - and he couldn't help thinking he might just have left them where they were, to become someone else's problem in the future. It was a question of priorities. And right now, his priorities were pretty much stretched to the limit.

He tossed the brandy down his throat and released his breath. Well, it was too late for any of that now. Natasha had seen them and he couldn't rely on her to keep quiet about the discovery.

Which meant he had no choice but to get on and report it.

***

They were there within fifteen minutes. Not bad for a Saturday, he thought, watching as two cars pulled up. He walked out onto the front drive, his face impassive as two figures climbed out of the front car and made their way over to him. Why did seeing the police always make you feel guilty?

'Mr Campbell? Detective Chief Inspector Murray, and my colleague, Detective Sergeant Briscombe. We were in the vicinity when the call went out and thought we'd take a look, if that's okay?'

He spoke abruptly; a stocky man in his mid-fifties with a brisk air of authority that sat somewhat oddly with his rather scruffy appearance. He was wrapped warmly in an ancient fleece and he peered at Adam through shrewd eyes before allowing his gaze to wander briefly over the attractive barn conversion and shingle courtyard surrounding it.

'So, a skeleton you say?'

His piercing gaze focused on Adam with a sharpness that was disconcerting.

Adam nodded. 'It looked like it to me. And possibly a baby. It was grim. Shall I show you?'

'If you wouldn't mind.'

Adam led him through the clematis-clad archway at the side of the house. When he reached the small orchard at the top of the garden everything was as he'd left it. He couldn't bring himself to look at that disturbed pile of earth again.

'It's there, beneath the mud. Do you need me for anything else?'

'A couple of questions, then you can leave us to it. I'll come back and see you when we've finished.'

Murray looked at how the garden backed onto open fields. 'Nice setting you've got here, but very open if someone wanted to gain access?'

'Yes, I suppose it is. Not that we've had problems with trespassing.'

'Was it you that found the remains?'

'Yes.'

The Inspector bent down and carefully probed the soil. Then he looked up. 'They're certainly very small bones, but what made you think they're human? Not that obvious just looking at them.'

'The remains of a skull are buried a bit further over to the left. I'm a vet, so I have a certain knowledge of the anatomy.'

'Ah, right. And did you touch anything or move it?'

'Yes, I suppose I did when I was trying to scrape the

mud off. Sorry.'

The Inspector shrugged, turning back to the hole. 'You weren't to know. I understand your wife also saw the remains. Did she touch anything?'

Adam shook his head.

'Good.' He stood up. 'I think that'll do for now. No need for you to stay any longer. I'll come back to the house when we've finished.'

'Right.' Adam cast one more look in the direction of the skull and turned away. He didn't need telling twice.

Murray watched him go, waiting until he was out of earshot before turning to his Sergeant. 'Are forensics on the way?'

His companion snapped his phone shut. 'Should be here any minute.'

'Good.' He bent down and had another careful poke. 'I think he might be right, Harry. They look human to me. And as he says, possibly a baby.'

He turned to look up at the other man. 'Are you thinking what I'm thinking?'

Harry Briscombe smiled. 'I'd never presume to guess what you're thinking, sir. But if you're referring to the identity of the skeleton?'

'I am.'

'There haven't been many babies gone missing in the area.'

'Precisely. Ah, looks like forensics are here.'

Harry followed his gaze to where a gowned-up figure, with a toolbox in his hand and covers on his shoes, was making his way purposefully towards them.

They waited in silence until the pathologist joined them. He nodded his head at Murray. 'Morning,' he said briskly. 'What have we got?'

'Phone call from the owners to say they'd found what looked like human remains. The husband's a vet, seems to know his stuff. Apparently, there's a skull under that lot there.'

The pathologist knelt and surveyed the scene before getting to work. Murray waited patiently as he went through the usual ritual.

'Yup,' he said, looking up. 'They're human remains all right. A very young baby, I'd say. I'll get this lot back to the lab and send my report through as soon as I can. But I warn you now, we're inundated. Nothing's going to happen in a hurry.'

Murray simply nodded. 'When you can.' Sighing, he turned to Harry. 'I think I'll have a chat with the husband. You keep an eye on things up here. I won't be long.'

Back at the house he saw Adam Campbell through the lounge windows, sitting staring out onto the garden.

He rose as the Inspector approached and opened the patio doors.

'Did you want to come in, Inspector?'

'Just a few questions if you don't mind, sir.'

He stamped his feet to dislodge what mud he could and stepped carefully onto the mat by the door. His gaze swept quickly around the cool elegance of the room before settling on the dark-haired man in front of him.

'You've got a nice home here. Doesn't quite fit my image of the typical country vet with muddy boots and a host of abandoned animals trailing after him, but...' he shrugged and smiled. 'I guess that's just another example of how things have changed these days.'

Adam's look was rueful. 'That's my wife's influence. If it were down to me the place would be just the sort of retreat you describe. But Natasha would have a fit. She doesn't do messy.'

'Right now, just a few questions, and then I'll leave you in peace. I'm sure I don't need to stress the potential seriousness of this situation?' His eyes bore into Adam's. 'The forensic team have confirmed that the skeleton's human, and, as you say, a baby. It'll need looking into. They'll be taking everything off to the lab, but it would be helpful to have a few facts.'

Adam looked shocked. 'Of course.'

'What were you doing when you made the discovery?'

'Clearing the space to build a new barbeque area.'

'And you and your wife have lived here how long?'

'Six and a half years.'

'Lovely house for a young couple to be starting off in. You must have been very young when you bought it?'

Adam's discomfort showed. 'Actually, it was my mother-in-law who bought it shortly before we got married. The plan was for her to live here with Natasha while I was away at university, but unfortunately it didn't work out that way. She died a couple of months after our wedding.'

Why did he feel the need to explain himself? It was nobody's business what sort of a house they lived in.

The Inspector merely nodded. 'What about the people who lived here before you? Do you know what happened to them?'

'I never met them, but I think they emigrated. We might still have their names amongst our papers if you want them?'

'Yes, please, when you've got a moment. Is your wife around? I'd like to speak to her now if I may?'

Adam hesitated. 'She's not been too well; she's sleeping right now. I just went and checked on her. Can it wait?'

Murray closed his book with a snap. 'Someone can drop by in the morning, if that's more convenient?'

'Thanks. We'll both be here unless I get called out on an emergency.' He looked at the Inspector. 'I know it's probably asking the impossible, but ... have you got any thoughts on why those bones might be there?'

Murray's response was guarded. 'Difficult to say at this stage, but the circumstances may well speak for themselves. In my book, you don't usually bury a baby in someone's back garden unless you've got something to hide.'

16

'You don't think it could be some sort of archaeological find then? There are lots of sites around here and I remember reading somewhere that in ancient times they sometimes buried their dead close to the house - something about keeping the spirit close.'

Murray's look was sceptical. 'I think, even back then, they usually buried their dead in coffins, and I didn't see much evidence of that. But it's possible I suppose. We'll keep you posted.'

He opened the patio door and stepped back outside, pulling his fleece tightly around him as the cold air bit in. 'Thanks for your time, Mr. Campbell. We'll need to excavate a wider area to make sure we don't miss anything I'm afraid. I'm sure it goes without saying, that nobody goes near the sealed off section until we've finished examining it?'

Adam nodded. 'That won't be a problem.'

'Good. I'll leave you to it then. As I say, someone will drop by tomorrow to speak to your wife.'

Adam watched him trudge back up the garden before picking up his empty coffee cup and carrying it through to the kitchen. A frown marred his face. Natasha was fragile enough at the moment – he recognised the signs all too well. The last thing they needed was a police investigation on their doorstep.

CHAPTER TWO

Hannah dumped her shopping bags on the floor and ran straight into the lounge, switching on the TV.

The remains of a baby, the Sergeant had said. They were just letting her know as a precaution. She flicked on the News and caught her breath as the first thing she saw was a haunting image of herself looking bewildered – and much younger – fighting her way through a horde of reporters. She didn't need any introduction as to what it was about, but already the picture was changing, moving on to where a reporter was standing outside a house with a couple of policemen standing guard.

'Yes, Malcolm. As you can see, I'm in this very pleasant village on the outskirts of Hertford where the residents enjoy one of the country's lowest crime rates. Certainly not somewhere you'd normally expect to discover the grim findings that police have uncovered here today. They've released no details except to confirm they have found, what they believe to be, the remains of a young baby. Suspicious causes can't be ruled out at this stage. Around here, conjecture is growing as to whether these could possibly be the remains of little Sophie Walker who went missing from her pram nearly six years ago when she was just three weeks old. She was never found and no charges were ever brought. Of course, until the remains are formally identified, the police won't be drawn, and we can only speculate, but...'

Hannah grabbed the tv remote and clicked it off before sinking down onto the settee. She wasn't interested in their speculation. She'd heard it all before.

She dropped her head into her hands as emotions she'd hoped never to experience again flooded in, threatening to send her spiralling back into the deep abyss she'd taken so long to climb out of.

She didn't remember much about those early days after

Sophie had been taken. Didn't want to remember. She'd felt that the whole world must be blaming her for leaving her daughter out in the garden, yet it was surprising how, in the face of tragedy, people had shown her nothing but kindness, assuring her, repeatedly, that it hadn't been her fault.

But, no one could shift the heavy burden of blame she'd piled on herself.

Then, inexplicably, hard on the early sympathy their plight had aroused, came the far more incomprehensible, and in her view, distracting accusations, that maybe it was her or Ben who'd done something to Sophie. And even though she hadn't really believed that Ben could have done something like that, it had sealed the impenetrable rift between them.

'Do you think I don't know that you're sitting there suspecting me?' He'd accused aggressively one evening, in the early stages of the search.

'Ben, I don't suspect you.' She was in tears. She didn't think she could take much more. 'Of course, I don't.'

He'd tossed his scotch back in one. 'Then why don't you stick up for me in the bloody media? Tell *them* that?'

'Because I don't want to talk to any reporters. They just twist everything you say. I want to be left alone.'

'But it's not just about you, Hannah. How do you think I feel being accused like some bloody criminal? I could do with some support here. You may not like me doing the tv interviews, but at least I'm doing something concrete to find our daughter, which is more than can be said for you.'

She shook her head. He was right, she knew. It had been the idea of the police to do the appeals, yet, she couldn't quite get it out of her head that a part of him was actually enjoying the media attention. Enjoying the importance of his role in all this.

'I'm sorry, I can't think straight at the moment...' She'd buried her face in her hands.

She felt *useless. Useless...*

She didn't know how long she sat there on the sofa, fighting off memories she'd thought long buried. It was the sound of the telephone, cutting shrilly into her thoughts, that finally dragged her back to the present. She moved in a daze to answer it.

It was as if thinking about him had conjured him up.

'Hannah? It's Ben. Have you seen the news?'

Dread curled in her chest, the image of his arrogant features swimming before her.

'I told you never to call me, Ben.'

'This is important. Have you seen the news? They've found the skeleton of a baby in a village near Hertford. They think it might be Sophie.'

It felt an age before she could muster the strength to find her voice. 'Yes, I saw it.'

'Well, what are we going to do about it? Have the police been in contact with you?'

'Yes, they phoned me about an hour ago.'

'Well, that's typical. They haven't called me – though why that should surprise me, I don't know. What did they say?'

Hannah hated how just the sound of his voice made her stomach churn. She took a steadying breath.

'Very little, other than that the skeleton of a baby had been found in someone's garden and they've no evidence at the moment to suggest it's Sophie. But, in the circumstances, it was their duty to let me know. There's nothing we can do at this stage, Ben. It might not even be her.'

'Well, the press seems to think it is. But I suppose you're right. I hope that bastard Hedges isn't still running things. If he comes sniffing at my door again, he'll get more than he bargained for.' He gave a short laugh. 'Bloody police think they know everything, but I'll be more than a match for them this time around.'

The phone in Hannah's hand began to tremble. Just the sound of his voice was enough to roll away the years and remind her of how it had been. She couldn't do this.

She felt the clamminess and suffocating tightness in her throat that indicated the onset of a full-blown panic attack. Something she hadn't experienced in over a year. She took a deep breath.

'I've got to go, Ben. My mum's here and we're about to eat...'

'Sure,' he said quickly. 'I should go anyway. It's been good talking to you, Han. You're the only one who really understands.'

Hannah couldn't put the phone down quick enough. Grabbing the back of the chair, she leant forward and forced herself to take deep calming breaths. Her body was shaking and her head felt fuzzy; her ears hissing loudly as the blood pounded in her head. She mustn't pass out. Clutching onto the chair and sofa for support, she stumbled to the sideboard drawer and pulled out a brown paper bag. She thrust it over her nose and mouth and began to breathe deeply in and out. After a few moments, she began to feel the benefit of her efforts. The ringing in her ears subsided, the fog in her head starting to clear as the attack receded.

Just as she'd folded the bag neatly and replaced it in the drawer, the phone rang for a second time. She picked the receiver up warily.

'Hannah? It's Mum.'

She released her breath. 'You've seen the news?'

'Yes. Are you all right? I tried to call you a few minutes ago but your line was busy.'

'It was Ben.'

There was a moment's silence at the other end.

'I didn't know you were still in touch with him?' Her tone was cautious.

'I'm not, but she was his child too, Mum.'

'I know.' Her mother's voice was hesitant. 'But you know what he's like. Don't let him use this as an excuse to...'

'I'm not you, Mum.'

The minute the words were out, she bit her tongue – where had that come from? 'I'm sorry,' she said quickly, 'I didn't mean that the way it sounded. But you don't need to worry. I have no feelings left for Ben.'

Or anyone else, she thought, hollowly.

'I'm glad,' her mother said quietly. 'And you're right – you're not me. You're much stronger.'

Hannah closed her eyes, and for a precarious moment felt the floor swimming beneath her feet. Once she had been strong – headstrong too, and so sure of herself. She'd sailed carelessly through life as all teenagers do with the selfish acceptance that it was her due.

Then reality had struck. Her parents' separation, Ben, Sophie. Now she was like a shell with its insides scraped out. She had nothing to give - let alone be strong for.

'I'm really not. I'm not strong at all...' she was in danger of proving that at any moment. 'I'd better go, Mum. Thanks for calling.'

'Do you want me to come over?'

'No, it's all right.'

'Darling?'

'Mum, I'm fine. Please don't fuss. There's nothing you can do. It might not even be her. I just need to be alone.'

She hadn't meant it to come out as abruptly as that, and she bit her lip, knowing her mother would be hurt by the rejection.

'I'm sorry,' she sighed.

'It doesn't matter. As long as you're okay?'

There was an awkward silence as they both realised that of course, she wasn't okay. She was about to go through the whole thing again, with all the heartache it would entail.

She looked out of the window, her eyes drawn by a set of headlights as a car pulled up outside on the road. She felt suddenly sick.

'I need to go – the police are here. I'll call you

tomorrow.'

She replaced the handset, an attack of butterflies gripping her stomach as she moved into the hall to open the front door. She didn't recognise either of the men standing on her doorstep, and for that at least, she was grateful.

'Miss Walker?'

It was the older of the two who spoke. He was in his mid-fifties and his voice was brisk.

'Yes.'

'Chief Inspector Murray, and this is Detective Sergeant Briscombe. He spoke to you earlier I believe? Can we come in?'

'Of course.' She didn't even bother to look at the card he offered. She stepped aside, her face impassive. 'I saw the news. Do you think it's Sophie?'

Hannah sensed she'd surprised him, and she wondered if it was because she looked so different now to the lost, ghost-like little waif she'd just seen peering out from the television screen. She didn't like the fact that she looked normal again; hated how her physical image could be so different to the hollow emptiness that still existed inside her, but there wasn't much she could do about that. Nature had its own way of healing and her body had betrayed her, filling out to its former curves, her blond hair looking healthy and shiny despite the fact she'd clipped it to within an inch of her scalp.

Murray's look was direct as he answered her question. 'We don't know if it's your daughter yet. I hope the news report didn't upset you too much. We didn't release specific details about the findings, but somehow the Press got wind of the fact it was a baby, and we were forced to confirm that fact.'

'But, do you think it's her?'

Murray hesitated, his gaze sympathetic. 'As I say, we don't know yet. But there is a chance it could be. You might need to prepare yourself.'

He paused, allowing her some space before continuing.

'I'm sorry to put you through this, but I need to ask you a couple of questions just to get things straight in my mind. Please appreciate I wasn't handling the original case.'

Hannah's voice was terse. 'I told them everything I knew back then. Nothing's changed.'

'I appreciate that. But we wouldn't want to miss anything.'

He pulled a small notebook from his pocket. 'Now. Your baby was three weeks old when she went missing and you say she was taken from her pram in the garden?'

'I don't just say it. That's how it happened.'

'Would you mind filling me in on the exact details?'

Hannah took a deep breath. 'There's not much to tell,' she said, slipping back with frightening ease into the horror of that day nearly six years ago. 'It was a nice day – the first proper spring day we'd had. I'd just got back from the baby clinic and my boyfriend suggested I put Sophie out in the back garden for her nap.'

'That would be Ben Short, right?'

'Yes. It was about ten-thirty in the morning – the time she usually had her sleep. I was keeping a good eye on her. She was only out there for about half an hour,' her voice caught.

'And you didn't see anyone at all in that time?'

She cleared her throat. 'No. One of my neighbours was out in her garden when I put the pram out, but she'd gone in by the time I realised Sophie was missing.'

'Which side is she?'

'Number 29, but she's not there any longer. She moved soon after it all happened to go and live with her daughter. Some family crisis.'

'And you saw no-one else?'

'No. The garage is at the back of the house. We thought maybe someone had spotted the pram when Ben left for his appointment.'

'Is Mr. Short around to talk to?'

'No, we're not together anymore.'

'It must have been a difficult time for you both?' His eyes were keen as he put the question to her and Hannah kept her returning stare cool. 'Yes, it was. And if you've read your predecessor's notes, you'll see that there were a number of people who seemed to think either Ben or I had done something to Sophie. Our relationship didn't survive the pressure.'

She hesitated, but there was no point going into the other reasons why they'd split up. They were personal and would only serve as a distraction.

'You say your partner suggested putting your daughter out in the garden. Was that something you regularly did?'

'No. I'd never done it before. She was only three weeks old.'

'I see. And you live here alone now? Or do you have a new partner?'

'I live here alone. I prefer it that way.'

He looked around the sparsely decorated flat.

'A lot of people in your circumstances feel the need to move. It can't be easy living with the memories?'

Hannah shrugged. He wasn't the first person to say that. People didn't seem to get that this flat was the one remaining link she had with her daughter. That if ever the abductors decided to return Sophie, it was the one place they might bring her back to. It might have sounded desperate, clutching at straws even, but it was how she felt. She'd never move away.

'You're right,' was all she said, 'it's not easy living with the memories, but moving away from them would be harder.'

His look was penetrating, and she found her own gaze sliding away from it. He slipped his notebook carefully into his pocket and stood up.

'Well, thank you for your time. We'll leave you in peace now. This is my card. If you think of anything else, just give me, or Harry here, a call. If we're not around we'll

25

get back to you.'

He hesitated. 'I should probably warn you that depending on what we get back from forensics, we might need to take a DNA sample off you next week. We'll let you know. In the meantime,' his gaze drifted to the window, 'the media can be more bloody trouble than they're worth at times like this. If you'll take my advice, a "*no comment*" response usually gets rid of them in the end.'

Hannah gave him a wintry smile. 'I'm sure I can remember how to do that. I got enough practice last time around.'

After they'd gone, she stared bleakly out of the window. It was going to start all over again. The phone calls, the anonymous letters, the accusations of blame. She wasn't sure she could handle it.

She yanked the curtains viciously together. Of course, she could. She wasn't a naïve, emotional nineteen-year-old any more. She was a twenty-five-year old woman who'd learnt to cope with the worst life could throw at her. If she could survive losing Sophie, she could survive anything. Even the final awful confirmation that her daughter might be dead.

***

'Hannah? Han, are you there? It's me, Jess.'

She jumped at the sound of the voice coming through the letterbox. Moving into the hall she opened the door and even managed a smile at the sight of her friend's unruly auburn curls sticking out in all directions from beneath the colourful winter scarf she'd wrapped around her head. She was sporting a bottle of wine in one hand and a holdall in the other.

'Thought you could do with some company,' Jess said. 'I didn't call because I knew you'd say no, but my beloved hubby is happy to baby sit if you want me to stay over?'

'That's really nice of you, Jess, but you don't need to.'

'I know, but it doesn't feel right you being on your own

26

tonight.' She dumped her stuff on the floor and gave Hannah a fierce hug. 'Come on. Let me stay and keep you company? You'll only mope if you're on your own.'

Hannah sighed, her lips twisting into a reluctant smile. 'Okay, thanks. It's kind of you. I've got a ready-made curry if you want to share it, but–' her eyes focused on the bottle in Jess's hand, 'a drink first might be good. I've just had the police around.'

'Your favourite public service, I saw them leaving. What did they say?'

She helped Hannah scoop up the shopping bags in the hall, and followed her through to the kitchen.

'Not a lot. Just that I should prepare myself for the worst.'

'Oh hon, I'm sorry ...'

Hannah shrugged. 'I almost want it to be her now – at least that way there'd be an end to it.'

Her words hung in the air between them for a moment, before Jess said softly. 'I can understand that. You've been incredibly strong, Hannah. I wouldn't have coped nearly as well.'

'I haven't always dealt with it brilliantly, as well you know.'

She hesitated, struggling over the words she knew she should be saying. That she didn't know how she'd have survived without her friend's support. That she'd been a real anchor through everything that had gone on. But, as always, the words stuck in her throat and the moment passed.

'Thanks for coming,' was all she said.

Jess moved over to the cupboard and pulled out two glasses. 'That's what friends do when they've known each other forever. You'd do the same for me.'

'I know, but even so...'

She watched as her friend opened the bottle of wine and poured it. It was crisp and chilled and it soothed her. But it wasn't enough. She set it restlessly down on the kitchen worktop and started unpacking the bags.

'Come on, I'm hungry. I'll get dinner under way. Do you mind if we don't talk about Sophie for a while? I'm trying to get my head around it all still.'

'Of course not.'

Twenty minutes later they were sitting at the kitchen table tucking into their chicken curry. Jess had insisted on making raita out of some Greek yoghurt and cucumber she'd found in the fridge, and Hannah had found it calming as they worked together.

It was only as they were finishing up with fruit and ice cream that Jess eyed Hannah across the table, her gaze gentle.

'Are you okay?'

'I feel like shit, if you really want to know, but …' She held her glass up. 'This is going some way towards making me feel better.' She took a sip and added abruptly.

'I don't really want it to be her.'

'I know you don't.'

'I've never lost hope that she's alive, but this news today's knocked me back. What if it *is* her?'

Jess reached out and took her hand. 'Then you'll deal with it like you've dealt with everything else. And maybe the person who took her will be brought to justice.' She squeezed Hannah's fingers. 'I wish I could say something to make you feel better.'

'You just being here helps. Mum offered to come over, but…' She sighed.

'I thought the two of you were getting on better now? She only wants to be a Mum to you, Hannah.'

'Maybe it's a bit late for that.' Hannah's voice was detached.

'It's never too late if it's something you want. And you and your mum were always so close.' Jess hesitated. 'You know, you don't always make it easy for those who care about you to support you.'

'I know I don't.' Hannah's smile was rueful. 'If I was you I'd have given up on me years ago.'

'You don't get rid of me that easily. Or your Mum, I'm sure. Has something happened between you?'

'Not really. I was just a bit impatient with her when she rang and I'm feeling bad about it.'

'She'll understand.'

'I know she will. That's what makes it worse.'

'Look, you can tell me to butt-out if you want to, but, this thing with your mum; you don't blame her in some way for what happened, do you? I've sometimes got that impression.'

'No.' Hannah's denial was instinctive. 'At least ... oh, I don't know. I blame myself mostly for putting her out in the garden. But sometimes I can't help thinking that if things hadn't been so awful at home, maybe, I wouldn't have moved in with Ben quite so quickly, and none of it would have happened.'

'Hannah, you were besotted with Ben. I don't think you'd have done anything differently whatever was going on at home. And you need to get rid of the whole guilt thing – there's only one person to blame for what happened to Sophie, and that's the person who took her.'

Hannah knew it was true. She wasn't hearing anything she hadn't told herself a million times. So, why was it so hard to accept?

She jumped up from the table and started to clear away the dishes. 'Thanks, Jess, and I know you're probably right, but can we drop it now? I can't think straight at the moment. Let's clear this lot away and get a film on. I think some distraction therapy would be good.'

Later though, as she lay in her bed, her thoughts wouldn't be distracted. The hostile feelings she'd experienced towards her mother had shocked her. And Jess was right, that wasn't fair – especially as the ultimatum that had led to their estrangement had come from her and not her mother.

Even now she could remember almost word for word, the terrible row they'd had that night, all those years ago.

'What do you mean you're taking him back? How can you, after all he's put us through?'

'Hannah, I know you're upset…'

'Of course, I'm upset. I come back from Uni to that news? Why didn't you tell me before I broke up? I wouldn't have bothered coming home then. We've been happy this last couple of years, haven't we? How can you want to undo all that? Can't you see what he does to you?'

'Darling, it's not going to be like that. Your father's promised the affair's over and I believe him.'

'Yeah – because he's *ill* and she can't be bothered to look after him.'

There'd been sadness in her mother's expressive blue eyes as she'd looked at her daughter and seen the hurt behind those words, but there'd been determination too.

'I can't turn my back on him. I can't write off nineteen years of marriage as if they never existed. Your father needs me now – needs us.'

'Mum, he uses you. Can't you see that? Why should we have to look after him just because she won't?'

Her mother's eyes had welled up. 'Oh sweetheart, I hate hearing you talk like that. I know how much you loved Dad before all this happened and it breaks my heart that he's destroyed all that. But he's still your father and he's still my husband. Please try to understand that I have to do this. I'll make it up to you, I promise…'

'Don't bother.' Hannah swung sharply away. 'I'll be out of your hair when I'm back at Uni anyway. I'm sure you'll both be much happier without me.'

'Hannah …'

The sound of a car horn outside the house had Hannah

grabbing her bag.

'That's Jess – she's giving me a lift. Do what you want. You always do anyway. I told Dad that I never wanted to speak to him again and I meant it. If he moves back in, then I move out.'

Hannah had stormed out of the house slamming the door behind her. She knew she was being a selfish cow but she couldn't seem to help it. How could her mother take him back after two years of being messed around? It was pathetic.

And now she'd lost Ben too. She hadn't told her mother about their break-up yet. She'd wanted to wait until she got home to pour her heart out, but now she knew she probably never would. The special relationship they'd had this last couple of years would be gone forever. Life was crap.

'Hey ... what's up with you? You look fit to explode.'

The twinkle in Jess's eyes as she'd watched her friend throw herself into the car had gone some way to diffusing Hannah's anger, but she'd still scowled her response.

'I don't want to talk about it. But I'll tell you something. Sod everyone. I don't need any of them. I'm getting pissed tonight.'

'Still not heard from Ben?'

'No. And I don't want to. It's over.'

'What did you fight about?'

Hannah had hesitated, knowing she could never give the reason for their split. Not even to Jess. She'd not got over the humiliation of finding her hands being handcuffed to the frame of Ben's bed and discovering that no matter how loudly she'd shouted at him to let her go, he'd completely ignored her wishes; whispering that he knew she didn't often come when they made love and that perhaps she needed more kinky sex to enjoy it. He'd used her body and taken his pleasure of her with a passion she'd never witnessed in him before. It had shocked her to the core and afterwards she'd stormed out of his flat telling him she never wanted to see him again.

'Just stuff,' she responded vaguely, not looking at her friend.

'Uh huh … and if you think I believe that when you're so hot for the guy? It must have been something mega to cause a bust up between you.'

Hannah had given her the benefit of one of her fiercest scowls. 'I really don't want to talk about it, Jess.'

'Okay.' Her friend had shrugged her shoulders and started the engine. 'Let's go get drunk.'

Now, as Hannah lay in her bed remembering, she switched on the bedside light and finally gave up all pretence of trying to get to sleep.

She carried tremendous guilt about both her parents; she didn't need any analyst to tell her that. She hadn't believed her father was that ill – had thought it was just a ruse to con her mother into taking him back. And when Helen Walker had chosen her husband over her, Hannah's hurt had been so deep she'd refused to have anything further to do with either of them – moving in with Ben when she'd discovered she was pregnant and leaving her mother to cope alone with a dying man.

The guilt, when her father had died five months later had been excruciating, and over the years she'd dealt with it the only way she knew how. She'd packed it up and filed it neatly away, alongside her guilt over Sophie. And though she and her mother had subsequently reconciled, that period was like a huge invisible barrier between them, and something they never discussed for fear of destroying the fragile relationship they'd rebuilt.

She threw back her bedclothes and moved restlessly over to the window, unsurprised to see that, at some point, night had turned into dawn. Reaching into the drawer of her dressing table, she pulled out a small bottle of sleeping pills. She hadn't taken one in a long time but she didn't hesitate to down one now. She'd done enough remembering for one night.

CHAPTER THREE

Natasha Campbell came too very slowly in her bed that Sunday morning, aware of a sick feeling in the pit of her stomach. Then she remembered why. That terrible sight of yesterday – the tiny skull, parts of it already crumbled away. She shuddered. What with finding those bones and the problems between her and Adam, it was no wonder she felt ill. Anyone would. It was nothing to do with her condition. She closed her eyes and took a deep breath as she'd been taught, and then another. Her thoughts drifted back to Adam. It had upset her when he'd stomped off up the garden like that yesterday. Even after seven years, she sometimes felt she didn't know him at all.

She turned onto her side and closed her eyes, Adam's image sliding away, to be replaced by a darker, more sinister one that nudged at her mind as if to torment her. The skull had been horrible; she didn't want to think about it. She hated anything to do with death. It triggered too many memories – like the speed of her mother's passing away, for example, despite the chemo.

Stop it, Natasha. Don't go there ...

With a determined breath, she flung back the bedclothes and headed for the bathroom. No point dwelling on stuff. If she'd learnt anything from her therapy it was that. In the shower, she turned her face upwards, letting the water flow over her – washing away the darkness of her thoughts.

Later, as she made her way to the top of the stairs, she was surprised to hear voices coming from the lounge. It didn't take long to work out that it was a policeman talking to Adam. She frowned. She didn't feel like entertaining anyone right now, but Adam had warned her they'd be coming back to ask a few questions. She'd just have to answer them as best she could so that they'd leave and she and Adam could have a calm day.

Adam looked up as she entered the room. 'Natasha! I

34

was just about to come and wake you. Are you feeling better?'

She pinned a bright smile onto her face. 'Yes, much, but I felt I'd go mad if I stayed upstairs on my own any longer.'

She turned questioning eyes to the slightly older and rather good-looking man who was standing by the window. Probably in his early thirties, he had sandy hair and a pleasant face that was somehow reassuring in the bizarreness of everything else.

'Tash, this is Detective Sergeant Briscombe. He needs to ask you a few questions.'

'Okay, though I'm not sure what help I can be.' She moved over to one of the chairs and sat down. 'It was awful. I can't get the picture of that skull out of my head.'

Harry Briscombe's smile was sympathetic. 'I can come back another day if you're not feeling up to it, Mrs Campbell?'

Natasha shook her head. 'No, no, I'm fine. Let's get it over with. I wouldn't say no to a cup of tea though, Ad, if you're making one?'

She watched her husband leave the room then turned back to the sergeant.

'So, how can I help? I wouldn't have thought there's much we can tell you. Adam said those bones could have been there for hundreds of years?'

'Well, it's possible, but we won't know for certain until we get all the information back from the Lab. And in the meantime, we like to gather all the facts while they're still fresh in people's minds. So ...' He consulted his notebook. 'Your husband tells me you've lived here for several years?'

'That's right.'

'And before that apparently it was occupied by a couple who he thinks moved abroad?'

'Yes. Australia, I think. Or maybe New Zealand.'

'Well obviously we'll be looking into that further. Do you remember if they had children?'

35

'Oh, no. I don't think so. They'd have been too old for young children I'm sure, though they could have had grandchildren I suppose.'

'And no history of any children going missing in the area that you're aware of?'

'No. Apart from that poor little baby in Hertford of course...' She broke off, her eyes clouding. 'I saw the news last night. They were saying it might be her. Is that what you think?'

'Well, the press do seem to have got ahead of us somehow on that one and we won't know for sure until the DNA results are back. It's a possibility'.

'That's horrible. How dreadful to think...' She looked out onto the garden, glad that the rhododendrons blocked that awful view. Then her eyes returned to the sergeant. ''How long will it take? Before you know for sure if it's her I mean?'

'That depends. It's much quicker and easier, for example, to process samples from a living person or a body, than it is from a skeleton; so, while we can possibly get some results back quite quickly, other bits could take a couple of weeks before we're able to do a statistical match.'

'I see. And if it is her, do you think it could have been one of the parents who killed her? That's what they were suggesting at the time, I seem to remember.'

'It's much too early to speculate at this stage,' Harry said cautiously. 'First off we have to establish whether or not it is their baby.'

'Yes, of course. God, I hope it isn't. It makes it seem even more horrible somehow, knowing the history behind it. I've been praying that Adam's right and it'll turn out to be some sort of ancient discovery.' She gave him a thin smile. 'You read about this sort of thing happening to other people in the papers but it doesn't seem real when it's your garden.'

'Did you know the woman?'

'No. I went off to boarding school when I was eleven.

I've not got many local friends.'

'One of the drawbacks, isn't it?' Harry's look was sympathetic and she looked at him surprised.

'Sounds like you speak from experience?'

He shrugged. 'Yup. I went when I was eight.'

'That's unusual for a policeman, isn't it? Though I probably shouldn't say that – not terribly PC to label someone like that.'

'I'll forgive you,' his smile told her that he wasn't offended and she recognised something else in it. Interest.

Her expression lifted, her eyes glinting mischievously. 'Anyway, no need to feel too sorry for me, I found ways of getting my fun. There was a boys' school just down the road.'

She could tell he didn't quite know what to make of her and the thought amused her. She watched as he made a pointed show of returning to his notebook.

'When your husband found the remains, did he call you to come and look?'

'No. In fact I don't think he'd have even told me if I hadn't happened to go out into the garden looking for him. He's very protective of me.'

'And what exactly was he doing when you went out to him?'

Natasha thought. 'Well I'm not sure ... just looking at them I think. He tried to cover them up as soon as he knew I was there.'

He had rather nice grey eyes, she noted inconsequentially, and she found her own engaging rather cheekily with them, despite the severity of the occasion. She watched, amused, as the colour crept into his cheeks.

Then Adam came in with a tray. 'Tea, Sergeant?'

Harry blinked, then cleared his throat. 'Erm, no thanks. I think that'll do for now. Thanks for your time, Mrs Campbell. I've given your husband a card in case you think of anything else?'

'Of course. We'll be in touch straight away.'

After he'd gone Adam and Natasha looked at each other.

'Are you okay?' Adam asked.

'No, I'm about to have a breakdown,' Natasha responded impatiently. 'For God's sake stop fussing over me the whole time.'

She lit a cigarette and took a deep drag from it, blowing the smoke slowly back out into the air. 'I think they suspect it's that little baby that went missing from Hertford.' Her eyes were keen as they fixed on him. 'You remember?'

'Sort of,' he dismissed vaguely, 'but I was backwards and forwards between here and university when it was all going on.'

'Well, it was in the news for ages. They never found her. It doesn't seem possible does it, that a child can just disappear like that?'

She put her cigarette down and looked at her husband provocatively. Something about the sergeant had channelled her thoughts towards sex and she didn't want to think about all this depressing stuff.

She slanted him a look from beneath ridiculously long lashes. 'Why don't we make the most of it while Katie's at your mum's and go to bed?' she suggested.

'I've got some work to catch up on.'

She rose from her chair and sidled up to him, ignoring the set expression on his face as she trailed her hand lightly over the front of his jeans. 'Oh, come on. It can wait surely? What's the matter with you? I always used to be able to turn you on. It's been a horrible couple of days. We need something to distract us.'

He stepped back, breaking the contact. 'I know you're upset, but I'm sorry, I really do need to get on with my report.'

She stared at him for a long moment, one eyebrow raised, then said in cool tones. 'Are you ever going to forgive me?'

He seemed to consider her words.

'I don't know.'

'Oh, for God's sake, it's been three months since I finished it and you know I was in a bad place in my head at the time. I said it wouldn't happen again and it won't. I just want things to go back to how they were.'

Adam shook his head. 'And as I've said – I don't know that they can. Do you think I can just forget you had an affair? Do you have any idea what it's like finding something like that out? And I'm not convinced it was the first time – that's what really gets me. Things like trust and loyalty don't seem to mean much to you, but they do to me. Things can never go back to how they were.'

Natasha held his gaze defiantly for a moment longer, then she shrugged and turned away. 'In that case, get me a glass of wine, will you? If I can't have a good shag to take my mind off everything I might as well bury myself in a bottle.'

'You know you shouldn't drink with your medication.'

'Oh, for fuck's sake get a life,' she shrieked, rounding on him. 'No sex, no alcohol – what else is there left for me in this bloody life? You make me sick.'

CHAPTER FOUR

DCI Murray was in the office bright and early Wednesday morning. He'd had two days leave and was raring to go. Harry could tell that, the minute he pinned him with his sharp gaze.

'So, what's new?' Murray asked.

'Not a lot. Things are reasonably quiet for a change. We finally got those fingerprints through on the Post Office robbery. They match the suspect, so we can turn that over to the CPS now.'

'Good. What about the skeleton?'

'Nothing's come through yet. But I'll chase it up,' he added hurriedly, recognising that look.

'Make sure you do. We can crack on with that if things are quiet. How did you get on interviewing the wife on Sunday?'

'She didn't have much to offer. Seemed pretty upset at the thought it might not be historical bones like they'd hoped.'

'That's not surprising. What's she like?'

Harry shrugged, remembering with a sense of discomfort the disturbing effect she'd had on him. She'd been quite stunning to look at with her dark hair and sultry eyes, and yet there was something quite fragile about her. Just for a moment, when she'd first walked in and fixed him with that slanting stare, he'd lost the plot - aware of an instant attraction that had disconcerted him.

Harry avoided Murray's eyes. 'Difficult to say. Posh, very attractive, but on edge somehow. That's the impression I got. The husband did mention she'd been unwell and still has to take things easy. I don't know what that's about.'

'What was your impression of him?'

'Seemed a straightforward sort of guy. Obviously concerned about her. I didn't know whether to think it suspicious or not that she reckoned he wouldn't have told her about the bones if she hadn't seen them for herself. She said he was very protective of her and tried to cover them over when she arrived on the scene.'

'Reasonable enough I suppose. The real question is; would he have told us? Where was he when the Walker baby went missing? Have you established that?'

'Touched on it briefly. Didn't want to make too much of that until the stuff's back from the lab and we know what we're dealing with. He said he was away in Glasgow at university over that period – coming back on and off to see his wife.'

'Hmm.' Murray's tone was impatient. 'We need to see what Edwards has come up with on the forensics. Give him a ring. Let him know we're on his case.'

Jeez, Harry thought, walking out of the room. They'd only been in half an hour and it wasn't even eight thirty. He could see what sort of a day it was going to be.

Two hours later Murray looked up as Harry entered the office. 'What's that?'

'Post Mortem. Edwards has come up trumps but you're not going to like it.'

He slapped the document down on the desk and Murray skimmed his eyes over it
before looking up.

'Suspicious causes cannot be ruled out or confirmed? What the hell does that mean?'

'If you look at page two it tells you. It seems there wasn't enough to go on to tell the exact cause of death. But there was a small fracture of the left arm. They're still working on the full forensics.'

Murray turned his attention back to the report and read it through. When he'd finished, he looked up.

'Okay, so we don't know cause of death and it's impossible to tell the sex from a skeleton that young – but we do know that it's a tiny baby, only a few weeks old. And they're not ancient bones. The time scale would appear to be around the time Sophie Walker went missing. I'd say there's a good chance it's her. What do you think?'

'Sad news for Hannah Walker, I agree. It's not as if there's a long list of missing babies to pick from.'

'Right. Well, first things first. Contact Hannah Walker and ask her if she can come down and give us a DNA sample, and while you're at it, do the same with the Campbells. Tell them we need to eliminate them from the enquiry if they're huffy about it. Did you get the address of the people that lived there before them?'

'Not yet, but we're working–'

'Well crack on with it,' Murray interrupted impatiently. 'We need as much information as we can get on who's lived there over the last ten years or so. Odds are it'll be the Walker baby, but we should also check the database and cross-reference for any other infants that may have gone missing in the area. Put Peterson onto that will you?'

'I already have. Erm … anything else you particularly want me to follow up today?'

Murray raised an eyebrow. 'Are you being facetious, Harry, or have you got plans?'

'Wouldn't dare be facetious, sir,' Harry grinned. 'But I thought I might try and track down Hannah Walker's ex and see what he's got to say for himself.'

'Good idea. And while you're doing that, I'll go see some of her neighbours. See if any of them were there six years ago when the child went missing. I've been reading through the file and there's bugger-all that's useful. Hedges seemed convinced it was one of the parents. He may be right of course, but you can't help feeling that someone must have seen something.'

Outside Hannah Walker's flat, Murray pressed on the bell that said, Applemore - 1st floor.

'I don't think I can be of much help,' the tall blond

woman who answered the door said, shooing her toddler ahead of them as she led Murray into the lounge. 'I told the police everything I knew back then, and it wasn't much. We'd been here about six months when he moved in. And then she joined him several months later. When she found out she was pregnant, I reckon.'

'How long had they been going out, do you know?'

Murray was busy scribbling notes as he fired the question and she watched him with interest, answering, 'A year or so I think. They told us they'd met at university when she was in her first year and he was doing his finals. Then he got a job in the City, which was when he moved in downstairs. She used to visit him at weekends and then she moved in.'

'And the day the baby went missing? You were at work I believe?'

'Yes. I'm a radiographer and it was before I had my little girl. I was working full time back then. My husband and I only heard about it when we got back. The place was swarming with your lot and she was in a terrible state. It was awful.'

'And nothing unusual had happened at any point previously that might have drawn your attention, or made you suspicious in any way?'

'No.' The woman hesitated, and Murray waited. 'At least, only what I mentioned to the last inspector who was handling the case.'

'Which was?'

'That they didn't seem to be getting on too well, both before and after the baby came along. We had to bang on the floor several times to get them to quieten down. It was mostly him and we reckoned maybe he drank more than was good for him.'

'Are you saying he was violent?'

'I don't know that he was violent as such. All I do know is that it wasn't very nice having to listen to it, and I did

43

worry about her being pregnant and everything. Things got worse after the child went missing – it was a blessed relief when he moved out not long after.'

'Did you ever talk to her about what you heard?'

'No way. I didn't know her well enough. Still don't. She keeps herself very much to herself.'

Murray stood to go. 'Thanks for your time, Mrs Applemore.'

'Do you think it could be her baby?'

'We don't know yet. It's a possibility.'

'Poor woman. I keep thinking maybe I should go down and say something to her but it's difficult, isn't it? You wouldn't wish what she must be going through on anyone. But as I say, she doesn't exactly encourage friendship.'

CHAPTER FIVE

Hannah walked along the deserted strip of beach and even though the wind blew bitterly cold in her face, she felt at peace for the first time in four days. She loved this stretch of the Suffolk coastline; felt an affinity with it. Slowly but steadily it was being eroded, just as she felt bits of her had been eroded over the last few years. Not visible from the outside maybe, but deep within the thinking, bleeding heart of her.

She hunched into her jacket as she looked out at the cold grey sea. It was rough today, a swirling mass of choppy white horses that rode the crest of the waves until they landed with a noisy crash on the shoreline. She imagined walking into the icy cold water, feeling it seep slowly through her clothes numbing her body, numbing her pain, until she simply disappeared beneath the surface. But it wasn't an option she ever allowed herself to contemplate. Even in her darkest moments, when it had seemed to offer a blessed route of escape, she hadn't seriously considered it. What if they found Sophie alive? What use would she be to her daughter then? But now it didn't seem likely they would find her alive, and the raw pain was devouring her.

Her feet crunched on the shingle as she walked. A sample of her DNA, the sergeant had said when he'd phoned her that morning. Could she come down to the station?

It didn't take much working out to realise they obviously suspected the remains they'd found were Sophie's.

The cold wind stung her eyes. She drew one last breath of the biting air, feeling it whip sharply down her windpipe, before turning back in the direction of her car. There was a new sense of purpose in her eye.

She was tougher now than she'd been before. And this time she'd keep up to speed with everything that was going on. Make a nuisance of herself if necessary. Do every damn thing she needed to make sure that if it was Sophie they'd found, then her abductor would be brought to justice.

She was due back at work tomorrow after three days off, and though she'd been grateful for that time to herself, she was glad that she'd have something to keep her mind occupied. But first there was something she needed to do...

It was raining hard by the time she got there. Pulling the collar of her jacket tighter around her neck, she cast a quick look about her before climbing slowly out of the car.

It hadn't been difficult finding it, she'd simply punched the name of the village into her Satnav and let it do the work, and once she'd arrived, she couldn't miss the collection of police and media cars outside the attractive barn conversion down the quiet country lane. Her steps quickened as she walked towards the house, oblivious to the punishing downpour that was soaking her hair and clothes.

A small crowd stood a short distance away, umbrellas raised and talking amongst themselves. Vultures, she thought contemptuously, hanging around for any bits of gossip they could take back to the supper table.

For a long moment, she stared at the house in front of her, logging every detail to her memory. It was modern with large windows and would be light and airy inside, she could tell. The sort of house she used to imagine she might live in one day, and probably would have done if she and Ben had stayed together. Was it possible her beautiful daughter could have ended her days here? Or were these people like her, innocent victims of another person's immorality?

'Sorry Miss, no-one beyond this point,' a young policeman informed her officiously, stepping forward to halt her progress.

'I need to speak to someone. I need to see where she was found.'

'We'll be issuing another statement in due course. You'll have to wait for that like everyone else I'm afraid. Now please go back to the road.'

Hannah's determination grew. It had to be Sophie, didn't

it? No other babies had gone missing in the area. She had a right to see where they'd found her.

'DCI Murray...' she said abruptly. 'Is he here? He'll speak to me I know.'

The man shook his head but she could see that the mention of the inspector's name had caught his attention, his dogmatic air of assurance wavering.

'Look, I must speak to someone. You don't understand. My name's Hannah Walker. It's possible it was my daughter they found here. I need to see where...'

She tried to choke back the emotion but now that she was here, possibly about to see where Sophie had been buried, it was fast getting the better of her. And it was certainly more than the constable could deal with.

'Wait here,' he said after a moment's hesitation.

He turned away from her, calling someone to take his place as he disappeared up the side of the house. A few minutes later he was back.

'I'm sorry, Miss Walker. DCI Murray isn't here at the moment and I'm afraid we really can't take you through to where the remains were found at this stage.' His expression softened. 'But if you give me your details I'll pass them on and I'm sure DCI Murray will get back to you as soon as he can. There's no point you waiting around here getting soaked.'

'But I need...'

'I'm sorry, Miss.' His tone was final and Hannah gave up, watching as he carefully wrote down her details.

She walked slowly away, ramming a fist into her mouth to check the sobs that were choking her throat.

'Miss Walker! Miss Walker, isn't it?'

A camera flashed, catching her tortured expression perfectly.

'Have they confirmed yet that it's your daughter? Have you got any comments to make?'

Covering her face with her hands she pushed past the

man and ran back to her car, driving off as quickly as she could before anyone else stopped her.

But she'd be back. Later, when it was quiet and everyone had gone.

***

Upstairs from the landing window, Natasha Campbell couldn't help but be moved by the anguish she saw reflected in the other woman's face – even while she felt intimidated somehow by her proximity. Was that her? The mother? Why else would all the press suddenly be swarming towards her? A shiver ran through her as she watched the woman make a dash for her car and drive swiftly away. It was horrible enough having faceless, nameless people tramping over her beloved garden, turning it from the beautiful haven it had once been into the sordid scene of a crime it had now become – without having the threat of a demented woman to contend with. And now she knew where they lived. What if she started hounding them?

'The police constable confirmed it was her,' Natasha said to Adam later that evening when he got in from work. 'You have to *do* something. She could turn up on our doorstep at any time and what would we say to her? How would we handle it? I think you should contact that Inspector Murray and tell him we want some protection.'

'For God's sake, Natasha. What from? She's hardly likely to attack us.'

'You didn't see her, Adam. She looked desperate. And she doesn't know that it wasn't us who harmed her baby, does she? Or what if it *was* her and her partner, and they take it out on us because we're the ones who found her? You're not here half the time. If you won't help me, then I'll call the police myself. It can't be right that she's just free to wander up to our house like that whenever she wants...'

'All right ... all right.' Adam threw his keys down on the table, his voice harassed. 'I'll call the inspector in a little while. Just let me have a shower first, will you?'

Natasha grabbed the phone and thrust it into his hands. 'Do it now, or he'll have gone home'

'I'll send my sergeant around to have a word with your wife tomorrow,' Murray told him a few minutes later. 'I'm quite sure she has nothing to fear from Miss Walker. I'm going to see her myself in the morning. I'll speak to her and make sure she knows not to contact you in any way.'

'Thank you. I hope you don't mind me calling, but Natasha was upset by her visit, and as I explained to your sergeant when he was here, things aren't straight forward with my wife's health at the moment. Anything you can do to make the situation a little easier?'

'Do you mind me asking what your wife's health problems are, Mr. Campbell?'

Adam hesitated, his eyes fixing on Natasha. 'It's complicated,' he said, choosing his words with care. 'She's had some issues with depression and is under the psychiatrist. She's on medication now which is helping, but all this stuff is unsettling for us both.'

'I can understand that. Thanks for explaining it to me. It does help if we know people's backgrounds.'

'So?' Natasha's voice was abrupt as he put the phone down.

'He's going to speak to her in the morning and make sure she doesn't come anywhere near us. And he's sending his sergeant over to have a word with you tomorrow, to reassure you.'

'You think I'm being ridiculous don't you ... *paranoid?*'

'Of course I don't, but I'm sure you have nothing to fear from the woman. She's just grieving like any mother would.'

'Well, it's not right that she comes around to our house and upsets us. It's bad enough that we found those remains without her making us feel worse. I don't want to get ill again, Adam. I saw Amanda today and she said that it's important for me not to get worked up over all this.'

'And haven't I been saying exactly the same?'

'But you're not my therapist. In fact, according to her, you're part of my problem. She said it doesn't solve anything you moving into another bedroom. You need to accept me as I am and both of us work on it from there. I could see she was annoyed that you didn't come today like she asked.'

'You know why that was. Jeanette's got flu and I had to cover two clinics.'

'I'm sure you could have sorted something if you'd wanted to.'

'Natasha, I couldn't.'

'Well, she wants a session with you on your own now. That's *if* you think you can find the time to fit her in? I think it's the least you can do, seeing as you're the one who sent me to her in the first place.'

'It was Dr. Graffe recommended her if you remember? Not me. Anyway, I thought you said she was good?'

Natasha shrugged. 'She's all right. I'm just sick of everyone treating me like I'm some sort of moron.'

'Tash, nobody's treating you like a moron.'

He broke off as Katie wandered into the room in her pyjamas. 'I'm ready now, Mummy. Can I watch television?'

'Have you tidied your room and brushed your teeth?'

'Yes.'

'Show me.'

The little girl opened her mouth.

'You haven't done a very good job on the top teeth. Go and do them again before you watch any television.'

'Ohh…' Katie's face fell and she looked like she was about to cry.

'Come on, Angel,' Adam said, swooping her up into his arms and tickling her. 'Show me how clever you are now that you can brush your teeth all by yourself.'

She started to squeal with delight. 'Will you read me my story tonight, Daddy? I want the one about the witch.'

'I might manage that.'

'I wish you wouldn't do that.' Natasha's voice was sharp

and Adam looked at her in surprise.

'What?'

'Undermine my authority. She has to learn to do these things properly.'

'And she will.' Adam spoke with more patience than he was feeling. 'But she's still young. Now why don't you relax in here for a bit while I have my shower and read her story? I know it's unsettling for you on the days you see Amanda. I'll serve up dinner when I come back down.'

CHAPTER SIX

Hannah switched her phone to silent and shoved her hands deep into the warm lining of her jacket pocket. It was cold in the car without the heater on, and night was drawing in, but she didn't want to draw attention to herself by leaving the engine running.

Ahead of her, camped outside the Campbell's front gate, a couple of photographers were packing their gear into a car, obviously heading home for the night. She waited until they'd driven off before getting out of the car and making her way cautiously towards the house. Through the windows she could see a shadowy figure moving from one room into what she guessed would be the hall. She waited for it to disappear before heading, heart pumping, for the archway at the side of the house. An owl hooted and she jumped, clutching her torch tighter as she made her way quietly around to the back.

The area was mostly grass with large bushy shrubs bordering the edges that afforded her some degree of cover. Something scuttled in the undergrowth making her veer to the left. Instantly the security lights came on. *Shit*. Ducking quickly into the nearest bush, she looked back towards the house. She didn't dare think what might happen if she were to get caught. The papers would make a field day of that one.

No one appeared, and after a couple of minutes she continued on her way, carefully hugging the edge of the shrubbery with the help of the torch. Ahead of her she could make out a row of large rhododendrons acting as a divider in the garden. There were no signs of any disturbance to the ground this side of them, therefore, what she was looking for must be beyond them, in the top part of the garden.

She moved purposefully on, being careful to keep to the shadows, her eyes scouring the darkness ahead of her.

And then she saw it.

There was no warning to prepare her for the stark little

scene she suddenly stumbled across, although the night's shadows cast a slight softening over the harsh reality of it. An area no more than three metres square cordoned off with white tape, surrounded by a larger area of bright yellow tape. Not much different to the countless, similar scenes she'd seen in detective dramas on the tv.

She came to a halt at the outer perimeter and flashed her torch. She couldn't see anything in any great detail, as the immediate area where she assumed the remains had been found was covered by a small plastic tent. It looked stark and bleak.

This, then, was where they'd found her.

She stared at it for several trembling moments, trying to imagine what they'd discovered here. She didn't really want to picture it. She still clung to the image tight in her mind of how Sophie had looked that last time she'd put her down for her nap, wrapped snugly in her shawl, her eyes drooping closed as she drifted peacefully off to sleep in the secure little world that had been created for her. But it had been a false security, her trust misplaced. She'd been let down by her own mother.

A twig snapped loudly in the night behind her making her jump. She spun round. The outline of a man's shape loomed large and threatening over her.

She gave a frightened gasp and without giving herself time to think, hit out instinctively with her torch, feeling the thud as it came into contact with solid, hard chest.

Strong arms grabbed her preventing her from lashing out again, but she fought fiercely, terror driving every thought from her mind except the instinct to survive.

'Stop struggling,' a voice rasped in her ear, 'and I'll let you go. I'm not going to hurt you.'

The cast iron arms were imprisoning her so effectively that her fear was threatening to bubble over into panic.

It wasn't Ben.

She felt the pressure on her arms relax just a little and

she took a gasping breath, forcing herself to be still. Immediately his hold eased. 'That's better,' he said cautiously. 'Let's be calm. Who are you and what are you doing in my garden?'

His voice was low and cultured. It calmed her, but she could feel the tension emanating from him as he stood in front of her.

She couldn't see much of him in the darkness of the night, only enough to know that he was taller than her and broad. It made her feel vulnerable, she realised, confronting the man who could quite possibly have murdered her daughter. Her hand tightened on the hard rubber handle of her torch. It gave her a feeling of reassurance even if it wasn't much of a weapon.

She took a steadying breath. 'My name's Hannah Walker,' she said. 'I needed to see where the baby was found. The police seem to think it might be my daughter.'

He'd known who she was of course, but what he hadn't been prepared for was the tear-stained face exposed by his torchlight. She looked heartbroken, with deep secretive eyes that looked like they harboured a thousand nightmares.

He kept his voice uncompromising. His main concern had to be Natasha. And it would freak her out to know that this woman was in their garden.

'And you had to come sneaking around like this in the dark?'

Even in that dim light he couldn't fail to see the impatience that flared in her eyes.

'So, tell me how you'd have done it? I tried to come earlier but there were reporters everywhere and the police wouldn't let me in. It could be days before they make a proper identification and I can't wait that long. Everyone's saying it must be Sophie. They asked me for my DNA today …' Her voice trailed away, her eyes fixing on that bleak little area again. 'Was it you that found her?'

'I can't discuss that with you.'

'Why not? Have you got something to hide?'

Her question made him feel uncomfortable. As if he did have something to hide.

'Of course not. My wife and I were as horrified as everyone else at the discovery, but the police have forbidden us from talking about it with anyone.'

He was annoyed that he'd allowed himself to be drawn into conversation instead of simply ejecting her from his property. He couldn't clearly see what she looked like in the darkness but there was a vulnerability about her that was getting to him despite the defiant attitude she was adopting. He stiffened his resolve.

'I'm afraid I must ask you to leave. I know how awful it must be for you, but my wife's not been well and all this has been very upsetting for her.'

'*Adam ...?*'

As if on cue, Natasha' voice carried on the night air. Adam flinched, his eyes flitting briefly in the direction of the house.

'I'd rather she didn't know you were here,' he said quickly. 'Do you mind? I'm sure the police will let you come back another time, in daylight.'

Hannah turned back to the excavated piece of ground and stared at it for a long moment. She could not – would not – believe that her daughter had ended her life here in this dump of a hole like some tossed out piece of garbage. She straightened her shoulders.

'It's all right. I don't need to come back. I'll know soon enough if it's Sophie or not. I'm sorry to have disturbed you.'

'Look...' Adam said more gently. He couldn't begin to think what she must be going through.

'*Adam!*' Natasha's voice was more impatient this time.

'You go,' Hannah said. 'I'll leave it a couple of minutes, then I'll follow.'

He hesitated, experiencing a bizarre urge to comfort her.

But really, what else could he say?

Without another word, he turned and headed back to the house. He felt unsettled by the encounter, as if by entering his domain she'd somehow sucked him into the drama that was about to unfold. Of course, whether he liked it or not, he was involved and he had only himself to blame for that. But they could get through it. Hopefully, the Sergeant's visit in the morning would reassure Natasha and then all they needed was to keep their heads down and wait until the police had finished doing their job. Then maybe life could get back to some semblance of normality.

He thought of a pair of eyes staring bleakly into his, and sensed that life hadn't been normal for Hannah Walker in a very long time.

CHAPTER SEVEN

Adam led Sergeant Briscombe into the lounge.

'Thanks for coming, Sergeant. I'm afraid I'm running a bit late and I need to drop our daughter off to school, so, if you don't mind waiting in the lounge my wife will be down in a moment? It threw her yesterday seeing Hannah Walker on our drive. Anything you can say to put her mind at rest?'

'I'll see what I can do, but I'm sure you've got nothing to worry about as far as Miss Walker's concerned.'

'I tried to tell her that, but …' he shook his head.

After he'd gone, Harry looked around the spotless room. It was attractively done, with old oak beams from the original barn still running across the ceiling and down the walls, and huge patio doors opening out onto the large garden. Not many couples in their twenties could afford a house like this. It was certainly a contrast to the semi-detached ground floor flat conversion that Hannah Walker occupied, which he guessed would be rented rather than owned.

He was sitting on the settee looking out of the window when Natasha came in, and once again, he was struck by the extraordinary appeal of her. What was it about her that was so different? She wasn't classically beautiful, but she was stunningly attractive with her delicate features and glossy dark hair swinging alluringly around her shoulders like that. And she was slender as a willow; with small rounded breasts and shapely hips that made a man want to smooth his hands over them.

But it was the expression in her eyes that somehow locked him in. Knowing, was the word that sprang to mind as their gazes met, as if she was drawing him into a world of promise where his every fantasy would be indulged. Sexy as hell - and he hadn't reacted to a woman like that in years.

Get a grip man! He almost laughed out loud at his fanciful imagination. What would she think if she could read his mind?

Natasha walked further into the room. 'Thanks for coming, Sergeant,' she said prettily. 'No, don't get up. I expect you think I'm as mad as my husband does, but all this business is getting to me. It's horrible enough having a discovery like that in your back garden but seeing that woman on my drive yesterday freaked me out.'

'It's understandable, Mrs Campbell. DCI Murray's seeing Miss Walker this morning. I'm sure he'll explain to her why it's not a good idea for her to be seen near here.'

Natasha motioned towards the daily paper lying on the coffee table. 'You've seen what the newspapers are saying? They're still pointing the finger at her and her partner. Have you got any more information yet on whether it is their daughter?'

Harry hesitated. 'We can't say too much at this stage, but I'm afraid I can confirm that they're not the archaeological find you were hoping for. The papers will know the basic facts by later today anyway, so there's no harm me telling you that they reckon the remains have been there a few years – anything up to ten. It's possible it could be Sophie Walker.'

Natasha sank carefully down onto the settee next to him. 'Oh, that's so sad.'

She shivered, the eyes she suddenly turned on him haunted. 'Adam thinks I'm being paranoid, but I do worry about our safety. What if whoever was responsible for that child's death blames us for exposing everything? If they can do it once...'

'I really don't think you need to worry. It's unlikely anyone would risk implicating themselves further like that. And as for Miss Walker, there's nothing at all to indicate that she had anything to do with her daughter's disappearance. I can't imagine for one moment that she'd want to harm you in any way.'

Natasha's frown eased a little, some of the tension leaving her. 'Well if you're sure? It's all so unsettling.'

She made a little movement on the sofa beside him, her leg brushing his, and he was aware of a knee-jerk reaction in his body.

'Do you have children, Sergeant?' she asked, changing the subject.

'Not married. Wedded to the job is the usual accusation I get, and probably quite rightly.'

'What a waste. You're very reassuring. You'd make a good husband, I'm sure.'

The swift change in her mood was disconcerting - the coquettish look in her eye so direct that it unnerved him. He should be putting a mile between them, he thought. But he didn't. The tension in his stomach fanned out pleasurably as he found himself holding that flirtatious gaze; allowing himself to be sucked into it for a brief indulgent moment.

'I'm not so sure about that. Policemen tend to make lousy husbands, the hours they work.'

'So perhaps you're always destined to be someone's lover? Even better. Most women get to a point in their marriage where they need a bit of excitement. Do you have a girl friend?'

He couldn't believe they were having this conversation, and this was where he should be putting an end to it, simply by saying yes, but...

'No, not at the moment as it happens. Too busy.'

She tutted. 'All work and no play.' she mocked softly.

Her hand strayed to his thigh and she grazed it deliberately, her eyes holding his. Harry sucked in his breath. He absolutely knew that if he were to lean forward...

He jumped up from the sofa, not allowing himself to even consider it. 'Makes Harry a dull boy,' he finished for her, grinning.

'Very dull indeed. And getting duller by the minute. Are you frightened of me?'

Now he'd put some distance between them he felt safer. 'Should I be?'

'No. I think we could have fun together.'

'I'm not sure your husband would be too happy about that.'

'Oh, Adam and I haven't been husband and wife in that sense of the word in ages. Ours seems to be more a marriage of convenience these days; though quite who it's convenient to is debatable.'

She crossed one leg delicately over the other and eyed him whimsically.

Harry looked shocked. 'I don't think you should be talking about this to me, Mrs Campbell.'

Natasha shrugged. 'I'm sorry if it embarrasses you but it's no secret amongst our friends that Adam and I have got marriage problems. Act in haste, repent in leisure and all that. Adam married me because I was pregnant with Katrina, and he felt sorry for me because my mother was dying. I'm not sure he ever truly loved me. It's no wonder I've got issues, don't you think?'

Harry looked uncomfortable, wondering how they'd ever got onto such a personal topic. 'I wouldn't want to add to them Mrs Campbell, and …' he took a deep breath, knowing he had to knock this on the head. 'I'd have issues of my own if I allowed anything to develop between us. Apart from anything else, it could cost me my job.'

Natasha's eyes dropped away and she shrugged, reaching for a cigarette. 'No problem. I thought there was something different about you. You looked like you could be up for a bit of fun. But obviously I got it wrong. Thanks for coming and reassuring me about that woman. Shut the door after you, will you?'

It was a dismissal and Harry wasn't used to being dismissed by women. In fact, his instinctive inclination was to grab hold of her right there and then and haul her into his arms – show her that he was more than capable of being up for a bit of fun. But he didn't do it. He looked bemused as he drew further back shaking his head, trying to regain some semblance of professionalism.

'I'm sorry.' He didn't understand why he was the one apologizing, when it was her who was out of line, but he felt wrong footed somehow and it was disconcerting. 'It's not that I don't find you attractive …'

'Don't worry about it, it's no big deal. No need to explain.'

At the door, he was forced to turn back as he remembered something else. His eyes were embarrassed as he cleared his throat. 'I, err ... forgot to say, we'll need to take DNA samples from you and your husband to eliminate you from our enquiries. Can you both come down to the station in the next day or so do you think? I'll get someone to call you to fix an appointment?'

Natasha nodded but her eyes were softly taunting, reminding him of the pleasures he'd just passed over. 'I'm sure that won't be a problem,' she said amiably. 'But I'd much rather you came here yourself; to take it personally.'

She grinned when he made no response to that, and got up to see him out. 'See you around, Detective Sergeant. And don't forget. I'm here if you're feeling lonely.'

The gleam in her eye lingered as she watched him go. Poor Adam didn't know the half of it, thinking she'd only had the one affair. He'd definitely leave her if he knew the full extent of it. She sighed. What it boiled down to was the fact that she couldn't give him what he needed and he couldn't give her what she needed. Simple as that. Two misfits struggling in a marriage that was falling apart. Adam needed someone who could be honest and open about everything, tackling and solving their issues together – presenting a united front as he put it. And while she rather liked the idea of all that, the reality was that she was incapable of doing it. She wasn't interested in delving beneath the surface of people's emotions – it was too dark a place to be. She liked to be admired, desired. It might seem shallow but it was how she functioned best. If someone

61

wasn't fancying her she felt worthless - and all the counselling in the world couldn't change that.

She felt a moment's panic. She didn't want to lose Adam, she relied on him so heavily for everything. But she'd given him his chance and he'd turned her down. If this flirtation with DS Briscombe came to anything – and she hoped it might, then he had only himself to blame.

Remembering the sergeant, she smiled. For some reason, he reminded her of Zach and that first time she'd gone with him at the Sixth Form Dance.

She shook her head. God things had to be bad when she was relying on memories for her thrills. But she couldn't help it, she'd felt so powerful. It had been the start of a whole new world for her …

'*Go on Tash, you can do it,*' her friend Penny had shouted over the sound of thumping music. 'We all know Zach fancies the pants off you. If you can get some dope off him I'll do your maths homework for a week.'

'You're on, it's a deal!'

Biding her time, she'd waited until she saw him head outside with a couple of mates in the direction of the football pitch. Then, making sure he saw her, she'd sauntered casually in the opposite direction towards the little copse that ran along the edge of the pitch. Once there, she lit a cigarette, and waited. It wasn't long.

'You know this is out of bounds?' he'd said, coming to a halt in front of her. He was tall and blond, and confidence oozed from every pore.

She'd feigned surprise. 'Is it?' She took a deep drag on her cigarette and looked around. 'How do you bear to live in this dump? Bet you're really glad this is your last year. It's all so old. At least our school was built in the twentieth century.'

His lip curled. 'You don't get it, do you? That's part of its tradition. Both my father and my grandfather came here. I expect my son will too.'

'God! Poor kid.'

'If you're going to be rude...'

'Sorry.' She laughed carelessly and sat down on a bench, crossing her legs so that he got a good flash of thigh beneath the skimpy skirt. 'It's just been such a crap evening I could really do with a joint. Don't suppose you've got any spare?'

He followed the movement of her legs with his eyes. 'I have as it happens. How much do you want?'

'Just enough for tonight. Only trouble is I've got no cash. Can I pay you next week?'

His eyes moved back to her face and the smile he gave her was disdainful. 'Are you kidding? I've only got a small amount spare and there are people queuing up for it. I'm not about to give it away.'

'So,' she'd turned her dark, provocative gaze onto him, 'perhaps we can come to some other arrangement for payment then?'

His look was suspicious. 'What do you mean?'

She rose from her seat and very slowly, her eyes not leaving his, her hands moved up to undo the top two buttons of her blouse. She may not have much to thank her father for and a lot of reasons to despise him, but if there was one thing he'd taught her well, it was how to manipulate men.

She heard his sharp intake of breath before he let out a derisive laugh. 'Don't be ridiculous, you can't persuade me like that.'

'Can't I? Why not? Are you gay or something?'

'No, I'm not!' His eyes locked on her chest. 'But I'm not stupid either. Certainly not stupid enough to be taken in by a tease like you.'

Her voice was softly taunting. 'I'm no tease, Zach. I never start what I'm not prepared to finish.'

She undid two more buttons and pulled the folds apart to reveal the gentle swell of softly rounded breasts – unencumbered by any bra and surprisingly full.

She took a step towards him. 'Are these ridiculous?' she

63

mocked softly.

He moistened his lips. He seemed unable to shift his eyes.

'What are you suggesting? Are you crazy or something?'

Her next action left him in no doubt of her intentions as she trailed her hand lightly over the front of his trousers and gave him a gentle squeeze.

'I'm suggesting I could take care of this for you,' she whispered.

She heard his sharp intake of breath as he jerked himself compulsively into her manipulating fingers.

A couple more squeezes and she knew she had him exactly where she wanted him. 'I'm just offering you a fair deal,' she murmured reasonably, withdrawing her hand. 'I want some dope and I'm prepared to pay for it. But it's up to you. Take it or leave it.'

Without another word, she'd turned her back on him and headed further into the woods. For a moment, there was silence. Then she heard his feet padding softly after her.

Afterwards she'd been stunned. She'd never experienced anything like it before – the sheer sense of power that had gone to her head with such dizzying effect. She'd never expected to enjoy sex after what she'd been through but she'd experienced her first ever explosive climax in that brief encounter.

Smiling at the memory, Natasha moved over to the hall window to watch Harry as he drove away. Yes, that had been the start of it, she realised – the powerful moment when she'd turned from being manipulated to becoming the manipulator. And men were so incredibly easy to manipulate.

But it had become something of an addiction and it was costing her huge. The biggest casualty being her marriage. All the psycho-babbling she'd undergone had blamed her problems on the abusive childhood she'd had. They talked about things like personality and attachment disorders. It was all a load of bollocks as far as she was concerned, but if it kept everyone happy thinking they'd got her labelled...

She lit another cigarette and took a deep drag. She should forget about this thing with Sergeant Briscombe really. It was undoubtedly asking for trouble getting involved with a policeman. Yet a fling with him might be just what she needed to distract her – keep her mind off everything.

And anyway, what else was she supposed to do when her husband had moved into another bedroom and showed no signs of ever coming out?

CHAPTER EIGHT

"Anguish or Guilt?" the headline screamed. Hannah stared at the picture horrified. It was the one they'd taken of her outside the Campbell's house the previous day.

'Is this the tortured face of a mother in anguish?' the article read, 'or the guilt of someone about to be exposed? Seven years ago, I followed the case of little Sophie Walker closely. I maintained then, and I still maintain, that the handling of that investigation was a shambles. There were a number of questions that were never answered adequately by either the police, or Hannah Walker and her partner. I sincerely hope that if these do turn out to be Sophie's remains, this time around, the police will leave no stone unturned in their quest for the truth. I'll continue to follow the investigation closely and do not intend to let excuses of poor resources and manpower be a justification for inefficient management of this case. Whoever was guilty of this heinous crime – and only they know who they are – must know that their days of freedom are numbered. We owe it to our children to protect them.'

The signature at the bottom of the article came as no surprise to Hannah, and she flung the paper angrily down on the chair. *Robert Lawrence.* It was almost as if the man had a personal vendetta against her and Ben. His sensationalist innuendos had done much to sway the public tide of opinion against them during the last investigation, yet they'd been powerless to do anything about him then, and no doubt she'd be powerless again this time around. Picking up her handbag she headed for the door. Once she was at work she could keep herself busy – clear her head of all this for a few blessed hours.

She opened the door and reeled back at the sight of DCI Murray on her doorstep.

'Ah ... Miss Walker. Sorry to call so early. Have I caught you at a bad time?'

'I was just leaving for work.'

'Shouldn't take too long if you can spare me a minute?'

Hannah looked at her watch impatiently. 'I don't want to be late Inspector. This is my first day back.'

'I'll be as quick as I can then.'

She opened the door wider to let him in. 'Look … if you're here about last night.'

'What about last night?'

'Oh, nothing.'

'Are you being bothered at all?'

'No, it was nothing.'

She picked the newspaper up from the chair and showed it to him. 'Have you seen this?'

'Yes. It doesn't exactly sing our praises either.'

'No, but this man caused enough trouble for us during the last investigation. Between him and DCI Hedges I think half the country thought Ben and I had something to do with Sophie's disappearance. Can he get away with insinuations like these? Isn't it libellous or something?'

'I think you'll find he'll be very careful about how he phrases things but you can always take advice from a solicitor?'

'Yes.' The look she threw at him said it all. She tossed the paper back down on the chair and turned to him.

'What did you want to talk to me about?'

'Perhaps you'd like to sit down?'

Her pulse raced. Was this it? Had he come to say it was Sophie?

'I've come to tell you that we've had some preliminary results back from the pathologist,' Murray said without preamble. 'In a nut-shell, they've confirmed that the remains that were discovered are those of a very young baby, only a few weeks old. They've been lying there for anything between five and ten years.'

His voice softened when he saw her expression. 'I'm sure you realise that means there's a possibility it could be your daughter?'

'Was it a girl?' Her voice was strained.

'We can't tell with a skeleton so small I'm afraid. We'll need your DNA to definitely confirm things one-way or the other. I believe someone's already rung you about that?'

Hannah nodded. 'I'm going down to the police station this afternoon, after work.'

'Good. In the meantime,' he paused, referring briefly to his notebook, 'I have a couple of things I'd like to clarify with you if possible, just to set the record straight? Your next-door neighbour, Mrs Morrison – the one you say was out in her garden at the time your daughter went missing. Do you know where she lives now? There's nothing in the old notes to show she'd moved and we may need to take another statement off her at some point.'

Hannah shook her head. 'We weren't close. The only thing we had in common was that her daughter was pregnant the same time as I was – though you'd never have believed it to look at her.' She shook her head reminiscently. 'I remember bumping into them once when I was six months pregnant and already huge, and she hardly looked pregnant at all. Then there was some family crisis not long after Sophie went missing and she went to live with her daughter to help out. Somewhere in Enfield is all I know.'

'Thank you.' He jotted something down in his notebook then looked at her piercingly.

'I spoke to a couple of your other neighbours yesterday. The tenants upstairs mentioned that you and your boyfriend were arguing a lot before your daughter went missing and that the rows escalated afterwards. My predecessor also mentions that he found Mr. Short to be very 'hostile' throughout the investigation. It's a sensitive question I know, but do you mind me asking if you ever suspected your boyfriend of being involved in your daughter's disappearance?'

Hannah tried to hide her frustration. She needed him to

stay focused on any new angles he might bring to the investigation, not waste time going over old ground.

She sighed. 'Things weren't good between us and we'd had a row that morning. I'd be lying if I said the thought never occurred to me. But that's the awful thing about situations like this. You end up being suspicious of everything and everyone. I never seriously considered it … not really.'

She broke off, thinking back to that time. Their grief had acted briefly as a unifier before it had driven the final, impenetrable wedge between them that had ended their relationship. She recalled the image of Ben bending over the pram. She'd turned away before he'd straightened up – hadn't actually *seen* him walking away. And he was a man of impulse. Especially when he was angry.

'No,' she said, more sharply than she intended. 'I can't believe he'd have done something like that.'

'Can't believe, or don't want to believe?' Murray asked.

Her eyes misted over. Was she now to accept that on top of all the other mistakes she'd made, she'd fallen in love with a man who could murder his own child?

'I notice he was very much in the public eye when it was all going on,' Murray continued, '– doing the appeals on the television, giving interviews. Did that bother you?'

It had. A lot.

'Yes. He felt it was the only way of keeping her disappearance fresh in people's minds and I got that, but I didn't like it. I felt there was a part of him that was enjoying the attention too much. He was a bit like that – loved the limelight.'

'These sorts of things put an incredible strain on a relationship, I know. It wouldn't have been easy for either of you.'

'No. We split up six weeks after she went missing.'

She could feel his eyes on her, penetrating. Seeing more than she wanted him to see.

'One more thing.' He pointed to the newspaper lying on the chair. 'One of my men told me you visited the house where the baby was found yesterday afternoon.'

'Yes. I'm sorry. I probably shouldn't have...'

'I must caution you against any contact with the couple living there, or visiting the place again without my strict permission beforehand. If confirmation comes through that it is your daughter, then I'll take you myself. Until then, all it does is give more fodder to the Press. I'm sure you understand?'

Hannah nodded. 'It was a stupid thing to do. I don't know what came over me. I just had to go when your sergeant phoned about the DNA. Up until then I'd been so convinced that Sophie was still alive.'

'Why do you say that?'

Hannah met his gaze. 'Because I feel I'd know if she was dead.'

Inspector Murray snapped his notebook shut and made to rise. 'Well, let's hope you're right,' he said gently. 'It shouldn't be too long now before we know.'

***

Hannah rushed into the warm, cosy staff room, stripping off her coat as she went. She'd missed the sights, sounds and smells of the school she realised as she hung up her coat. They washed over her now like a soothing balm, shrouding the other darkness in her mind.

The door opened and Harriet, the school secretary, popped her head around it.

'Hey, Hannah. I thought I saw you come in. Miss Williams asked if you could go and see her before lessons start.'

'Sure...' It was an unusual request and a flicker of unease trickled down her spine. 'Shall I come now?'

'If you're ready.'

'What about the kids?'

'Don't worry, Maggie's standing in for you.'

'Oh … right.'

Ten minutes later she was staring at the Headmistress in disbelief.

'You're firing me?'

'Absolutely not. I'm suggesting you take some extended leave. I'm sorry, Hannah. I tried to talk the Governors out of it but they were adamant. They called an emergency meeting last night and decided it was their only option until we know more about the facts of the case.'

'But that's so unfair. The police haven't even confirmed that it's my daughter yet, and there's no evidence to say I've done anything wrong. And I haven't...'

'Don't you think I know that? I put your case as strongly as I could but some of the Governors felt you should have mentioned your history at your interview.'

'It was nothing to do with them,' she said heatedly. 'Or my job. I was trying to put it behind me.'

Miss Williams sighed. 'I get that, and I promise I'll fight your corner as hard as I can. But at the moment my hands are tied. I hate to say this, but we've already had two parents expressing concern that you're teaching their children...'

She held up her hand when Hannah would have interrupted.

'I'd stress that I've had a lot more parents go out of their way to say you have their full confidence and support – including the parent representatives on the Board. So, don't think all is lost. But for the time being, all I can suggest is that you make the most of taking some leave on full pay. I'll keep you updated on what's going on. I'm sorry.'

Hannah lips tightened. 'This'll be something else the press will have a field day over, you realise that? It's tantamount to saying the school doesn't have confidence in me.'

'It's nothing of the sort,' Miss Williams stated firmly. 'And I'll make it my business to reflect that in my statement. I'm sorry. I wouldn't have done this to you for the world if I could have avoided it.'

Hannah got up from her chair. She was hardly aware of clearing her belongings from the staff room. Sophie's abduction had robbed her of two years of her life. It had been an enormous step for her to go back to university and then do her teacher's training. Her job was the one thing she'd been depending on to carry her through this latest development. Now that had been stripped away it left her vulnerable to the depression she knew could be so destructive. She needed to talk to someone before she locked herself up in her flat and never came out again.

Half an hour later she was pulling up outside Silver Lining Interior Designs in Hertford.

She could see Jess working on the window display, a frown of concentration on her brow as she carefully draped a swathe of brightly coloured material so that it hung in soft folds from the ceiling. Seeing her friend at the window Jess waved and beckoned her in.

'What's up?' she said seeing Hannah's face.

Hannah told her.

'Oh, Hannah. That's terrible. What are you going to do about it?'

'Not a lot I can do. I'll just have to sit it out. But it'll drive me nuts sitting at home all day doing nothing.'

'Come here and work with me.' Jess said straight away, abandoning her task and moving into the little kitchen to put the kettle on. 'I can't afford to pay you much, but there's always plenty to do.'

Hannah was taken aback at the offer. 'But I don't know anything about interior design.'

'What's to know? It's only a question of going through the books with the clients, helping them choose materials and the like. You've got a good eye for fashion. It's no different.'

She grinned. 'And if the practical side doesn't grab you, there's always plenty of invoicing and paperwork.' She waved a mug in the air. 'Not to mention making coffee. You won't be idle, believe me.'

'I don't know...'

'You might even enjoy it,' Jess suggested gently 'dealing with Joe public. I know you love your job but you have rather buried yourself in it this last couple of years.'

'I haven't exactly felt like partying.'

'I know you haven't, and I'm not trivialising what you've gone through. But you know, you've got your whole life ahead of you still. It would be nice to see you let your hair down a bit sometimes.'

Hannah's look was indignant. 'I do let my hair down.'

'Compared to what you used to be like, you don't.'

'Well you may not have noticed, but things have changed, Jess. We've grown up for a start.'

'I know, but...'

'What?'

'Forget it, now isn't the time with all this going on.'

'Come on. You obviously need to get something off your chest.'

'Look, it just upsets me seeing what's happened to you, that's all. You're young and you should be out there having a good time, meeting men even. What happened with Sophie was terrible and I'm not suggesting for one minute that you *ever* get over something like that. But you can't go on punishing yourself forever.'

Hannah stiffened. 'I'm not punishing myself, and I certainly don't need another man complicating my life.'

'Not all men are like Ben – or even your Dad. There are some good marriages out there.'

'And there are some crappy ones too. You and Fraser are lucky.'

'Yes, we are, and that's why I hate it when you dismiss your own chances of finding someone decent. We can all manage on our own but it's a million times better when you've got someone who loves you at your side.'

'Well…' Hannah got up from the table and walked over to the sink with her cup. 'We'll just have to agree to differ on that one. I'm not interested in meeting anyone and that's all there is to it. I'll come and work with you though if you're serious about that? As long as you think you can put up with me – miserable cow that I am!'

Jess grinned. 'I think I can manage – and that's brilliant news. We'll have a ball.'

'And the even better news for you is that you don't need to pay me anything, because I've been suspended on full pay. I'd feel bad about if I didn't feel so angry over the injustice of it all. So, when can I start?'

'Today if you like? Unless you'd prefer to start after the weekend?'

'No. Today would be great, otherwise I'll only go home and drive myself mad thinking about everything…'

She broke off; frowning as a thought suddenly struck her. Jess eyed her quizzically. 'Now what?'

Hannah shook her head. Something had been bothering her all morning, plucking away at her subconscious like an irritating itch. Something to do with the inspector's visit that morning.

And she'd just realised what it was.

'I don't know,' she said cautiously, giving the thoughts in her head time to form some clarity. 'It's probably nothing, but … something the Inspector said to me this morning. Do you remember that woman, Joan, who used to live next door to me? The one who was out in the garden the day I put Sophie out there?'

'Vaguely. I think I may have seen her once or twice.'

'Well, her daughter was supposedly pregnant the same time as I was. Joan told me our due dates were almost identical. But I was telling the police how I bumped into them once when I was six months gone and huge, and she hardly looked pregnant at all. Joan said later that she'd been the same with *her* first child – hadn't shown until the last couple of months. But…' she drew a breath, excitement in her eyes, 'what if she wasn't pregnant?' What if it was Joan who took Sophie for her daughter?'

Jess's look was dubious. 'The police would have checked that out, hon, surely?'

'They never told me, if they did.'

Hannah's face was fierce with concentration. 'They might not even have known Joan had a daughter if she didn't tell them. And why should she? As far as I know all she did was give a statement to the fact that she saw me put Sophie out in the garden. And then she moved out about three months later. There was nothing suspicious about her behaviour. But I'm telling you … the more I think about it, the more I don't believe her daughter wasn't pregnant at all that day. I can't believe I didn't think of it before'

'Hannah,' Jess looked uncomfortable, clearly awkward about challenging her friend. 'I know you're desperate to find Sophie, but it's not that easy for someone to simply conjure a baby up out of thin air. There's so much red tape these days. I know you're desperate to find Sophie, but –'

'You're right.' Hannah's eyes glinted passionately, 'I am desperate to find her. Wouldn't you be? It never goes away, Jess. Sometimes I'm back there in the garden that day putting her down for her nap, just wishing I could have that time over again so I could do things differently. But I can't …the only thing I can do is try my hardest to find her. I'm not saying it *was* Joan who took her; all I'm saying is that it's a possibility. Surely you can see that?'

'She'd have had to have planned things very carefully.'

'Of course she would, but she had plenty of time while I was pregnant.'

Jess's concerned features were still doubtful as Hannah pulled out her phone and switched it on.

'What are you doing?'

'Phoning the police,' Hannah said purposefully, looking up the number that DCI Murray had given her. 'To see if they'll look into it. And if they won't, then I'll do it myself.'

CHAPTER NINE

Murray looked up as Harry walked into his office with mid-morning sandwiches and a couple of coffees on a tray.

'Ah – good lad. I missed breakfast this morning so I could get to Hannah Walker's before she left for work.'

'How did you get on interviewing her old neighbours yesterday?'

'Nothing new. They just confirmed what's already on file. Nobody I spoke to, who knew her, believed she could have been guilty of anything. Interestingly the same couldn't be said for the boyfriend. He was described as a bit of a good time boy; moneyed stockbroker with a taste for the high life and a bit of a temper on him. The people upstairs said the shouting had come from him more than her, and had been going on both before and after the baby was born. It's much as Hedges documented. I've still got a couple of people to see, but here...'

He fished his notebook out of his pocket and copied something onto a slip of paper. 'See if you can track down this lady, Joan Morrison. Might be living in the Enfield area. She's the witness who saw Hannah Walker put the baby out in the garden. It's probably a complete waste of time but I've just had a call from Ms. Walker who now seems to think that it might be her who took her baby. Apparently, Mrs Morrison's daughter was pregnant at the same time as Hannah Walker; only Miss Walker reckons she bumped into them in the town centre and that the daughter didn't look pregnant at all. Now she says that having thought about it, she doesn't reckon she was pregnant.' He sighed. 'It's a long shot but Hedges doesn't make any mention of interviewing any daughter so we might as well check it out. There's nothing in the original file other than Joan Morrison's pretty brief statement about the events of that day.'

Harry took the paper. 'I'll look into it. Did you speak to Miss Walker about not visiting the Campbells' house?'

'Yes. I don't think she'll bother them again. What about you? How did you get on with the wife this morning?'

Harry got busy with some papers on the desk. 'Fine ... I, uh, think she was reassured. I get the impression all's not as it could be between her and her husband though.'

'Oh?'

'Just something she said.'

'I suppose I ought to go and see her myself. I'll get around to it in the next day or two. How did you get on yesterday tracking down Hannah Walker's boyfriend?'

'His parents have given us his address but apparently he's away on business, due back this evening they thought. I've left a message on his answerphone.'

'Good. It would be interesting to see what sort of bloke he is and I'd like to know what the cause of their split was. I reckon she gave him the elbow because he was enjoying too high a profile with the media. Here ... I've had the notes typed up from my interviews with Miss Walker's neighbours. Take a look at them and see if I've missed anything. Two sets of eyes, and all that.'

Murray was putting his coat on that evening when the phone rang. It had been a long day and he frowned. He'd been looking forward to getting home at a reasonable time for a change and Thursday night was the only good night for television as far as he was concerned.

He picked the handset up with a flourish. 'Murray.'

'Oh Inspector, it's Adam Campbell here. I understand your Sergeant visited my wife this morning?'

'That's right sir. He reassured her I hope?'

'Yes, she was very grateful. We were just wondering how long it might be before we get our garden back to ourselves? It's not very pleasant looking out of the window and seeing your men traipsing around.'

'That's a difficult one. Obviously, forensics need to do a thorough job and we have to keep the area clear from contamination, but I'll speak to them, see if they can give me a rough idea. I wouldn't have thought it would be long now.'

'Thanks. My wife also mentioned about giving DNA samples. Is that really necessary at this stage?'

'It's to help us eliminate you both from the investigation, Mr. Campbell.'

'Well, to be frank, we're not comfortable with the thought of it. You hear all too often about people's DNA sitting around on some database or other for years to come.'

Murray sighed; it wasn't an unfamiliar path to him. 'I hear what you're saying sir, but it's not an unreasonable request. We could be dealing with a murder enquiry here and we need to eliminate you. I have to ask myself why you'd want to refuse. It might not look very good for you.'

'I'm not interested in how it looks. We've got nothing to hide but I'm afraid the System doesn't inspire confidence, and the fact remains that once you've taken our DNA, that's it, you've got it. One more area of our civil rights eroded. And if the previous investigation is anything to go by it could be another six years – if ever, before this case gets solved. If it's all the same to you I'd like to take some legal advice.'

Murray sighed, his voice becoming curt. 'If that's how you feel I can't force you at this stage of the investigation. I can assure you though that we're working hard to solve this case and all I can do is stress that it would be very helpful to us if you'd agree to undergo a DNA test.'

There was a short silence on the other end of the line.

'Noted, Inspector. I'll get back to you once I've taken some advice.'

The line clicked and Murray slammed the phone down his end. 'Bloody human rights,' he muttered.

On the other end of the line, Adam also replaced the receiver.

'What did he say? Will they be leaving soon?' Natasha's eyes as she looked at him were intent.

'He's going to speak to the forensic team. He seemed to think it won't be too long now.'

Natasha shook her head. 'It's a bore, and it's not healthy for Katie seeing all this going on. What's she supposed to make of it all? I think you should have stressed the impact it's having on her more strongly.'

Adam's lips tightened at the criticism. 'It's not upsetting her; she's too young to know what's going on.'

'Don't you believe it. Kids take in more than we adults realise and it's our duty as her parents to protect her. You should have told him.'

'Natasha, the police aren't going to put a stop to whatever they need to do just because of Katie. If you're worried about the impact it's having on her then let her stay over at Mum's for a few days. She'd be happy there and mum would love to have her.'

'Then what would you and I have to talk about?' Natasha asked coldly. 'No thanks – I'd rather keep my daughter here where I can keep an eye on her. All this stuff's making me jumpy.'

Adam's gaze was deceptively casual. There'd been a suppressed nerviness about her this last couple of months that made him wonder if she was teetering on the edge of another attack. And none of this was helping. It had occurred to him that she might be back on the weed but he couldn't ask of course. She'd take that as him not having faith in her, not trusting her.

'You are still taking your tablets, Tash?'

'Of course, I am. What do you take me for?'

She ground her cigarette out viciously in the ashtray. 'All this is your fault, you realise that? If you hadn't found those bloody bones we wouldn't have the police traipsing about everywhere and I wouldn't be feeling like this. I'm beginning to think you did it deliberately just to get at me.'

'Don't be so bloody ridiculous. Why would I do that?'

She shrugged, her look dispassionate. 'I don't know

Adam. I really don't. But sometimes I think I don't know you at all.'

'Oh, for Christ's sake!' He took a deep breath and modified his tone. 'Look, you're tired and stressed ... we both are. How about I go and give Katie her bath while you get the supper on? Then you can listen to her doing her reading homework before she goes to bed. It'll cheer you both up.'

'No!' Natasha's voice was sharp as she rose from her chair. 'I'll bath Katie from now on. She's getting to an age where she might not like you doing it.'

Adam felt every muscle in his body stiffen. 'Don't be ridiculous. She's a child. It'll be a few years yet before she starts going shy on us.'

'I don't care.'

Adam's eyes narrowed. 'What are you saying, Tash? That I can't even bath my own daughter now? Because if you are ...'

'You'll what?' Natasha challenged, her chin lifting defiantly. 'Leave me? Leave your precious daughter? I don't think so, Adam.'

She held his gaze just a little longer before turning away and heading for the door. 'You can peel some veg while I'm bathing her. The casserole's already in the oven.'

CHAPTER TEN

The pub was a warm haven after the bitterly cold weather outside and surprisingly full for a Thursday night. Hannah rubbed her hands and scanned the throng, until her eyes came to rest on a figure sitting at a table close to the fire.

He hadn't changed much, she thought grimly, taking in the sleek fashionable hairstyle and pinstripe suit. He'd always presented a flawless image to the outside world. And just seeing him sitting there was enough to unsettle her – bring the memories storming back.

She hadn't spoken to Ben for two weeks the summer they'd split up over the handcuff episode, and with that and the tensions surrounding her father moving back in, she'd gone a little mad, finding herself hanging around with a crowd she didn't usually mix with, smoking, drinking, partying hard – wishing the holiday away so she could get back to university. Trying to forget about those handcuffs and how terrified she was that he might be right. What if she was one of those oddballs who needed weird sex to enjoy it?

She'd tried to erase him from her mind but with the strained silences between her and her parents, it had only made her miss him the more. And when one Friday lunch time she'd found him waiting for her outside the pub where she had a holiday job – leaning nonchalantly against the side of his shiny Audi convertible, her heart had flipped, even though she made a show of ignoring him and walking past.

In a flash, he'd moved swiftly around to block her path, his smile rueful.

'I've missed you, Han ...'

Somehow his hand had found hers. 'Why didn't you return any of my calls? Don't you think you've punished me enough? At least come for a ride with me so we can talk?'

'There's no point.'

He smiled beguilingly. 'Of course there is. Please...?'

She'd allowed him to edge her over to the passenger door, maintaining her frosty silence as she climbed in and waited for him to join her.

'How's your dad?' he asked solicitously. 'I heard from Ed that he's not good.'

She shrugged, not looking at him. 'He's got something wrong with his heart, so he says. He's been having tests at the hospital but they haven't shown anything. I think it's just a ploy to get mum back because his fancy woman's had enough of him.'

The tears welled in her eyes. It was such a strain trying to be normal when all the time she felt her life was in tatters. She hated the fact that her anger against her father was destroying her relationship with her mother. Hated the fact that she knew she was acting like a stroppy teenager all over again. Yet she seemed unable to do anything about it.

'Oh, babe,' he'd pulled her into the curve of his shoulder, 'I bet your mum's busy looking after him, but who's looking after you?'

'I don't need looking after...'

His arm had tightened. 'Of course you do. What's your mum thinking about that she can't see that?'

He comforted her, drawing her head down onto his shoulders, and she felt herself relaxing for the first time in what seemed like ages. Ben always seemed to know how she was feeling. He tapped right into the heart of her unhappiness. If he could understand it, why couldn't her mother?

'Why don't you come back to mine for a while?' he asked finally, breaking the silence. 'We can talk things through there.'

She pulled back from him and looked at him solemnly. He held his hands up with a flash of his easy smile.

'No handcuffs I promise, just you and me, talking. I've

83

missed you so much, Han. I haven't had a good night's sleep since you left. You belong to me. You know you do. I want to look after you and put a smile back on that gorgeous face.' He leant forward and kissed her gently on the lips.

And that was all it had taken, she realised later. Back in his flat she'd tried to explain how his actions had made her feel, but he'd seemed nonplussed, putting her reaction down to her naiveté.

'Loads of people mess around with stuff like that ... it's nothing to be ashamed of. It makes things more exciting.'

'It doesn't!' she flashed angrily. 'Can't you understand that? I hated it. It made me feel humiliated, like you had no respect for what I wanted. And you didn't even use a condom. How could you have done that?'

He shrugged. 'Got a bit carried away I guess. It feels so much better without. But I'm sorry.'

'You should be. I had to go down to the chemist and get the morning-after pill. And then I was ill so I don't even know if it will have worked. What if I'm pregnant?'

She was sitting next to him on the settee and he'd pulled her stiff body closer. 'I'd love it,' he whispered, nuzzling her hair, his lips grazing the soft hollow in her neck. 'It would make you mine and tie you to me forever.' He tightened his grip. 'I've missed you so much.' he whispered huskily. 'Have you missed me?'

She stifled a stab of guilt at just how off the rails she'd gone this last couple of weeks. She'd been so unhappy she'd acted like a tart. But it was his fault for pushing her to it.

She could feel his heart beating through his shirt. She drew back and looked into his eyes – those incredibly vivid blue eyes, and knew she was lost. She *had* missed him. Missed him like hell. She felt as if he was the only one who really cared about her. And all couples had their ups and downs, didn't they? He might not be perfect, but then, neither was she.

A month later she'd known she was pregnant. And

within two days of doing the test she'd dropped out of her university course and moved in with him.

Dismissing the memories, Hannah braced herself before pushing her way through the crowded room to where he sat. It was the first time she'd seen him in over five years.

'Hello Ben.'

He jumped up, his eyes sweeping over her before returning to her face.

'I ordered you a Pinot Grigio,' he said, indicating the glass on the table. 'I know it's your favourite.'

She tried not to resent that he was controlling her already. 'Thanks.'

She stood by the fire, warming herself for a few moments before taking the chair opposite him.

'You look good,' he said, watching as she removed her jacket. 'I like your hair.'

'You didn't get me here to tell me that.'

'No.' He looked nervously around. 'The police rang. They want to interview me.'

'So?'

'So, I need to know what to say. How much you've told them. Do they know ... everything?'

She was tempted to let him stew on it, but, 'I didn't tell them you knocked me around, if that's what you mean. I felt it would probably only complicate matters when we need them to concentrate on any new leads they might find.'

'Good. My thoughts exactly. I don't want the bastards wasting their time knocking at my door again.'

Hannah stared at him, her eyes hard. 'If anything were to come to light that made me begin to doubt you, I'd tell them everything – you know that don't you?'

'Well you won't find anything,' he dismissed. 'And neither will they. Anyway, what about our agreement? You agreed to keep silent if I moved out. Are you going back on your word now?'

There was a hint of menace to his tone that instantly jabbed at the ball of unease coiled in her stomach.

'No, but...'

'Good.' His voice was perfectly smooth again. 'It's irrelevant anyway. You know I wouldn't have hurt her. And I've changed. Only you seemed to have that effect on me. I was just stressed with the new job and everything. I still think about you, you know.'

Incredibly, his voice had softened, his eyes doing that thing of looking at her as if she was the only woman in the world. 'What we had was really special,' he said, reaching for her fingers. 'They say you never forget your first love.'

She moved her hand before he could get a grip.

'What we had was toxic and destructive,' she said coldly, 'and it was the best thing for both of us that we got out of it. Was there anything else you wanted to talk to me about before I leave? I don't want to see you again after this.'

She saw anger flicker briefly in his eyes before he masked it again.

'I don't know what to say to the police.'

'Say what you want. You could even try telling the truth, though I doubt that somehow. They'll probably ask you why we split up. I told them the pressure of it all got too much for us.'

'Well, that was certainly true.' His expression was bitter as he took a swig from his beer. 'Anyway, it probably won't be her so there's no point getting worked up about it. I'm getting married by the way – in September. I could do without all this rearing its ugly head.'

She wanted to ask him whether he hit his fiancée too, but she refrained. It all seemed such a long time ago now and irrelevant. Looking at him, it suddenly dawned on her. She was over him. She was free.

No-one, when she'd finally told people what he was like, had been able to comprehend the incredible power he seemed to wield over her. Neither had she. And breaking free of it

86

had been hard, especially with all the problems surrounding Sophie's disappearance. Yet somehow, she'd done it. Found the strength to tell him it was over.

And now she could see him exactly for what he was. A manipulating bully. She felt a sudden sympathy for the unknown woman.

'How's your mother?' Ben asked, changing the subject.

Hannah's response was curt. 'She's fine. Everything's good.'

'You got over your nervous breakdown then?'

'It wasn't a breakdown, Ben. I reacted no differently than any other mother in those circumstances. I'm fine now.'

She felt an urgent need to escape. Seeing him tonight was bringing everything back, tightening that twist in her gut. 'I can't stop long, so unless there's anything else you wanted to say?'

He shrugged. 'Not really. I just wanted to know what you'd said to the police and to see you again – for old time's sake.'

Before she realised his intention, he snaked a hand out to trace a finger lightly along the back of her hand. 'You're still in my system, Han. You'll always hold a special place in my heart, you know that don't you?'

'Don't.' She snatched her hand away, scraping her chair back as she arose abruptly from the table and stared coldly down at him.

'Don't contact me again, Ben. I have no feelings left for you and there's certainly no place for you in my heart. I don't think I can state the situation any clearer than that.'

She didn't wait to see his response before she turned and walked away.

It took her the whole journey home to calm herself down. He hadn't changed at all, she realised. It left her feeling deeply unsettled.

Climbing out of her car, her mood took a further dive

when she saw a rather disgruntled looking police sergeant waiting for her outside her house.

'Ah, Miss Walker, at last. Sergeant Briscombe, if you remember?'

The fact that she was still on edge made Hannah's voice sharper than she intended. 'Of course I remember. But it's late. Is it urgent? I have to be up early in the morning.'

'I won't keep you a minute and I have been waiting here the last hour or more. Did you not get the voicemail I left? I asked you to call me back if it wasn't convenient for me to come tonight.'

'Oh. No, I'm sorry. My phone must be on silent.'

She walked up the path and he followed her into her flat, waiting patiently while she switched on the lights and removed her coat.

'Meeting a friend, were you?'

Did he somehow know?

'Yes. Do you have a problem with that?'

'Not at all. I'm sure socialising at a time like this helps keep your mind off things.'

He made it sound as if she'd been out partying for heaven's sake.

'I don't know what you expect me to say but I was suspended from my job today and I needed to get out. And I'd have been a hermit for the last six years if I'd put my life on hold waiting for all this to be resolved. Now what can I do for you?'

He looked at her and she saw genuine sympathy in his eyes. 'I'm sorry to hear about the job, that's tough.' He pulled out his notebook. 'It's regarding the post mortem on the baby.'

Hannah blanched. 'Have ... have you identified it?'

'No not yet. But I do need to ask you something. Did your daughter sustain any physical injury that you were aware of?'

Hannah frowned. 'No. Why?'

'I just need to ask. Was she a good baby?'

'What do you mean by that?'

'Well, did she cry a lot? Keep you awake at nights?'

'Sometimes.' Hannah's voice was guarded as if she suspected him of trying to trip her up. 'But no worse than any other baby, I'm sure.'

'Did you ever get angry with her?'

'No.'

'You sound very sure. Not many mothers could be as unequivocal as that.'

'Well, not many other mothers only have their babies with them for three weeks,' Hannah retorted. 'I remember every day, every hour of the time I had with Sophie. And yes, I did get tired, and yes, she did cry sometimes. But I never got to the point where I felt I couldn't cope, if that's what you're asking.'

'I suppose it is, Miss Walker. You've admitted that she kept you awake at night, and we all know how exhausting that can be. You never got ... impatient with her?'

'No.'

'Or your boyfriend?'

Hannah's stare was direct. 'No.'

'I'm sorry I have to ask these questions but the post mortem's revealed that one of the baby's arms was fractured. Obviously, we'd like to get to the bottom of that.'

Hannah found she was trembling so much she had to sit down.

'She was so tiny,' she whispered. 'How could anyone have hurt her?'

'No accident that you can think of that might have caused such an injury?'

'No! I'd have known if that was the case.'

The thought of it ... of someone being violent towards Sophie.

'Are you all right, Miss Walker?'

'Yes.' She pulled herself together with an enormous

effort. 'Was there anything else you wanted to ask?'

'No. I'm sorry if this has upset you, but obviously it's a line of enquiry we have to pursue.' He snapped his notebook shut. 'Thanks for coming down with your DNA sample earlier. We'll process it as quickly as we can, but it can take a while I'm afraid.'

'I thought that sort of thing was quite quick these days?'

Harry's hesitation was noticeable. 'It's the circumstances,' he said gently. 'I'm afraid it takes longer matching DNA to a skeleton than it would to a living person or body. But we'll do our best to get it processed as quickly as possible and we'll let you know as soon as the results are through. Thanks for your time.'

Hannah shut the door behind him and sank back down onto the settee. A fractured arm? Could that have happened without her knowing? Or maybe it had happened after she'd been taken? She couldn't bear to even think about that. She tried to think back. Had Sophie been crying more? A little maybe. She remembered one day in particular when she'd been difficult to settle; but surely not as difficult as she would have been if her arm had been broken?

A small moan escaped her. She'd always convinced herself that it was someone who loved Sophie that had taken her; someone maybe who couldn't have a child of their own. But what if her daughter had been condemned to some terrible life where she was desperately unhappy, physically abused? Or, even worse, what if she really was dead? The desperate hope she'd been clinging to all these years crushed forever in the harsh reality of that tiny grave?

She jumped up from her chair. No! She wouldn't believe it. Sophie was alive. And until she had proof to the contrary, she wouldn't even consider the alternative.

CHAPTER ELEVEN

She woke exhausted and sweating the next morning. For the first time in months her nightmare had returned. It had always been the same – Sophie being snatched by a stranger, her chasing after them screaming, trying to get her back. Only the faster she tried to run the more it felt like she was wading through deep, thick mud, her leaden legs dragging impossibly behind her as the gap between her and her daughter widened.

But this time the dream had been different. It was no stranger running off with Sophie. This time he had a face. It was Ben.

No. Why was she thinking this now? She hadn't seriously considered it before – had totally rejected the notion that Ben could have murdered his own child – that she could have fallen in love with a man who was capable of doing something like that. But could she have been wrong?

She peered at the alarm clock by her bed. Half past five. She knew she wouldn't be able to get back to sleep now and there was no way she was going to lie here tormenting herself for the next two hours.

Throwing back the bedclothes, she swung herself out of bed. It was Friday - not her usual cleaning day; but she spent the next two hours spring-cleaning the flat until it gleamed.

Only one room missed her ministrations. She opened the door hesitantly and stood on the threshold. One day, she thought looking around, she'd have to deal with this, but – she closed the door quietly and headed for the kitchen. It wouldn't be today.

The postman came just as she was about to leave for Jessie's and she flicked idly through the envelopes intending to leave them on the hall table for her return. But one pink envelope caught her attention, the handwriting slanted and messy, unfamiliar. She flipped it open, pulling out the contents and staring at them in bemusement.

Several locks of blond hair tied neatly in a pretty pink bow. The note was short and to the point.

I thought you might be worried by all the media attention. Your daughter is happy and thriving. If you want her to stay that way don't take this letter to the police.

Hannah's eyes fixed on the words in disbelief, reading them over and over again. Then her gaze shifted incredulously to the strands of hair in her hand and she lifted them slowly to her cheek. She could still smell the faint clean scent of shampoo and just for a moment she allowed herself the indulgence of believing that these really were Sophie's locks. She breathed in deeply, seeking a connection however tenuous, to a little girl – possibly her little girl – growing up somewhere out there, without her. Was it some sick hoaxer, cashing in on the publicity? God knew there'd been enough of them the first time around. She fingered the strands gently. She couldn't get enough of them. They were so silky.

Her lips began to tremble. How could anyone be so cruel?

The tears gathered pace and for once she let them run their course - her hopeless sobs echoing through the empty silence of her flat. When it was over she rubbed her eyes roughly and sat for a long time just looking at the locks of hair in her hand - at those few scrawling words so carelessly written.

If you want her to stay that way, don't take this letter to the police.

She didn't know what to do. She didn't want to risk any harm coming to her daughter if she was still alive, yet on the other hand, maybe there was something there that was relevant that the police could trace. The handwriting for example, or fingerprints? Maybe they could match it up to some other sample on their records, far-fetched though it may sound?

Or the postmark? Quickly she scanned the envelope, but the postmark was illegible giving nothing away as to where the letter had originated from.

She needed time to think.

Replacing the contents carefully in the envelope, she put them on the hall table and moved into the kitchen to refresh her face with water from the tap. Then picking up her bag she headed for the front door.

**

Harry walked down the road of large converted Victorian houses in Hampstead and decided that Ben Short was obviously doing all right for himself. It was an upmarket area. Stockbrokers were still obviously making a bob or two despite the bad press. And still obviously enjoying a relatively non-taxing life-style – Harry had offered to visit him in the evening after work but he'd been perfectly happy to be interviewed at home during the day. It was a different world, no two ways about it.

The front door was opened by a pretty young woman with mousy brown hair. She was dressed casually in jeans and a warm jumper and looked no more than about eighteen.

'Ben's just changing,' she said, looking at him curiously when he explained who he was. 'I'm his fiancé, Becky Davies. Is he expecting you?'

'Uh … yes. He didn't tell you?'

'He never tells me anything,' she said sulkily. 'But you'd better come in. He won't be a minute.'

On the mantelpiece was a photo of the girl with a man. Blond hair was combed carefully back from a smilingly handsome face as he stood with one arm draped carelessly around her shoulder. He was dressed impeccably in expensive looking trousers and an open necked shirt. He also looked a good ten years older than his fiancée.

'Is that Mr Short?' he asked the girl.

'Yes. What do you want to see him about? Is it to do with the baby that was found?'

'Get the Sergeant and myself a cup of tea will you, Becky?' Ben's voice interrupted smoothly from the door, 'and then perhaps you'd like to take Bruno for a walk? Ben Short,' he said, walking into the room and offering Harry his hand. 'What can I do for you?'

Harry took quick stock of him and decided that the profile they had of him on file was right. He was a smooth customer.

'Just a few questions if you don't mind. I believe someone's been in touch with you about the baby's skeleton that was found near Hertford?'

'Yes … eventually. They took their time about it. Do you think it's Sophie?'

'We don't know yet. I'm afraid there's a chance it could be which is why I'm here. Just wanted to straighten up a few facts. You were living with your girlfriend Hannah Walker at the time of your daughter's disappearance?'

'Yes.'

'I'm aware you've already answered these questions and I'll try to keep them brief, but it helps if we form our own impressions in cases like these. It sometimes enables us to view things from a different angle. Can you confirm to me where you were when she went missing?'

'In my car on the way to see a client.'

'And how did you learn of her disappearance?'

'Hannah left a message on my mobile. I picked it up when I pulled into the client's car park.'

And did you meet up with your client?'

'Of course not. I drove straight home. Hannah was distraught.'

'I should think you were pretty upset yourself?'

'Of course. I was I didn't mean that I wasn't. It's just that she was hysterical.'

'I see. So, nobody actually saw you arrive at your destination before you turned around and went home again?'

'No.'

'Can you tell me the last time you saw your daughter?'

'That morning before Han put her out for her nap.'

'Are you sure about that?'

'I think so. It was a long time ago now, but...'

'Only according to our previous notes Miss Walker saw you leaning over the pram on your way out to the car, when you were leaving for your appointment.'

'Oh, yes, that's right. It was a long time ago now, as I say.'

'And she was definitely in the pram when you left?'

'Yes.'

'So, in fact, you were the last person to see her before she disappeared?'

Ben's eyes met his coolly. 'I'll tell you what I told the last lot. When I left the flat Sophie was safe in her pram. I have no idea what happened to her between then and when I got the call from Hannah.'

'And you didn't notice anyone hanging around when you left?'

'No.'

'Can you tell me why you and your ex-partner split up, Mr. Short?'

He would have had to be blind not to see the caution that entered Ben Short's eyes.

'Everything got to be too much. Hannah more or less had a nervous breakdown and became very difficult to live with. It wasn't working for either of us.'

'Some of your neighbours have talked about quite serious rows between you and your partner over that time?'

Ben shrugged. 'Have you got children?'

'No.'

'Well, you can take it from me it's not always what it's cracked up to be. Hannah changed when she got pregnant and once it was born it felt like the baby dominated our lives. I make no bones about the fact that I believe children should come second to the parents. That's what's wrong with society today. Parents are too bloody indulgent. And your lot are too bloody easy on kids when they get into trouble, letting them off with cautions left right and centre instead of making them pay consequences for what they do.'

He caught the look on Harry's face and added smoothly. 'That doesn't mean to say that I didn't love Sophie. Of course I did. All I'm saying is that children can come between you as parents if you don't handle things right.'

'And was that something of an issue between you and Miss Walker – your different approaches to parenthood?'

Ben hesitated. 'Maybe. Sometimes. Hannah seemed to think the world revolved around Sophie.'

'So, you felt pushed out, did you?'

Ben gave him a supercilious smile. 'Putting words into my mouth Sergeant? That's not what I said.'

'I know you and Miss Walker came under a lot of suspicion from the Press during that time. That must have bothered you quite a bit?'

'Too right it did. And most of the flack seemed to come my way. Easier to blame a bloke, isn't it? But we only ever had Hannah's word for it that the pram was empty when she went out to get her in, don't we? No-one ever thinks to question that.'

Harry raised an eyebrow. 'Are you saying you suspected your girlfriend, Mr. Short? Did she ever give you reason to believe she might have hurt Sophie?'

'No. I'm just saying that no one even seemed to question it. In my view, the press had a lot to answer for, interfering the way they did and trying to pin it on me. And the police weren't much better. The whole lot of them had hang-ups about me being a rich stockbroker if you ask me. They loved getting their teeth into that one.'

He shrugged, his eyes meeting Harry's. 'I'm telling you now, you won't find any evidence linking me to Sophie's disappearance so you might as well save yourselves the trouble this time around and concentrate on something a bit more productive.'

He held Harry's gaze challengingly and Harry returned

that look for a long moment, before closing his notebook with a snap.

'Well thanks for your time, sir. I take it you have no objection to giving us a DNA sample to help eliminate you from the enquiry? Miss Walker's already given us hers.'

Ben scowled. 'Well, I'm not sure about that. I didn't have to give one last time.'

'There was no body last time.'

'Can't you identify the baby from Hannah's sample?'

'We can, but for the sake of completeness it would be helpful to have yours as well.'

Ben scowled. 'I thought you were innocent until proven guilty in this country.' Then he shrugged. 'I don't see why not. I was her father for God's sake – it's not as if it would be incriminating if my DNA was found.'

'Thank you.' Harry handed him a card. 'My number's on here if you think of anything else you might have forgotten.'

Ben took the card and made a show of studying it. 'I'll look forward to seeing if you're any better than the last lot, Detective Sergeant Briscombe. They couldn't organise a piss-up in a brewery.'

His manner was deliberately goading but Harry made a point of keeping his voice pleasant. 'We'll do our best to do a better job this time around, sir.'

***

Helen Walker's gaze moved in disbelief from the letter in her hand to her daughter's face.

'Hannah. I can't believe you haven't told the police.'

Hannah wasn't even sure why she'd decided to confide in her mother. She hadn't intended to. But after her conversation with Jess the other night she'd accepted an invitation to go for Sunday lunch and somewhere between desert melding into coffee, she'd found herself pulling out the envelope and its contents.

'I haven't kept it from them deliberately. I just needed time to think it through. Anyway, it's bound to be a hoax, so what's the point taking it to the police?'

Her mother looked at her, her expressive blue eyes incensed. 'Because people shouldn't get away with this sort of thing. It's disgusting. And anyway, you may well be right, but you don't know for sure that it is a hoax – and this could be the last chance the police get to look into everything thoroughly. You need to know you gave them every fact at your disposal to help them. At the very least they should test the hair sample and ease your mind that it isn't Sophie's. If you don't get that done, you'll never put it fully to bed. There'll always be a part of you that wonders.'

Hannah knuckled her eyes. She missed that it was at times like these in the olden days when she would have been sitting on the sofa with her mother's arms around her, comforting her as they had this discussion. Yet she just couldn't make the move to bridge that gap.

'I know you're right,' she said abruptly. 'But I also know that if I take it to the police, it'll raise my hopes. And I don't want to put myself through that again. I'm not sure I can take any more setbacks.'

It was the closest she'd ever come to voicing her real fear – that there'd be one setback too many, and she'd go under.

'Hannah, whatever the outcome of all this, you'll come through it. You're stronger than you realise. And things are different this time around – you don't have the issues with Ben for a start. But if you're worried that everything's going to get on top of you at some point, well, maybe it will, there's nothing to be ashamed of in taking a few tablets to help you through a difficult time if that's what you need to do. You won't be alone in doing it. Life's a balancing act love and it's not always easy getting it right.'

Her words hung in the air between them before she added hesitantly. 'You know there's always a bed for you here if you want one?'

'Thanks, Mum.' Hannah could feel the tears beginning

to well up in her eyes again and she blinked them away furiously. What was the matter with her?

She jumped up from her chair and started to clear the table. 'I'm sure I'll be fine…'

'Well, the offer's there if you need it. Now, what are you going to do about the letter? Would you like me to take it to the police for you if you don't want to do it yourself?'

Hannah shook her head. 'No, it's okay. I'll drop down to the station tomorrow – see if I can grab an appointment with the Inspector in charge of the case.'

Later, as Hannah showered and got ready for bed, she thought back on their conversation. Her mother was right, she realised, life *was* a balancing act and you couldn't always get everything right. Everyone made mistakes.

It just felt like her mistakes were much bigger than most.

CHAPTER TWELVE

Murray picked up the Morning Post on his desk and made room for his coffee. 'Good weekend Harry?'

'Not bad, what about you?'

Actually, it had been a bloody boring weekend. He hadn't even gone out for a drink with his mates. He was in danger of becoming a hermit.

'My wife and I went to the theatre Saturday night, she told me I needed to earn some brownie points after – *shit!*'

He almost spilled his coffee. He was staring at the newspaper in his hand.

Harry looked over. 'Problem?'

'Tell me that isn't Adam Campbell's wife!'

Harry got up and looked at the picture in the newspaper. He felt a tightening in his groin just looking at her and it wasn't even a particularly good photo. She was looking startled into the camera as if she'd been caught off guard – that knowing, sensual look discernible even though the picture was in black and white.

He forced his voice to sound casual. 'I'm afraid it is. What does it say?'

'I'll tell you when I've read it.'

A minute later he flung the journal down on the desk, his expression furious. 'Jesus! Didn't anyone tell the family not to talk to the press? We haven't even confirmed it is the Walker baby yet.'

"We were distraught to find such a discovery in our garden,' Harry read. "and it's been very upsetting, but all we can hope is that the poor child's identity can be confirmed as soon as possible and the truth of what happened all that time ago established. And if the parents are innocent - then hopefully this will help them lay their grief to rest..."

Harry looked up when he'd finished and grimaced. 'They probably caught her unawares. You know what reporters are like. They've been hanging around their front door since all this started. There's nothing too damaging in there.'

'Maybe not but it's hardly going to help the case. Go there and explain to Mrs Campbell that we only give press releases when we're sure of our facts. And *she* doesn't give them at all. And while you're at it, see if her husband's got his legal advice yet. The sooner we can get on with that the better. Talking of which...'

He rose from his seat and went into the outer office. 'Rosie ... is the post sorted yet?'

'I'm just doing it, sir.'

'Anything from Forensics that you can see?'

She rifled through the enormous pile in her basket and finally looked up shaking her head. 'Doesn't seem to be. I'll check the emails.'

'Thanks. And if there's nothing there, get onto Edwards and chase him up, will you? I don't care how short staffed they are, we need to get on and confirm if that baby is Sophie Walker or not.'

Harry looked at him as he walked back into the office, and said, 'I spoke to Edwards on Friday. He assured me they'd have something for us this week.'

'Good. How are we getting on pursuing other angles? What about the previous owners of the house – any luck tracing them yet?'

'The Campbells were right. They were a middle-aged couple who moved to Australia – a Mr. & Mrs Lewis. The Aussie police have tracked them down and are interviewing them. We should hear back any day now.'

'Good. Any other leads?'

'Not really. We've been interviewing the Campbells' neighbours to see if they can shed any light on anything, but it was probably a bit much to hope that someone might remember unusual digging going on in the garden.'

'Did any of them know the previous owners?'

'Not well. Seems they kept themselves pretty much to

themselves. Considered they were above everyone was the general opinion, and took off in a bit of a hurry. One minute there, the next minute gone. But no kids on the scene.'

Murray sighed.

'Well, keep on it – and get around to see Mrs Campbell, will you? Make sure she knows I'm not happy about that article – or the fact they haven't given us their DNA samples yet.'

***

'I'll certainly pass your message onto my husband, Sergeant,' Natasha said, smiling at Harry as she invited him into the kitchen. 'Would you like a coffee? I've just made some.'

'Thanks, just a small one then. White, no sugar.'

She was dressed in tight fitting jeans tucked into boots and a navy-blue polo-neck sweater. Her dark hair was swept neatly up into a ponytail. She didn't look old enough to be married with a child.

'Adam's seeing the solicitor about the DNA issue today,' Natasha said, pouring the coffee, 'so we'll probably have some news for you by this afternoon, if you want to call back?'

'Thank you. Obviously it would speed things up to be able to eliminate you and your husband from our enquiries.'

She handed him his coffee and sat down opposite him. Harry couldn't help noticing that like everything else in the house the kitchen table was spotless – not a crumb to be seen. He realised she'd probably have a hissy fit if she ever saw his own personal tip that was his bedroom.

'You do understand that it's not because we've got anything to hide that we're reluctant to give the DNA? It's just the thought of being 'marked' people afterwards that doesn't sit easily with Adam.'

She pointed to the newspaper on the table and grinned. 'I'm a celebrity ... did you see?'

She sounded almost childlike in her excitement about it. Harry felt harsh having to prick her bubble.

'Erm yes ... my boss wasn't too happy about that I'm afraid. He asked me to request that you don't give any more interviews for the time being.'

'Oh. Right. I didn't see there was any harm in it.'

'We've not established the identity of the baby yet. It may not even be Hannah Walker's child.'

'Oh, come on! Who else is it likely to be?'

'We don't work on *likelies,* Mrs Campbell. We work on facts. And until they're established - those are the orders I'm afraid.'

'Okay,' she tossed her head and looked at him teasingly over her cup. 'I promise I'll be a good girl and not speak to any more of those horrible reporters. I didn't particularly want to in the first place, but they promised they'd go away and leave us in peace over the weekend if we gave them an interview. It seemed like a good deal, and I have to say I feel much better having had the break from them.'

She shrugged holding his gaze. 'But I wouldn't want to upset the Inspector. What's he like ... is he scary?'

Harry laughed. 'He can be. You wouldn't want to get on the wrong side of him, that's for sure.'

'I'm more interested in getting on the *right* side of you.'

Her eyes flirted openly with his and Harry shifted uncomfortably, thinking for the hundredth time that it was pathetic the way his body responded as if it had a mind of its own, to her very obvious feminine charms. He'd only ever reacted to a woman like this once before, and that had been when he was eighteen for God's sake.

She dipped her biscuit into her coffee cup, and placing her elbow on the table, leaned cheekily forward as she placed it slowly in her mouth. How could an action as mundane as that seem so sexy? It made him think of the last time he was here, when they'd sat so close on the sofa.

'Have you been thinking about me at all?' She could

almost have been reading his mind. 'I have about you.'

'Maybe ... but I know I shouldn't.'

'That's half the fun of it though don't you think? The naughtiness?'

'I've seen too many marriages break up because of affairs, to call it fun.'

She pouted. 'Oh Harry, you're so serious. Sounds to me like you need a bit of sparkle in your life. Haven't you ever done anything you shouldn't? And anyway, I told you – Adam and I have an understanding about this sort of thing, so who's it harming? You and I could have fun, and I could do with a good time at the moment.' She tipped her head to one side, looking at him saucily.

There it was. The offer was down on the table. All he had to do was reach out and take her hand. And he was tempted. It had been too long. But it was a golden rule not to mix business with pleasure.

He smiled ruefully. 'You're a temptress Mrs Campbell ... all right, Natasha,' he said seeing the look on her face, 'I can see that. But it'd be more than my job's worth to get involved with you. And I think I'd better take myself off before I forget that.'

At the door, she brushed an imaginary speck of dirt off his lapel.

'Bye then...' she grinned impishly. 'Think of me when you're lying all alone in your bed, consoling yourself with the knowledge that you did the right thing. I'll be thinking about you ... and all the things I could be doing to you.'

Harry's heart was pumping. She was so close he could have whisked her to him. Nearly did in fact. But he didn't. Instead he smiled awkwardly and walked away, knowing even as he did so that there was a sense of inevitability about all this. He couldn't help it; despite knowing he would be mad to even entertain the idea, a tingle of anticipation ran along his spine at the thought.

Natasha closed the door behind him and looked at her watch. Four hours to kill before her session with the psycho-babbler. And she felt fidgety.

She shouldn't, she knew – she was getting to be too reliant on the stuff – but she couldn't help thinking about the package she'd got hidden away in her sewing box. And she had the rest of the morning to herself.

***

'So, what do you think is the main cause of the problems in your relationship with Adam?'

Natasha stared impatiently at the therapist across the desk, her eyes glittery and over-bright. Christ, hadn't the woman been listening to anything she'd been saying over the past couple of months?

'I'd have thought that was obvious ...'

The therapist waited.

'Oh, I don't know.' Natasha felt uncomfortable being put on the spot. 'Anyone would have problems being married to me, wouldn't they? I make a mess of everything.'

'And why do you think that is?'

God, she hated all this skirting around. 'I thought that was why I was paying you Amanda – so you could tell me.'

The therapist smiled. 'You know that's not how it works. My job is to try and help you pinpoint where you feel things have gone wrong for you and why. Once we've identified that, hopefully we can start to move forward and put things in place to improve your situation. But we can only do that if you're serious about confronting your issues in the first place.'

'Of course I'm serious. I wouldn't be here if I wasn't.'

'Okay ... let's see if we can narrow things down a bit. Over the course of our sessions you've identified two big problems that have affected your relationship with your Adam – and I can probably add a third. One is the abuse you suffered from your father, the second is the affair which Adam has now found out about, and the third significant one,

105

which I'd tag on to those two, is the fact you're still taking drugs – which you've somehow managed to conceal from him.'

'The drugs don't affect anything.' Natasha said defensively. 'I only take them sometimes – when I feel the need to escape for a while. And it's only pot.'

'Yes, but we've talked about this,' Amanda said gently. 'Some people can get away with dabbling in drugs with no long-term affects; others can't. I'm not being judgmental Natasha, but we already know that you fall into that second category. I think I'm right in saying that the fact you took drugs was partly responsible for you being sectioned a couple of years ago?'

Natasha didn't answer.

Amanda flipped through her notes. 'At our last session, you said you were going to try to stop the drugs. How have you got on with that?'

'Look – it's not that easy okay? And I thought about going to the GP like you said, but if I do that, I'll probably end up on some sort of Watch register. What if they took Katie away from me? Adam would never forgive me and then our marriage really would be over.'

She could feel the therapist's eyes on her hands where they plucked agitatedly in her lap, and she made a concentrated effort to still them.

'Natasha, I think you'd benefit from getting some professional medical help,' Amanda said quietly. 'If not from your GP, then maybe from the doctors at the hospital? They already know your case and–'

'I don't need help. I can stop on my own.'

'But you've been trying for a while and it's not happening, is it? I know it's hard but if you had someone you could turn to?'

'It wouldn't make any difference. You don't know what it's like being me. Sometimes I need to escape.'

She wrung her hands wretchedly. 'I have such horrible

dreams,' she whispered. 'And when I'm on my own my head just fills with all sorts of dreadful thoughts and I can't control them.'

'What sort of thoughts?'

Natasha didn't answer and after a moment Amanda said gently. 'Surely you can see that taking drugs is only making things worse? You've told me how dark your moods get when you're on them. It's not a sign of weakness to ask for help, you know.'

'I don't want to go back into hospital. I don't need to. I know I'm not that bad.'

'No one's talking about putting you back into hospital. But I don't feel these sessions with me are working. I think you need more specialised help than I can give you. What about the psychiatrist you're under at the hospital? When's your next appointment with him?

'Next month.'

The therapist leaned forward in her chair. 'Bring it forward,' she said gently. 'You've got a lot going on at the moment; it's not surprising that it's taking its toll. But from what you tell me you've got a good husband and a beautiful daughter – the sort of life most women would crave. Don't you think it's worth doing everything you can to hang on to that?'

Natasha's eyes filled with tears but she brushed at them angrily. 'It's too late – I've lost it already. I knew *that* the day Adam moved out of my bedroom. I can't fool him into believing I'm someone I'm not any longer. My father's the only man that ever really loved me for the person I was – and that was a sick love, wasn't it? What sort of man could say to his own daughter that she's so beautiful he'd like her to have his child? And what sort of sick daughter would actually feel flattered by that?'

She grabbed a tissue from the box on the desk and stabbed at her eyes. Amanda's regard was compassionate as she watched, but her manner was coolly professional.

'Natasha, if you take one thing away from these sessions it's that you mustn't blame yourself for what your father did. You were a child. Adults have a way of manipulating their offspring that those children can't even begin to understand. But you're an adult yourself now and you have the option of either trying to deal with your past and move on, or let it cripple you forever. You took the first step, even if you didn't realise it, by choosing a decent husband. Make the second step, putting everything you've got into making your marriage work and kicking your drug habit. And if you really can't face going to your doctor for help then perhaps you could think about telling Adam? Trust him. Don't shut him out. Let him help you.'

'He'd just be disappointed in me,' she said in a low voice. 'He thinks I stopped the pot when I came out of hospital.'

'I'm sure he'll understand. He's made an appointment to come and see me next week. If you like, I could broach it with him, have a chat about how best he can—'

'No.' Natasha scraped back her chair, ending the session. 'I'll think about it. But you mustn't tell him anything. Not unless I say you can.'

***

'Hannah, why don't you go home early? Mondays are always quiet, and you're not looking good, hon.'

Hannah looked at Jess over the length of material she was rolling up. 'Sorry, I've been rubbish today I know.'

'You're thinking about the letter?'

Hannah nodded. 'I can't help it. It's on my mind the whole time. I know it's just going to be another hoax, but I can't help thinking, what if it isn't?'

'What time's your appointment with the police tomorrow?'

'Nine-thirty.'

'Well, don't come in after that if you don't feel like it. You're doing me a favour and I'm grateful for whatever you can offer, but I don't want to take advantage.'

'Thanks, Jess.'

She didn't deserve her friend, she knew that. She'd taken her support totally for granted these last six years and not once had Jess ever complained, or let her down.

She took a deep breath and said awkwardly. 'You've been so great through everything. I don't know how you've put up with me sometimes. I feel ashamed of myself. I know I don't say it very often, but I couldn't have managed without you. Our friendship means a lot to me.'

'It means a lot to me too,' Jess said, 'you know that. Now, come on … get off early for a change and just remember I'm here if you want to talk about anything. I'm on tenterhooks as much as you are over all this. And give the school a ring about your job. I know for a fact that some of the mothers have started a petition against your suspension and that's what you really need – to get back to doing the job you love.'

Hannah knew she was right. 'Maybe I'll drop round there now. I could pick Emma up for you at the same time if you like?'

'You don't need to do that.'

'I know I don't, but I love giving her a lift, you know I do.'

'Well …' Jess grinned. 'Who am I kidding – that would be great. I could go to the supermarket on my way home.'

'Take it as done then. I'll need a bit of light relief after I've spoken to Miss Williams. Just pick her up from mine when you're ready.'

She was doing the right thing telling the Inspector about the letter, Hannah told herself, as she shrugged into her coat and headed out to the car. Her mother was right, this might be the last chance the police got at taking a fresh look at everything, and it was only right they had all the facts.

***

'I'm working on trying to get your situation resolved as

109

quickly as possible,' Miss Williams said, her eyes sympathetic. 'I know how difficult it must be on top of everything else you're going through. But these things can't be rushed I'm afraid. There's a due process that has to be gone through. I'm seeing the governors on Thursday and hopefully I'll have some more news for you then. I'm sorry …'

"They're not going to change their minds, are they?' Hannah said. 'They won't do anything that might involve putting their necks on the line.'

'I'm on your side, Hannah. I promise I'll do everything I can to fight your corner.'

But as Hannah headed home with Emma, she couldn't help thinking about the cases she'd read in the papers where people had been suspended for months on end, years even.

'Aunty Hannah?'

'Yes, Sweetie?' Hannah looked in the mirror at Emma's frowning little face.

'Why aren't you at school anymore? We miss you.'

'And I miss you too, darling.'

'Sarah said it's 'cos you hurt your little girl. But I told her that was silly 'cos you don't have a little girl and you wouldn't hurt anyone.'

Hannah smiled. 'Thank you for saying that, Emma.' She didn't know how much to say – what, if anything, Jess had told her. 'Has Mummy said anything to you about it?'

'She said you used to have a baby but it went missing and you didn't know what happened to her and that was very sad for you. That's why you're like another mummy to me.'

'And she's exactly right. I still miss my little girl, and that's why I sometimes give you an extra big hug to make me feel better.'

'I love you, Aunty Hannah.'

'I love you too, Emma.'

'Do my mummy and daddy love each other?'

Hannah looked at her in the mirror and smiled. 'Of

course they do. They love each other very much.'

'They were cross this morning. Daddy said mummy's getting too ... too...' she frowned, trying to remember the word. '*Involved*,' she managed triumphantly. 'I don't like it when they're cross.'

Hannah felt her heart dip. The last thing she wanted was to come between Jess and Fraser. 'I'm sure it was nothing,' she said. 'Mummies and daddies argue all the time and it doesn't mean they don't love each other. Now ...' her eyes twinkled as she firmly changed the subject. 'A little fairy tells me it's your birthday soon. What special things have you got on your list this year?'

CHAPTER THIRTEEN

Tuesday morning, Adam woke early and stretched his uncomfortably aching limbs. If he was really planning staying in this room he'd need to do something about getting a more comfortable bed, which was something that wouldn't go down well with Natasha. He frowned, knowing they couldn't go on like this forever. They needed to resolve things one way or the other, but he didn't seem to have the energy at the moment to instigate the discussion they needed to have. The decisions facing them both were massive, and the repercussions if they couldn't sort themselves out were too devastating to get his head around.

He threw back the bedclothes. *No.* Cowardly though it may be, he wasn't ready to face all that yet.

After showering, he woke Katie and put his head around Natasha's door to see if she wanted any breakfast. She was still flat out, her luscious dark hair spilling over the pillow, her face for once relaxed in her sleep. It made her look younger; reminding him of how things used to be in the early days. Never perfect, but they'd had some good times together. Could they recapture anything of that? Was it still possible to try and save something from their marriage?

Downstairs in the kitchen he was deep in thought as he got the breakfast under way. On the radio, the presenter was saying there was a chance of snow but he didn't really register her words. It was eight o'clock. Turning the volume down, he picked up the phone and dialled the mobile number they'd been given.

'Inspector Murray?'

'Yes.'

'Adam Campbell here. Sorry to ring so early but I understand your sergeant dropped by yesterday and asked my wife about the DNA samples?'

'That's right, sir. We really need to move on with all this.'

There was a pause. 'I've taken advice now. My solicitor tells me that although we can refuse to undergo testing at this stage, there really doesn't seem much point. He did say though that once our records are on your database it can be difficult getting them off again?'

'If the investigation gets solved we'd have no need to keep them and you can apply to have them removed. I'm sorry. It's a hassle I know but that's the way the law stands at the moment.'

'And if it doesn't?'

'Then I'm afraid we'd want to keep your details on file. Certainly, for the foreseeable future.'

Adam made up his mind. 'Okay. I've got a window of opportunity around ten o'clock this morning if that works? I'm a bit concerned, as I know my finger prints will be on some of the remains we found. Can they tell the difference between fresh and old DNA?'

'I'm not sure how it works. But obviously we'd take into account the fact that we know you handled the bones. I'll get someone to call you to confirm the time. Will your wife be coming with you?'

Adam hesitated. 'She's not too bright at the moment. Would it be possible for someone to come here and do it? Perhaps your Sergeant? She seems to feel quite comfortable around him and when she's like this...'

He was barely aware of the Inspector's response, remembering how he and Katie had come in yesterday and found Natasha curled up in her chair by the window, quietly mumbling to herself. She'd snapped out of it quickly enough when they'd approached her, scowling at Adam's concern; telling him she was fine – she'd been pissed off by the therapist, that was all. But Adam's heart had flipped uneasily. He hadn't seen her like that in a long time.

'I'm sure we can arrange something. I'll get it sorted for either today or tomorrow. Thanks for that Mr. Campbell. It'll make our job easier.'

Always so polite Adam thought as he hung up. But he wouldn't like to get on the wrong side of him.

'I've done mummy's tray, daddy...'

Adam looked at his daughter and smiled at the carefully made up tray just waiting to have some food added to it.

'The flower's a nice touch,' he said ruffling her hair. 'Is that from the garden?'

'No. I took it from over there.'

Adam looked over at the huge bouquet of flowers sitting on the window ledge. He hadn't noticed it yesterday.

'They're nice,' he said. 'Where did they come from?'

Katie looked at him solemnly, eager to show off her newfound vocabulary. 'Mummy said they were from a secret admirer. They came yesterday and the card just said; *"Remember Me."* It's got three kisses. Look ...'

She ran excitedly over to the vase and withdrew the card. It was just as she said and Adam compressed his lips. So much for thinking they might yet salvage something of their marriage. He was shocked to discover that he didn't give a toss about the fact his wife might be seeing someone else.

***

Murray was in his office with his jacket on. 'It's bloody cold in here. Can't we get some heating on?'

'Problem with the boiler,' Harry said, handing him a steaming cup of coffee. 'They're onto it as we speak. At least you're secluded in here – it's even colder out there in the main office. What time's Hannah Walker coming in?'

Murray shifted his basket of post to make room for the cup. 'Any time now. She asked for an early appointment.'

'Any idea what it's about?'

'Nope. When I called her back she just said she had something to show me to do with the investigation.'

He looked up as someone tapped on his door. 'Looks like we won't have to wait long to find out. Here she is now.'

Murray stared at the note and locks of hair on his desk.

114

'These came on Friday, you say?'

'Yes, I did try to get an appointment to see you yesterday, but they told me you weren't free. I didn't want to leave it with anyone else.'

'And how many people have seen and touched them? Apart from you?'

'Only my mother.' She was appalled at her stupidity, remembering how she and her mother had fingered the contents over and over 'I'm sorry. I didn't think.'

Murray sighed. 'Well, I'll get the hair tested for you and we'll send the letter off for analysis, but I won't encourage you to hold out too much hope. The chances of anyone running the risk of having the case re-opened because of evidence they've freely provided...'

'I know it will probably prove that it's just another hoaxer. But you know...' her eyes followed his actions as he replaced the contents carefully in the envelope, 'my hair used to be that colour when I was little.'

Murray put the envelope to one side. Then he leaned forward and looked at her intently.

'As it happens, I'm glad you've come in. There was something else I wanted to talk to you about. I'm not sure you've been entirely honest with me about your relationship with your ex-boyfriend.'

'Oh?' Hannah's expression became guarded.

He picked up a sheet of paper from his desk. 'I have a report here from your doctor from several years ago. You apparently visited him displaying evidence of having been physically assaulted. You claimed at the time that it was your boyfriend.' His eyes were sharp. 'It was around the same time you and Ben Short separated.'

She should have guessed they'd find out. And now it would look suspicious that she hadn't come clean in the first place and told them Ben could be violent.

She sighed. 'I'm sorry. I didn't want to muddy the water by having you suspect Ben - like DCI Hedges did.'

115

'I'd remind you, Miss Walker, that it's my job, not yours, to decide what is and what isn't relevant in this case. You should have let me be the judge of that. I'd like to hear what happened please.'

She hesitated, throwing a quick glance at Harry before saying quietly. 'We had a row. A big one. I felt Ben had got too involved with all the media people and I accused him of sensationalism. He was furious. He stormed out and I knew when he came back he'd be drunk. I ... I barricaded myself in the spare room hoping he'd have cooled off by the morning – only that maddened him even more. He took an axe to the door and once he'd broken it down he grabbed me by the throat. I thought he was going to kill me.' Her voice had dropped almost to a whisper. 'He'd been violent before when he was drunk – but never to that extent. The next day I went to my GP so there'd be an official record of the attack and I told Ben that if he didn't leave I'd apply for a restraining order and tell his work what he'd done. He knew I meant it, so we parted.'

Murray stared at her in shocked disbelief. 'And this is the man who you've been quoted as saying would never have hurt your baby?'

'But it was only me that he used to get angry with, and usually only when he was drunk.'

'Miss Walker ... you were how old? Twenty? How could you possibly have been able to judge what a man like that was capable of? Where exactly was your boyfriend when Sophie disappeared?'

'On his way to work.'

'But he wasn't in work, was he? And it says in the paperwork that he never actually got to see his client.'

'No. But that was because I called him to tell him about Sophie.'

'And how much later was it that he called you back, after you left your message?'

'I don't remember exactly. About half an hour.'

'And how long after that before he arrived back home?'

'I don't know. About another hour I suppose.'

'So, in fact he could have been anywhere when you called him? And he would have had plenty of time to…'

'No!' Hannah jumped up from her chair, looking confused. 'He wouldn't have done that … he wouldn't.'

But she was looking less sure of herself all of a sudden. *He'd been jealous of Sophie.*

'Well, I hope you're right, but we'll certainly be re-interviewing him. Is there anything else you've not told me? I'd suggest that now would be a good time to get everything out in the open.'

His manner was curt and Hannah couldn't blame him for being angry. She shook her head.

'Right, well in that case…' he rose from his seat.

'I know you're busy,' Hannah said quickly, swallowing hard but determined to forestall him before he terminated the interview, 'but before I go … I was wondering if you'd managed to speak to my old neighbour yet, Mrs Morrison?'

'Ah yes, Mrs Morrison.'

He re-opened her file and pulled out a piece of paper. 'My sergeant did manage to track her down and pay her a visit.'

'And?'

Murray shook his head. 'Not what you want to hear, although you were right about one thing. Her daughter wasn't pregnant when you saw her. But there was a plausible reason for that. She was adopting a baby and they didn't want everyone knowing. Said it was their business and nobody else's. Only close family and friends knew the truth.'

Hannah's face dropped. 'Did you check their story out with the adoption people?'

The look he threw her was impatient. 'Naturally. And it all stacks up. It had taken them a long time apparently for the process to go through, but they got their baby – a little girl – around the same time as you had yours. Joan Morrison wasn't your abductor, Miss Walker.

Disappointment flooded through her.

'Will you be confirming that by taking DNA from their little girl? Just to make sure?'

'No.' Murray's response was curt. 'Why would we? There's no reason at all to suspect the Morrisons of anything.'

Hannah clamped her lips together. She hadn't realised how much hope she'd been pinning on the possibility of Joan Morrison being the person who'd taken Sophie. She picked up her bag, damping down her disappointment.

'Thank you for your time, Inspector.' Her eyes settled one more time on the envelope on his desk. 'You'll let me know when…?'

'Of course.'

'Thank you.'

Harry saw her out then walked back into Murray's office. He was sitting at his desk staring at the envelope in his hand.

'What do you make of this then, Harry?'

Harry shook his head. 'The publicity could have dragged the real abductor out of the woodwork I suppose, but it's unlikely. I'll send it off for testing though. You never know.'

'Whilst we're on the subject of testing, Adam Campbell's coming down this morning to have his DNA taken. What's happening about the wife?'

'I'm going over to take hers tomorrow morning.'

'Good. The sooner we get that lot bagged the better.'

Harry hesitated. This was probably where he should be saying that it was inappropriate for him to do it – but he didn't.

'I'm seeing her at twelve o'clock,' he added, glad of something positive to report.

'Well, make an appointment to see Ben Short again as well. Let's turn the screws a bit.'

His eyes fixed on the scarf draped over the chair opposite him. 'Is that Hannah Walker's scarf she's left behind?'

Out in the reception Hannah was just about to exit the building.

'Miss Walker?'

'Yes?' She turned to see Sergeant Briscombe holding out her scarf.

'You left this behind, I think?'

'Oh, thank you.'

She didn't notice the intent stare of the man walking past her as she retraced her steps and retrieved her scarf.

He was waiting for her outside the station.

'Miss Walker?'

She looked at him in surprise. There was something familiar about him but she couldn't put her finger on it.

'Adam Campbell,' he said. 'We … met in my garden the other night?'

His expression held a glint of amusement, as if he recognised the incongruity of the situation, but Hannah's clear green eyes remained solemn.

'Oh, right. Hello.'

She recognised him now despite the fact it had been dark when they'd met. He was a good-looking man, average height, strong, rugged – very much the country type in his Barbour jacket. His casual appearance was in complete contrast to Ben's city-slick perfection. In the dark, he'd appeared intimidating. In daylight, he looked – reassuring.

'I've just been giving a DNA sample to eliminate myself from the enquiry. That's how they phrase it anyway.'

He smiled at her full on and the effect was startling, as if someone had winded her. She looked quickly away, knowing even as she did so that she carried every inch of that image in her mind. The generous mouth curved upwards in a smile, the golden-brown eyes – the dark brown hair pushed carelessly off his brow rather than meticulously combed like Ben's would have been. It was disconcerting to feel a connection with a complete stranger like that.

'I'm glad we've bumped into each other,' he said. 'I'm sorry, I was rude the other night. You didn't need that with everything else you've got going on at the moment.'

Hannah shrugged. 'I shouldn't have been there.'

'Would you ... that is, I was just going to head over to Mario's for a coffee if you'd like to join me?'

She hesitated, casting a quick glance at her watch. 'DCI Murray would probably have something to say about that,' she said wryly, 'but actually, that only makes me want to say yes even more, the way I'm feeling right now. A coffee would be good. Thanks.'

Probably not be the best of ideas, but she felt he was a link – even if it was a tenuous one – to Sophie, and what was going on at the moment. She needed to explore that.

'Do you know where Mario's is?'

'Yes. I've got my car. I'll meet you there.'

In the coffee shop they ordered and sat down.

'I really am sorry about the other night,' Adam said.

'Don't be.' She pulled her scarf off and shook her hair free. 'It's not every day you find a strange woman in your garden in questionable circumstances.'

'No. But it must be difficult enough for you and your husband at the moment without having some lunatic rant at you.'

'I don't have a husband.' She looked up, making space for her coffee as the waiter put it down on the table. Then realising that may have sounded a bit bald, added. 'My boyfriend and I split up after Sophie was taken. She'd been the only thing keeping us together.'

'I'm sorry. That must have made things doubly hard for you.'

'If you really want to know, it was a relief. We should never have got together in the first place.'

Her eyes held his - challenging him to think the worst of her. But how could he when he could so easily relate to that?

'Relationships can be difficult,' was all he said.

'Yes. How's your wife?'

'Fine thanks, a bit up and down. It doesn't sound much, but she suffers from quite severe mood swings and they can knock her back. That's why I was so abrupt with you. I'm sorry.'

'She's lucky to have your support.'

Hannah could have kicked herself for the wistful note she suspected had crept into her voice. She studied him covertly as he picked up his cup. His face struck her as an honest one. It complimented the broad shoulders and capable hands, and something deeply female within her responded to that package. She drew in a breath, acknowledging the irony of the situation. The first man to catch her interest in years and not only was he married, but he was involved in the case – could even be involved in Sophie's disappearance. It just went to prove there was something fundamentally wrong with her sense of judgement.

He took another swig from his coffee and looked at his watch. 'I'll need to make a move in a minute. My work colleagues will be wondering what's happened to me.'

'Me too. What do you do?'

'I'm a partner at the Pet Haven Veterinary Surgery. Do you know it?'

'Yes, I do as it happens. I take my cat there. But I usually see Jeanette?'

He nodded. 'She's been there for donkeys' years – she's great. What about you? What do you do?'

'Primary school teacher.' Then she remembered and pulled a face. 'At least I *was.* I've been suspended until all this is over. It would appear that the Board of Governors doesn't approve of a possible child-murderer teaching their children.'

Adam frowned. 'That's harsh.'

'Yes, but there's not much I can do about it, so I'm helping a friend out in her shop at the moment. She's an interior designer – could come in handy if I need to retrain.'

A ghost of a smile curved her lips and Adam found himself smiling back. 'I hope it doesn't come to that. It would be their loss I'm sure.'

She took a sip of her coffee. 'Have the police come up with anything new that you know of?'

He sighed. 'I'm beginning to think we'd be the last people to know if they did. They've said they should have more information by the middle of the week, which by my reckoning is tomorrow, but I'm not holding my breath. It's impossible getting on with your everyday life when you've got something like this hanging over you. You must find that even more than us.'

Hannah shrugged. 'You get used to it, but this recent stuff's not been easy, I must admit.'

Her gaze dropped to her cup – an unspoken termination of that conversation, and Adam found himself drawn to her as he studied the picture she presented. He didn't know what had prompted the suggestion of Mario's. It had been difficult enough finding the time to come down to the police station in the first place – he certainly didn't have time to sit around drinking coffee. But there was something about her. She looked rather lost sitting there in her thick winter coat, with a few strands of blond hair poking out from beneath the scarf she wore – as if she could do with a good laugh to blow away the clouds that hung across her face, but that wasn't likely to happen any time soon. Although she was nothing like Natasha, she reminded him of his wife in her more vulnerable moments. He had an urge to cup her face in his hands and smooth the lines of worry gently away with his thumbs. It was a totally inappropriate train of thought, and it threw him.

He stood up abruptly, pulling out his wallet. ''Well hopefully they'll get their skates on and you'll be back in your job before you know it. Sorry to dash off but I've got an op list to prepare for. Thanks for coming. It's been good to talk. I was feeling quite fed up to tell you the truth.'

He put some money down on the table. 'I'll keep my fingers crossed that things get resolved for you. Please let me pay for the coffee?'

She shook her head pushing the money awkwardly back at him. Their hands clashed and they both snatched their fingers back.

'Really it's not necessary...'

Their eyes locked and he noted her heightened colour with something suspiciously akin to pleasure.

'I insist,' he muttered. 'Good luck with everything.'

**

Natasha was in the kitchen when he got home that evening and Kate was sitting at the kitchen table frowning with concentration over one of her workbooks. He ruffled her hair.

'What are you up to, mischief?'

'I'm doing my homework,' she responded proudly, holding up her book.

'I've cooked us dinner,' Natasha called out gaily, turning around. 'Roast pork, your favourite.'

He walked through to where she was vigorously mashing the potatoes.

'Uh, that's great, but have you forgotten we're going to Andy and Lisa's tonight?'

'Are we?' She frowned. The over-bright glitter in her eye that had worried him yesterday was still there.

'Yes. They're introducing us to their new neighbours?'

'Oh, God. I forgot.' She dropped the masher into the pan and buried her face in her hands. 'Stupid of me. Stupid. Stupid.'

'Hey, don't upset yourself,' Adam said. 'It's easily done with all that's going on at the moment. Kate can have the pork tonight and we can have it cold tomorrow. Come on, Katie, clear your stuff away and mummy and I will sit and chat to you while you have your supper.'

He turned back to Natasha, giving her a moment before asking. 'Anything more from the police?'

As he'd hoped, the question diverted her. 'No. As if they'd tell us anything anyway. How did you get on with the DNA thing?'

'It was fine. I explained about you not feeling great at the moment. They said they'd send someone round to the house for yours tomorrow.'

He didn't mention about going for a coffee with Hannah Walker – not that he had anything to hide.

'What's DNA?' Katie's voice was curious as she packed her books away and climbed back onto her chair.

'It's too grown up for little girls to understand,' Natasha said dismissively. 'Here you are, I've given you some extra crackling as daddy and I are eating out.'

As Katie munched her way through her dinner Natasha's mood lifted again. What with that and the spaced out look in her eyes, it made Adam feel uneasy. Her mood imbalances seemed much more pronounced these days; it reminded him of the last time that had happened when she'd been doing the drugs. Was she taking them again? Hiding it from him? His heart sank at the thought.

She was smiling animatedly around the table, her manner forced as she started up a non-stop dialogue of chatter about the other 'inmates' on the hospital ward she'd occupied a couple of years back. '*They were completely loony,*' she laughed. 'Did I tell you that? I remember thinking I'd never get out of there.'

She broke off, looking suddenly anxious from one to the other. 'You did *want* me to come home, both of you, didn't you? You don't prefer it when I'm not here?'

'Of course we don't,' Adam said quickly. 'We much prefer being a proper family, don't we, Kate?'

Katie nodded, but her face was thoughtful as she picked a carrot up in her fingers and took a nibble from it.

'*How many times have I told you not to do that?*' Natasha shouted, banging her fist on the table.

Katie dropped the carrot as if it burned her, her eyes shooting apprehensively to her mother, and then for reassurance, to her father. Her lower lip started to wobble.

'Sorry...' she said in a small voice.

'It doesn't matter, sweetheart, it's not the end of the world,' Adam said easily. 'It's just not very good manners. Use your knife and fork like we've shown you.'

'Oh, that's right ... stick up for her, like you always do. You think I don't know the two of you would be much happier without me?'

Tears filled Natasha's eyes and Katie's look darted worriedly from one to the other.

'And you can stop looking at me like that,' Natasha shrieked. 'As if I'm some sort of freak.'

The little girl's eyes widened even more. She sat as stiff as a board in her chair, her own eyes beginning to well up.

'Tash...' Adam said carefully.

Damn, damn, damn ... Natasha thought hysterically. Why did she always have to ruin everything? She took a deep breath, holding her hands tightly in her lap, willing her facial muscles to relax. 'I'm sorry darling – I didn't mean to shout like that. How about I read you a story later when you go to bed? You'd like that, wouldn't you?'

'Daddy's reading me Secret Tales,' Katie said sullenly. 'I like him reading to me.'

Natasha's expression tightened.

'Perhaps Mummy can do it tonight,' Adam intervened quickly. 'Mummy and I are going out for dinner to Uncle Andy's later and I've got some work I need to do first. It'll be nice for both of you.'

For a moment, it looked as though Kate was going to argue, her little face set in a mutinous line that was becoming all too familiar, but then perhaps sensing her mother's unhappiness she relented.

'All right. Will you do the funny voices like Daddy does?'

'I'll try,' Natasha said stiffly. 'Hurry up and finish your dinner, then go and get undressed. Call me when you're ready.'

In the kitchen, as she stacked the dishwasher, Natasha fought back the tears. She shouldn't have shouted at her like that, it wasn't Katie's fault that she was feeling like crap, just like it wasn't her fault that Natasha had never really wanted children. She'd been gutted when she'd broken up from school and realised she was having Zach's baby – it had come as such a shock. And if she hadn't been going through all the stuff with her mother's illness she'd have had an abortion, no doubt about it. But her mother had been so pleased at the thought of seeing her grandchild before she died and with Adam there believing the baby was his, it just seemed right to go ahead and have it.

She shuddered, remembering the onslaught endured by her body giving birth. Really, it was no wonder so many mothers found it difficult bonding with their offspring. The whole process was disgusting. She remembered it as if it were yesterday …

'*Come on, Natasha* ... don't give up now. One more push ... you can do it.'

'*I can't ...* '

The contraction tore through her, ripping her stomach apart until she felt she'd split in two. 'I want an epidural,' she screamed.

'You left it too late coming in for that,' the midwife said cheerfully. 'Oh, I can see the head. It'll be out in two shakes.'

'I hate it. I don't want this baby and I'm never going through this again.'

'That's what they all say, you'll soon forget. Come on, *push ... good girl.*'

And suddenly it was as if she no longer had any control at all over her body, the urge to push so strong that with one huge groan and a heave, the head was finally through.

'Now *stop!* Stop pushing and start panting ... look, here she comes ... and it *is* a she ... a beautiful baby girl!' She held her up, a delighted smile on her face. 'Here you go. Congratulations ... have a cuddle.'

But after a quick glance Natasha had turned completely pale, shying away from the blood splats on her daughter's tiny body with a flinch of abhorrence. 'For God's sake take her away and clean her up,' she said shakily. 'I can't stand blood. She looks revolting.'

The midwife hesitated, looking at her in concern. 'Okay dear ... if that's what you want. Is there anyone you want to ring, to let them know you're here? Your husband perhaps?'

'No. I'll call him later when I feel up to it.'

It was going to be a difficult conversation. And the moment of truth. Would Adam realise the baby wasn't his? Thank God she'd looked quite small. She'd have to tell him that she'd come early – but would he believe her? One thing she did know for sure, he'd be on the next plane home once she'd rung him.

Later that evening she'd held her breath as he lifted the tiny bundle gently in his arms and cuddled her, but she let it out slowly again when she realised there was no hint of suspicion in his eyes.

'She's beautiful,' he said in awe. 'And not *so* tiny considering she's come early. How can we have produced something so perfect?'

'Thank God she *wasn't* any bigger. I'm not going through that again.'

Adam smiled. 'You'll forget ... that's what they say happens.'

'No, I won't.' She paused, then said straight out. 'I've decided I'm not having any more children.'

'What do you mean? We've always talked about having a big family.'

'I know we have, but that was before I went through the childbirth experience.'

'But Tash…'

'I mean it, Adam. I've changed my mind and that's all there is to it. It's all right for you – you're not the one who has to go through it.' She looked at him archly. 'You didn't marry me just to have children, I hope?'

'Of course not, it's just such a big decision, and too soon after the birth to lock yourself into it. You might feel differently a year or two down the line.'

Natasha shrugged. 'Maybe, but I doubt it.'

She turned the subject firmly. 'Gail said she can come in every day to do the cleaning and help out, while I'm getting used to the baby. I've still got quite a bit of Mum's money left and I think I'll take her up on it. That way you can get back to Uni with a clear conscience. You can't afford to fall behind this far into your course.'

Adam looked doubtful. 'I know I can't, and I know we talked about it … but I hate that I can't be here with you.'

'I'll survive, Ad. You're only a phone call away if I need you.'

By the end of that first week she'd waved him back off to university. And although she'd promised him she'd think about the children thing, her mind was made up. They had Katie now and Adam would just have to get used to the idea of her being an only child.

'I'm ready Mummy. Can I have a hot chocolate in bed while you read to me?' Katie's voice in the doorway jolted her sharply back to the present.

Natasha forced a smile.

'You go on up sweetheart … I'll make some and bring it with me.'

But up in the bedroom, Natasha reeled at the sight that confronted her, her mood switching in an instant. Her eyes fixed condemningly on the small pile of books and toys on the floor and the two dolls propped up against them.

'How many times have I told you *everything* must be put away before you go to bed? This room's a mess. My mummy would have smacked me if I'd left my bedroom like this.'

She strode over to her daughter's bed and yanked back the bedclothes. 'Come on, out you get and clear it up. You know the rules. No story for you tonight.'

Later, at Andy and Lisa's house, Natasha looked around the table enjoying being centre of attention.

'God. You poor things. It must have been dreadful discovering something like that in your garden.'

The woman was staring at her in awe - hanging on Natasha's every word.

'Well, I've known Adam long enough to guess he took it all in his stride,' Andy said, with a wry look at his friend. 'I remember when we were at school in the science lab and that chap splashed acid in his face, Ad, do you remember? You were the quickest to react and the only one to know that you had to keep splashing it with cold water until the medics arrived. You're a cool customer in an emergency.'

'It was a shock finding it of course,' Natasha said, drawing the attention back to herself, 'and at first we thought it might have just been some old relic from years ago. But it seems not...'

'Do the police think it *is* that woman's baby?'

Natasha shrugged. 'They're not saying, but I think we'll all be surprised if it isn't. I just want it to be over so we can get back to normal. Adam's walking on eggshells around me at the moment – driving me nuts. I think he lives in fear I'm going to be whisked back into hospital again. What he doesn't realise is that he's going to push me into it, the way he's treating me.'

The look that accompanied this remark was malicious and Adam's lips tightened. 'I'm just trying to make things a bit easier for you.'

'I don't need protecting Adam – it's been two years since my suicide attempt. I'm fine now on this new medication. Sometimes I think it *suits* you, the thought of having an invalid wife.'

There was a shocked silence around the table and Natasha couldn't help the contemptuous smirk that curved her lips at the awkward exchange of glances. God, people were so *predictable* in their cosy little lives. They had no idea what *real* life was about.

'Who's for more wine? Andy asked quickly, reaching for the bottle. 'That was delicious Lisa. What's for pud?'

Natasha let him change the subject without comment. It was no more than she'd expected. Their friends hadn't known how to handle the suicide thing and her being sectioned any more than Adam had, and their response had been to pretend nothing was wrong. But that was all right. In the end, she'd come through it on her own and clawed her way back to sanity without any help from any of them.

For a brief moment, her eyes clashed with Adam's across the table, then she tossed her head, and turned to the man sitting at her side. 'So,' she said, flashing him her brilliant smile, 'you're in research? That sounds fascinating. Tell me all about it ...'

CHAPTER FOURTEEN

Harry pulled up outside the Campbell's house and drew a breath. This was stupid. He felt like some lunatic teenager. So, Natasha Campbell was an attractive woman and had made it obvious she wouldn't be averse to a bit of a fling; that didn't mean he should be tempted by it. In fact, he definitely *shouldn't* be. He was a thirty-two-year old man. Too old to be letting a woman get under his skin like this. He needed to remember that it was nothing more than hormonally driven temporary insanity, and intoxicating though it may be, it could ruin his career if things got out of hand.

Keeping that thought firmly in his head, he rang the bell.

She answered the door with a smile. 'Hi … thanks for coming.'

She was wearing a cream coloured satiny dressing gown, her dark hair hanging seductively around the collar. 'Sorry I'm not dressed. I took a sleeping pill last night and only woke up half an hour ago.'

Her gown was open at the neck offering him a tantalizing glimpse of black lace and frills. He averted his gaze as he followed her through to the lounge.

'Perhaps I should come back?'

Even though Murray would murder him.

'No, no. You're here now. We might as well get it over with. It doesn't hurt, does it?'

'No, not at all.'

'Good. Can we have a drink before we begin? Can I tempt you to a beer? I'm a bit nervous about all this.' She indicated a tray where drinks were already laid out.

'Bit early for me thanks.'

'Oh, go on … live dangerously! I was about to pour myself a glass of wine. Keep me company.'

Her look was enticing, her bright eyes gleaming audaciously into his.

'Well, ok ... just a very small one then.'

He regretted the words the instant they were out, recognizing his weakness for what it was – a desire to please; to be sucked into the forbidden world she was tempting him with.

He pulled out the DNA kit and made a point of appearing to study it. She poured the drinks, then sat down next to him on the sofa, drawing her legs comfortably beneath her as she took a sip from her glass and watched him.

'How's the investigation coming on?'

He shrugged looking anywhere but at that cleavage. 'Slower than we'd like but it often drags out like this to start with. It's all about trying to establish pieces of the puzzle and collecting whatever background information we can from everyone. Once we've done that, the interesting part kicks in, where we try to fit the pieces together and make some sense of it all.'

'So, this DNA thing. Where do you take the sample from?'

He withdrew the swab from its wrapper and cleared his throat. 'The inside of your mouth usually. It's very quick.'

She shifted her position unfurling a shapely leg so that she could lean closer to him as she tilted her chin and parted her lips. Harry had never viewed this procedure as erotic before but the way she swirled her tongue lazily round those lips – giving him a wicked smile before opening her mouth fully - did funny things to his heart rate. He swabbed the area gently, being careful not to meet her eyes, and replaced the stick in its container.

'There ... all done.' He caught an intoxicating wisp of perfume as she drew back and looked at him. She was eyeing him saucily.

'That was quick. How long is it since you've had sex, Harry?'

He blinked at her directness, then laughed. 'Longer than I care to remember…'

'Me too. How about we do something about that now?'

'Mrs Campbell…'

'It should *definitely* be Natasha if we're talking about something so personal, don't you think?'

She grinned, her eyes burning into his as she untied the belt to her robe and let the sides fall open. Beneath it the wispy black silk of her camisole clung seductively to her slender curves. 'Come on, let's have a bit of fun.'

His gaze dropped to the creamy whiteness of her breasts, the taut nipples protruding delicately through the thin material, and he knew he was in danger of losing it. All he could think was that he wanted to lose himself in the soft rise and fall of that delectable body.

He was hardly aware of her hand taking his, moving it slowly to cover her breast, rubbing it sensuously over the nipple. 'Where's the harm in it?' she whispered. She leaned in, brushing her lips tantalisingly over his, as her tongue slid out to trace the outline of his mouth.

This was madness. 'Natasha …'

The pressure of her mouth on his increased, her arms slipping around his waist to draw him closer. 'Kiss me,' she breathed against his lips. 'You know you want to.'

But even as her kiss deepened, one part of his brain was clinging onto sanity – trying desperately to find a way out of the hole he'd dug for himself. It was with huge relief that he suddenly realised that the buzzing sensation in the region of his groin wasn't passion, but his mobile phone going off.

He struggled to disengage himself, simultaneously reaching for the phone in his pocket. She clung onto him, her voice a feverish whisper. *'Leave it.'*

'I can't. I'm sorry.'

He looked at the ID. *Murray. Shit.*

'I have to take this.'

He pulled back from her, rising from the settee to move over to the window. He took a deep breath before snapping the phone on.

'Where the fuck are you?' Murray barked.

'Uh ... I'm over at the Campbell's house getting the DNA sample from Mrs Campbell.'

'Well get your arse back here now.' Murray didn't often lose it, but when he did, it was impressive. *Christ, did he somehow know?*

'Uh ... right ... yes ... I'm on my way.' He cleared his throat. 'What's up?'

'Just do it, Harry.' And the line went dead.

He hung up and looked at Natasha. 'Something's come up. I have to get back.'

'Oh, for God's sake.' She swallowed her obvious frustration with difficulty. 'When can you come back?'

But Harry wouldn't meet her eyes. It was dawning on him what a complete and utter idiot he'd been, and how his boss had just saved his bacon.

'I don't know. I'll call you.'

'Come over tomorrow or Friday,' she said quickly. 'Adam will be at work. I'm sure you can think of an excuse as to why you need to see me.'

She sidled up to him and gave him a parting kiss, seemingly unaware of how rigidly he was holding himself. Then she smiled seductively up at him and drew back.

'Don't leave it too long,' she murmured. 'I've enjoyed what I've experienced so far.'

***

Murray jumped up the minute Harry entered the office. 'You took your time,' he growled. 'No, don't take your coat off we're going out again.'

Harry took one look at his face and fell into step beside him.

'What's up?'

'The DNA results are back. It's not Sophie Walker.'

134

'What?'

'You heard me.'

'But ... *shit!* Are they sure?'

'Absolutely, according to Edwards. And he's run the information past all the other samples they've got on the computer – and nothing. What the hell's going on, Harry? I was convinced it would be her.'

'Well, we all were ... everything fitted. No other babies have been reported missing. Peterson's checked that out. It doesn't make sense.'

'Well let this be a lesson to you – to all of us – never assume anything. Christ, I can't believe I allowed myself to fall into that trap. We let ourselves be overly influenced by the media and now we need to do some serious rethinking.'

Outside he looked at Harry over the roof of his car.

'Speak to Peterson to find out how wide an area he covered when he did his search on missing babies. Get him to widen it to Countrywide if he hasn't already. Europe-wide if he has. And find out where we are with the previous owners of the Campbell's house. The Aussie police must have interviewed them by now.'

'I had an email yesterday. They were typing up the report and said they would be sending it today. I'll chase it up.'

'Do it. We need to pull our fingers out. I've got a meeting with Harrison this afternoon and he'll be breathing down my neck once he hears about this. No, don't come with me. You get on over to Hannah Walker and give her the good news. I guess she and the boyfriend are out of the loop for now.'

'What are you going to do?'

'I'm going over to forensics to speak to Edwards in person. I need him to prioritise that lock of hair just in case it *is* Sophie Walker's. I can't think for one minute that it will be, but at least then we'd have something to show for our efforts. And whether it's the abductor or a hoaxer, we need to get that established and decide if there's an argument for reopening the Walker case. After that I'll go and see the

Campbells and update them. I've not met the wife yet. How was she when you saw her this morning?'

Harry felt himself break out in a sweat. He needed to go over himself and see her – let her know that what had happened between them had been a mistake that mustn't be repeated. He suspected she might not take too kindly to that.

'She seemed fine today, but she's pretty up and down I think.'

'That's what the husband said. Perhaps I'll try and see him first. Catch you later.'

***

Harry pulled up outside Silver Lining Interior Designs in Hertford. He could see Hannah Walker replacing something in the window display, and getting out of his car he stopped to admire her efforts before nodding at her and entering the shop.

'Sergeant Briscombe.'

'Miss Walker.'

She looked at him apprehensively. 'Have you come with news?'

'Yes. I won't waste any time beating about the bush. The remains we found weren't your daughter's.'

Hannah gasped, staring at him in deep shock for a moment, before stumbling out of the window and sinking into the one and only chair on the shop floor. She buried her face in her hands. 'Oh, thank God, thank God...'

He gave her some time, saying nothing as she rocked gently back and forth in her chair. When she finally looked up, her expression was once again the expressionless mask she seemed to have perfected so well.

'Who is it then? Do you have any idea?'

'Not at the moment, no.'

'But you're positive it's not Sophie?'

'Absolutely.'

She let out a sigh. 'I prayed it wasn't of course, but it's such a relief to have it confirmed.' She threw him a sharp

136

look. 'So, what happens now? Does it mean the investigation into Sophie will stop?'

'We'll still process the letter and hair sample you brought in, but our main priority now has to be to try and identify those remains. If the hair sample's not a match to your DNA, then I'm afraid there's probably nothing new to go on that would justify us reopening the case. I'm sorry...'

'So, I just go back to my normal life? As if none of this has happened?'

Harry didn't know what to say. He couldn't begin to imagine what it must be like. She'd been through so much. 'It's an impossible situation, I know. I'm sorry.'

She shook her head, the depths of her distress palpable. But her shrug was dismissive. 'I've done it once; I suppose I can do it again. At least I can hopefully get my job back now there's no link to Sophie.'

'I'll keep my fingers crossed for you. If there's anything I can do to help with that?'

He wasn't entirely sure what influence he might bring to bear on anything, but there was a vulnerability to her prickly independence that got to him.

She looked at him in surprise and the glimmer of a smile transformed her face.

'That's kind of you but you'll have more than your work cut out trying to discover who that poor baby was. I don't envy her parents when you do find out.'

She watched as he drove away; then went to put the kettle on, surprised to discover that her hands were shaking. *It wasn't Sophie.*

She felt drained, not exhilarated like she felt she ought to feel. She was back in the no-man's land she'd inhabited for the past six years, but with an added complication.

She'd changed; she sensed it even if she didn't understand it, and she wasn't sure she could settle back down into the empty shell-like existence her life had become. What had previously been a refuge felt more like a prison now.

CHAPTER FIFTEEN

Natasha Campbell was looking tired and fidgety as she answered the door, her long fingers twisting agitatedly as she looked at Murray suspiciously.

'Mrs Campbell?'

'Yes.'

He showed her his card. 'DCI Murray. We haven't met yet. I tried to see your husband at his work but, apparently, he's out on a call. Alright if I come in for a moment?'

He saw her eyes flicker briefly past him as if expecting to see someone else and then she shrugged, standing aside to let him pass.

In the lounge, she offered him a seat and sat down opposite him, perching stiffly on the edge of her chair.

'What can I do for you Inspector?' Her eyes seemed unnaturally bright and she held herself with a tautness that belied the calmness of her enquiry.

'I came to tell you that we've had an update on the forensic results today. I thought you'd like to know that the remains we found in your garden aren't Sophie Walker's.'

She looked at him in shock, her eyes snapping to attention.

'*What?* But that can't be right surely? Who else could it be? It had to be her.'

'Well, we've all allowed ourselves to slip into that misapprehension I'm afraid, but now we have to start widening our investigation.'

Natasha seemed to sink into herself before his very eyes. 'It's so awful,' she whispered, her gaze shifting hauntingly to the garden. 'That skull – those tiny little bones. I'll never forget that sight as long as I live. I keep dreaming about it. Adam tried to cover them up so I wouldn't see them but he wasn't quick enough. It was horrible.'

Her eyes turned back to fix on him almost pleadingly. 'Are you absolutely sure they're not just some old relic? I mean - maybe your Lab got it wrong? It might all have a perfectly innocent explanation?'

'I'm sorry, Mrs Campbell, but that's not the case. We reckon the bones have been there an absolute maximum of ten years, and there are indications that it may not have been a natural death. We're keen now to track down the previous owners of this house. Are you all right? I didn't mean to upset you.'

She'd started to rock backwards and forwards on the edge of her chair, her fingers plucking restlessly at the material of her trousers. She stilled suddenly, her eyes fixing on him with an intensity that was disturbing. 'Death is a *horrible* thing, Inspector. You'd know that more than most. It creeps up on you unawares when you least expect it and there's no escape. It's sitting out there - waiting for us all.'

She broke off and reached for an inhaler that was sitting on the coffee table.

Murray looked at her in concern. 'Mrs Campbell, would you like me to call your husband?'

She shook her head vehemently. 'No! I don't want him back here. He'll only dose me up with more tablets and I don't want any more. They make me feel so tired.'

Murray rose from his chair, wondering how Harry could possibly have described her as simply *on edge*. It could be the medication he supposed, but the woman looked like she was on the verge of some sort of breakdown to him. She was out of it. He hesitated, wondering if he should over-ride her wishes and contact her husband. But really, it wasn't for him to interfere. For all he knew, she spent most of her days like this.

'Perhaps you'd better rest then. I'll take myself off, leave you in peace. I'm sorry if I've upset you. We'll try not to disturb you any more than we have to.'

She nodded her head, her voice shaky as she responded. 'Thank you. I'll tell Adam when he comes in.

He'll be interested to know, I'm sure, though he'll probably only start fussing over me again. He drives me mad.'

'Better than having someone who doesn't care,' Murray said gently.

'Is it?' Natasha asked darkly. 'I sometimes wonder.'

She was barely aware of him leaving. It was all so *unfair*. Just when she'd felt she was beginning to get a handle on everything.

Her eyes darted compulsively to the little sewing box in the corner. She'd already smoked one lot today and she knew Amanda was right, it wasn't doing her any good, but she needed it. It was the only way, apart from sex, that she could lose herself - and she certainly wasn't getting any of *that* at the moment. She jumped up from her chair and crossed the room. She had plenty of time before she needed to pick Katie up from Adam's mother. Raising the lid, she retrieved the small package tucked neatly beneath the cotton reels.

The first thing to hit Adam when he walked into the lounge later that day was the lingering smell. He'd recognise it anywhere.

'Natasha?'

She was sitting staring moodily out of the window, her diary on her lap. Her eyes jumped to his when he walked in. She shook her head as if to clear it. 'You're early,' she said.

'No I'm not. It's six thirty. Where's Katie? Did you pick her up from Mum's?'

'Oh!' She started guiltily. 'No. I ... forgot. I'll go now.'

'Not like that you won't. What the hell are you playing at? How long have you been back doing drugs?'

'I'm not. Don't be ridiculous.'

'Natasha, I'm not an idiot. I smelt it as soon as I walked in.'

Her eyes were unfocussed as she looked at him. 'It's only hash,' she said sulkily. 'I need an escape from all that's going on. It's all right for you – you can get away from it during the day. I'm here the whole time, looking out at the garden and thinking about that poor baby.'

'For God's sake - smoking weed isn't going to help. And what about *our* baby? She needs a mother who's capable of looking after her. Haven't we got enough problems without you adding to them? No wonder you've been getting your moods back.'

Her face took on a cornered look. 'Oh, fuck off, Mr Perfect. I don't have to answer to you. You go and get Katie from your Mum's if you want. Just leave me alone.'

Adam's lips tightened. Without another word, he spun around and headed for the door.

'By the way … it's not the Walker baby.'

He stopped in his tracks and turned back to stare at her. 'What do you mean? Who told you that?'

'That Inspector Murray. He dropped around earlier.'

'Christ. He didn't see you like this I hope?'

'Of course not,' she snapped irritably. 'But that's why I needed it. It was bad enough thinking we knew the story behind that baby's disappearance. But not knowing's even worse. There was someone outside earlier, I saw him – watching the house.'

'There's no-one watching the house, Natasha.'

'There *is*. I saw him, I tell you.'

'It was probably just a rubber-necker. You know what people are like.'

Natasha glared at him. 'You think I'm being paranoid, don't you – that I'm going nuts again.'

'Of course I don't...'

'There's someone out there, I tell you. I can sense their eyes on us all the time.'

Her gaze strayed fearfully to the window, as if expecting a face to suddenly materialise there. She shivered and rose from her chair. 'I'll come with you to get Katie. I don't want to be left here on my own.'

'Natasha, there's *no-one out there*. Okay ...' he caught her look and shook his head. 'Come if you want to. But you wait in the car. I don't want Mum seeing you like this.' He looked at her keenly. 'You *are* still taking your tablets?'

'I don't know,' she said vaguely. 'I may have missed this morning's but I hate taking them. They don't agree with me.'

Adam somehow stopped himself from snapping back that it wasn't surprising, if she was mixing them with Weed. He went straight to her bag and withdrew a bottle. 'You need to keep taking them like your doctor said. Here, take one now, so at least we know you've taken your evening one.'

She took the tablet reluctantly but he noticed her eyes had softened as she looked up at him. 'You're too good for me Adam Campbell – you know that?'

He found he couldn't meet that look. 'No I'm not, but all this stuff has knocked you. We need to get you through it.'

'And *then* you can leave me you mean?'

Her stare was intent.

'Of course not.'

But her words cut straight to the chase of his deepest disquiet. He didn't know how much longer they could go on like this.

CHAPTER SIXTEEN

Hannah lay in her bed listening to the relentless patter of rain on the windows. She didn't seem to have the energy to get up though she knew she'd have to make a move shortly. Why wasn't she feeling more jubilant? She should be walking on air now that she knew it wasn't Sophie.

Her mobile rang and she reached out for it.

'Hannah?' It was Ben, his voice agitated. 'I need to talk to you. The bloody police interviewed me at work yesterday morning asking me all sorts of questions about us. Have you been talking to them? Because if you have–?'

She felt her stomach muscles tighten. 'Don't threaten me, Ben. I didn't need to talk to them because they already knew. They had my doctor's notes.' She hesitated. 'Anyway, it doesn't matter now, does it? I assume they told you it wasn't Sophie they found?'

There was a stunned silence on the other end.

'*What*? Well, bloody marvellous. I'm the child's father and they don't even consider me important enough to share a little fact like that with! When did you find out? *Thanks* for letting me know.'

She took a breath. 'I'm sorry. I thought they'd have told you. They told me yesterday afternoon that it wasn't Sophie. They'll probably contact you today.'

'Or not! I told them they were probably barking up the wrong tree and it wouldn't be her. They're probably too bloody arrogant to admit they're wrong to someone like me.'

Hannah didn't respond.

'*What are you doing creeping in on me like that?*' he suddenly shouted. '*Have you been listening in on my conversation?*'

Hannah could hear a woman's voice in the background, sounding incredibly young.

'*No – of course not. I'm sorry ... I just wondered if you wanted some breakfast?*'

'I'll be down in a minute.'

Hannah felt sick – it was like being back there again - in the room with him. Except now she was older and he didn't frighten her any more.

'You shouldn't speak to her like that, Ben. I thought you said you'd changed.'

'I told you it wouldn't be her,' he said, ignoring her. 'All that hassle for nothing. I'm tempted to sue them for harassment.'

She couldn't listen to any more. 'I have to go to work,' she said calmly. 'Don't call me again.'

She frowned as she replaced the handset. She'd sounded so young, his fiancée. Was he violent with her? She thought back to when she'd been trapped in that situation – no-one to talk to – to confide in. She found herself feeling sorry for the girl.

She threw back the bedclothes dismissing her thoughts. Ben wasn't her problem anymore and neither was his girlfriend. She'd get dressed and ring the school. It was Thursday, the day they were having the Governors Meeting. She needed to tell them it wasn't Sophie.

***

The sound of the doorbell jerked Natasha out of her reverie. She'd just finished preparing Adam's lunch. It wasn't something she often did these days but she always felt the need to make it up to him when she was playing away. Not that she was yet of course, but it wouldn't be long. She smiled to herself as she walked to the door – remembering that kiss with Harry yesterday. It was so long since she'd experienced passion like that, she'd almost forgotten what it felt like. Maybe this was him now. Not a good time to be calling because Adam would be home any minute; but they could fix a better time to rendezvous – one when she'd make sure they weren't likely to be interrupted next time.

She wiped her hands on her apron and opened the door.

'Hello, Natasha.'

The smile on her face froze as she stared at the blond-haired man standing on her doorstep.

He grinned. 'Remember me?'

'Zach?'

His greeting words stirred her memory. 'Was it *you* who sent me the flowers?'

'None other.'

And she'd thought they were from Harry.

He allowed her a few seconds before saying casually. 'Aren't you going to invite me in? I've travelled a way to come and see you and I sure as hell could do with a drink.'

She opened the door wider, her mind in a daze. 'But, what are you doing here? How did you know where I live?'

He laughed, walking past her into the hall and looking around. 'That wasn't difficult. I face-booked Miles Packham and asked him for your address. Nice place you've got here. Your husband must be doing all right. What does he do?'

'He's a vet.' She led him into the lounge, her mind racing. *What was he doing here? Why would he come after all this time?*

His eyes focused on a photo frame on the table and he moved over to pick it up.

'Is this your daughter?'

'Yes.'

'Pretty girl. What's her name?'

'Katie.'

'Pretty name too.' He was studying the picture closely and she sensed a new urgency in him. 'They mentioned her in the paper. Said she was six years old. It sort of got me thinking …'

Shit.

'Oh?'

Now she knew why he was here, her mind went into overdrive. She didn't have long to get rid of him before Adam got back. She could feel the beads of perspiration beginning to form on her forehead.

'Yes ... such lovely blond hair she's got. Not unlike mine, is it? What colour is your husband's hair?' His voice was deceptively casual.

'Brown,' she said, moving over to the drinks cabinet. 'But his mother's very blond just like Katie. She hasn't inherited my colouring at all. What can I get you to drink?'

'A beer would be good if you've got one. Thanks.'

She went out to the kitchen fridge, using the time to gather her wits. She could handle this; she just needed to keep her cool.

By the time she'd returned to the lounge he'd put the photo down and was sitting in a chair. His gaze on her was intent.

'So, what have you been up to?' she asked, turning the conversation as she passed him his drink. 'Are you married?'

'Not any more – separated.'

'Wow, you've been busy! But sorry to hear that.'

'You ruined me for anyone else,' he mocked. 'What we had those last few weeks of summer ...'

Now they were on ground she was comfortable with.

'Yeah ... fun days.' She twirled the stem of her glass in her fingers.

'My wife and I couldn't have children.'

'Oh. I'm sorry to hear that.'

'Well, it was a blessing in the end seeing as the marriage didn't last more than a couple of years. But she was desperate for a baby as soon as we got together and when it didn't happen we had tests. Reduced fertility apparently, the both of us, so together it wasn't going to happen.'

'That's tough.'

'Yeah... it didn't help things.'

He set his glass carefully down on the table beside him and looked at her calmly. 'Let's cut the small talk, Tash, shall we?' His eyes locked with hers. 'If that newspaper article was right and your daughter's six, then that puts her being conceived around the same time you and I were an item.'

Natasha met his gaze coolly. 'I know what you're thinking Zach but it's not the case. You knew I had a boyfriend back home. Katie's Adam's daughter.'

'Yeah, well maybe, maybe not. There were a couple of times when we didn't use protection and I'd just like to know for sure. I'm not perfect but we do things right in our family and if your daughter's mine then I have a right to know and I'll want some say in her upbringing. If she's not, then I'll take myself off and you need never see me again. But I want a paternity test.'

'*A paternity test?*' Natasha's face drained of colour. She felt as if she was hanging onto her sanity by a thread. '*She's not yours, Zach.* Don't you think I'd have told you if you'd got me pregnant? It would serve no useful purpose at all to have a test. And it could destroy my marriage.'

'You don't need to tell your husband.'

'I wouldn't have to. Katie would. She's six years old. Not some baby that we can bundle up and take for a test without her even knowing it.'

'I need to know, Natasha.'

'But I'm telling you the *truth*. Anyway ...' she looked him straight in the eye. 'If what you say about having a low sperm count or whatever is true, then a pregnancy wouldn't have happened with me either. Why do you think Adam and I only have one child? I have a condition that makes it extremely unlikely I'll ever get pregnant again. It was apparently a miracle that it happened the first-time around.'

She sounded so convincing she almost believed it herself.

The sound of a key in the front door had them both looking in the direction of the hall.

'That's Adam – he's come home for lunch.' Natasha grabbed his hand. 'Look. Where do you live? I'll come to you. We can talk – have lunch, whatever you want – but please don't say anything to upset things now.'

'*Tash?*'

'*In here...*'

She dropped his hand, but not before he'd squeezed it back. He reached into his pocket and pulled out a card.

'All my numbers are on here. Call me. I've got the day off tomorrow. We could meet up then if you're free. But if I haven't heard from you in the next couple of days…'

'You will, I'll call you tonight. I promise.'

She turned with a brilliant smile as the door opened. *'Babe, you're early –* we're one extra for lunch. Let me introduce you to an old school friend of mine, Zach Baker. He's visiting in the area and dropped by.'

After Zach had gone, Adam looked at Natasha.

'How come he looked you up?'

'Saw that article in the paper apparently. And as he had a meeting in Welwyn he decided to pop over.'

'So … what was he? An ex-boyfriend or something?'

'God No! Nothing like that.'

He only happened to get me pregnant.

'Just someone who went to the boys' boarding school down the road. We used to share some of our A Level classes with them.'

Her gaze slanted away from the warning in Adam's eyes.

'Tash … if you're thinking about seeing this man, think very carefully about it. I can't go on like this.'

Natasha tossed her head. 'I'm not as it happens, but perhaps if *you* were to show a bit more interest I might not need to look around.'

'That hasn't stopped you in the past, has it? Even when our sex life was good it wasn't enough.'

'You're right, it wasn't. All part of my personality disorder according to the shrink in the hospital. *It's not my fault!'*

She threw back her head and laughed. 'God, he was such a patronising prig I was tempted to try it on with him. Why can't you understand, it's nothing personally lacking in you Adam. I'm a flirt, it's just the way I am. It doesn't mean anything. If I thought you could be the same I'd encourage it. But I know you can't. If you had an affair it would be the whole champagne and roses thing and you'd probably want to leave me. Do you think I don't know that you only stay because of Kate?'

She stared at him, challenging him to deny it. As usual he backed down. She knew exactly what he was thinking. His daughter was the one good thing that had come out of all this.

But if he ever found out the truth ...

'Remember we said we'd go over to Mum's for supper tonight,' Adam said, his tone cool as he picked up his jacket and headed towards the door. 'I should be through by about five thirty if you can come and pick me up? There's no point taking two cars.'

'Fine.' Natasha's voice was sulky. 'Just make sure you're ready when I get there for a change.'

***

Murray walked into the main office and looked around. It had been a long day and he was ready to head off.

'Where's Harry?'

'I think he may have gone home, sir,' someone volunteered.

'No. He was in the canteen five minutes ago,' Peterson said. 'I saw him.'

'Okay, I'll check it out. Tell him where I am if he comes in.'

In the canteen, he found Harry mulling over a cup of coffee. He bought one for himself and went over to join him.

'What's up? You look about how I feel,' he said, pulling out a chair.

Harry snapped himself out of contemplating how he was going to stop this thing with Natasha and looked at his boss, a gleam in his eye.

'Just pondering the case. You got my message?' There was a suppressed air of excitement about him.

'Yup ... what's got your juices going? It sounded big.'

'Something that's going to put a smile on your face I hope. Our first breakthrough and I think it could be pretty significant.' He pulled some papers out of his pocket and slapped them down on the table in front of him. 'That's the report from the Melbourne police. I think you'll find it very interesting.'

Murray picked up the papers and read them as he sipped his drink. When he'd finished he looked at Harry thoughtfully.

'Seems to me this case is getting more intriguing by the minute. I distinctly remember Mr Campbell saying he didn't know the couple.'

'Yes – and Mrs Campbell said the same. Why would they lie?'

Murray downed his coffee and stood up. 'Well, there's only one way to find out. We'll go and ask them, shall we?'

But when they called at the Campbells' house half an hour later it was deserted.

'We'll meet back here tomorrow morning, eight fifteen, sharp.' Murray said briskly. 'Catch them before they head off anywhere. Could be an interesting day.'

He looked at his watch. 'I'll drop you back to the station so you can pick up your car, then we might as well head off home for the night – not often we get the chance to bunk off early.'

CHAPTER SEVENTEEN

'Where are you off to today?' Adam lifted the porridge off the stove, his look suspicious as Natasha walked into the kitchen dolled up to the nines.

'London. I fancied doing a bit of shopping. Well done for getting the breakfast organised.'

'I helped Daddy,' Katie said proudly. 'I made the toast, didn't I daddy?'

'You certainly did. And laid the table,' he smiled, as he dished up the porridge and they all took their seats.

'Will you bring me a present when you come back mummy?'

'I might,' Natasha said indulgently. 'If you're a good girl at school today.'

Adam looked at her. 'I thought you had problems with the underground and the whole *crowds* thing? You haven't been up to London in over a year.'

She sipped her coffee. 'I'll be fine. I really think things are getting better. I'm actually looking forward to it.'

She wasn't sure how convincing she sounded but her claustrophobia was a necessary evil she needed to overcome. She had the nasty premonition that her past was about to blow up in her face and she couldn't let that happen. So, first things first, she needed to deal with Zach.

The doorbell rang and Adam's surprised gaze met hers.

'I'll go,' Katie said springing up from her chair.

'No, you run upstairs and brush your teeth before we leave,' Adam said. 'I'll get it.'

He moved into the hall and opened the front door.

'*Inspector.*'

'Mr Campbell. Is it all right if we come in for a moment? I have a couple of questions I'd like to clear up with you and your wife.'

'Well, we're only just finishing breakfast...'

'We can wait,' Murray said. 'I'd like to get this sorted this side of the weekend if possible.'

Adam frowned, but opened the door wider. 'You'd better come in then.'

In the kitchen, Murray's gaze was drawn to Natasha Campbell, still sitting at the breakfast table. She looked stunning. There was no other word for it. She was dressed in chic brown trousers and a cream silk shirt, a wide leather belt with an ornate buckle emphasising the slightness of her waist. Her face was beautifully made up and her hair was drawn into an elegant chignon that emphasised the line of her neck and accentuated the delicate slant to her eyes. A colourful silk scarf draped tastefully over her shoulder finished the look to perfection. She looked nothing like the fragile woman he'd seen only two days previously.

'Inspector.' she greeted him. 'And Sergeant ... Briscombe, wasn't it? What can we do for you?'

On closer examination, Murray could see she wasn't quite as relaxed as she appeared. Her eyes were darting back and forth from him to Adam in an agitated manner and the smile that was pinned to her face looked forced.

He pulled out his notebook. 'I was wondering if you could help us out with something, Mrs Campbell?' He paused staring at her keenly. 'We were wondering why you didn't mention the fact that the man who lived here before you, was your father?'

'What?' There was no doubting Adam Campbell's shock. He turned to his wife, his eyes confounded. Then he swung back to Murray. 'That's nonsense. Whoever told you that has got their facts wrong.'

'No, they haven't actually.' Natasha's expression as she looked at Adam was deceptively calm. 'It *was* my father's house, Adam, as it happens. I just never told you.'

He stared at her in disbelief. 'But you told me he was dead. Your mother said the same.'

Natasha's eyes were expressionless. 'As far as we were concerned he *was* dead. He was a bastard to us and it was the least he could do, to settle the house on her. As he'd already left for Australia we decided you didn't need to know all the facts. You were touchy enough about sponging off my mother as it was.'

Adam stared at her stunned.

'I can't believe you'd keep something like that from me. Why would you feel the need to?'

She shrugged but made no response.

He turned back to Murray. 'I had no idea. *Christ* ... not even the surname was the same.' His eyes swung back to his wife, sharply questioning.

'My parents never married,' she said coolly. 'His name was Lewis, my mother's, as you know, was O'Hanlon.'

Murray was studying her face closely. 'So, the truth of the matter is, Mrs Campbell, you had access to this house for several years prior to your occupation of it? And therefore, potentially, you or a member of your family could have information surrounding the infant that was found here?'

'I have no information for you Inspector,' Natasha said impatiently. 'I've already told you that. I haven't a clue how that baby ended up in our garden. Maybe you need to speak to my father and stepmother about it. Nothing they'd do would surprise me.' She glanced at her watch. 'Look, I'm sorry but was there anything else? I'll miss my train if I don't make a move.'

Murray's eyes were penetrating as he fixed them intently on her. 'Mrs Campbell, I have to ask you this. Do you know the identity of the baby we found in your garden?'

It was a direct question. She met his gaze full on. 'No Inspector, I don't.'

'And you, Mr Campbell?'

'Of course I bloody don't.'

He was still looking stunned and Murray inclined his head. He doubted they'd be getting much more out of either of them today.

'You have to realise, Mrs Campbell, it doesn't look good for you that you've deliberately lied during a police investigation. Obviously, we'll be following things up with your father, but I think it very likely that I'll need to come back and ask you some more questions and I'd be grateful if you could make sure that you're available over the next few days. It would have been a lot more helpful if you could have advised us of these facts at the start of our investigation – as I'm sure you're aware.'

'If I'd thought they had any significance I would have done, but I don't have any contact with my father and I prefer to keep it that way.'

Her tone was cold, and signified, as far as she was concerned, an end to their conversation. She rose from her chair.

'I need to make sure Katie's ready for school. So, if that's all for now, Adam will see you out.'

Up on the landing she looked from the window as the Inspector said something to Adam before he and Harry climbed into their car. She took a steadying breath. How she'd managed to keep her cool she had no idea. Their visit had made her think of things she'd long since buried and put behind her. She didn't want to start thinking of her father again – the things he'd done to her – the baby.

'Natasha?'

Adam was waiting for her as she came out of Katie's bedroom. She made a show of shepherding the little girl in front of her. 'Not now, Adam, we're both in a rush and I really don't want to miss my train. We can talk about it tonight. Neither of us is going anywhere.'

CHAPTER EIGHTEEN

Natasha wrapped her scarf more warmly around her neck and checked the map on her phone. It had been a long time since she'd come to the West End and she felt a mixture of excitement and apprehension as she threaded her way through the crowds, drinking in the window displays, realizing that she'd actually missed all the buzz of shopping and doing *feminine* things like that. But despite her therapy, the thought of going on the tube had been the one hurdle she hadn't been able to overcome. She felt proud of herself now as she consulted her phone again and located the address she was looking for.

Peacock Avenue was a quiet little cul-de-sac in Kensington. She looked at the row of pristine Mews houses and searched for No. 16.

On the doorstep, she took a deep breath before raising her hand to ring the bell. She could deal with this. She *had* to deal with it. She'd managed to keep a handle on things reasonably well up to now but the police visit this morning had shaken her - and so had the expression on Adam's face when he'd realised she'd deceived him over her father. How much worse would it be if he found out he wasn't Katie's father? She didn't want to lose him. He was the one bit of security she had in her life. Without that she'd fall apart. She knew she would. She needed to deal with Zach.

'Hi.' Zach's smile was confident as he opened the door. 'Good to see you.'

Her returning smile was radiant. 'And you.'

His house was surprisingly roomy and tidy – orderly in a masculine way. Natasha liked it. No children's toys littering the place here.

'Drink?'

'Wine would be good, thanks. White if you've got it.'

He poured out a glass and handed it to her. 'Have a seat. I just need to give the casserole a stir. I'm cooking – thought it would be nicer than eating out. Then afterwards we can talk.'

Natasha sat down on the large settee and took a sip from her drink as she looked around the elegant room. He was obviously doing well for himself. Houses in this part of London didn't come cheap whether they were bought or rented. She noticed a large collage of photos on the wall and got up to take a look at it.

'Have you spotted yourself there?' Zach's voice came from behind her shoulder.

'No.' She studied it more closely, then grinned. 'Oh, there I am. I remember that day. It was an Exeat, only neither of us went home for the weekend, we went to Dorset instead.'

'And you told your boyfriend you were staying at school to study for your exams.'

Their eyes met. 'Yes,' Natasha admitted. 'I'm not proud of my behaviour over that time but it was difficult with him being away at Uni.'

Zach shrugged. 'His loss was my gain.' He looked at the picture of Natasha on the beach, then switched his gaze to her face.

'You've hardly changed at all, unlike me.'

'Oh, I wouldn't say that. You're looking great, but far too young to have been married and divorced.'

'I met Susie my first year at Uni. I was married at twenty-two and separated at twenty-four. Not a great track record but I think her parents were more pissed off about it than we were. They spent a fortune on the wedding. I felt bad about that. I'll certainly think twice before I leap into matrimony again.'

He flashed her a grin and gestured back towards the seating area. 'Come and sit down. I want to hear what you've been up to the last seven years.'

'That must have been tough,' he said sympathetically, after hearing about Natasha's mother dying. 'And quick.'

'It was. I don't know what I'd have done without Adam through that time, and then of course, I got pregnant too.'

Surprisingly, he didn't pick up on the subject of Katie, showing more concern over how she'd fared at the time. But later, after lunch, as they sat on the settee in front of the fire, he took her hand in his as he broached the subject.

'I don't want to cause trouble in your marriage, Tash. Well, no … actually, I'm not sure that's true. Now I've met up with you again, I rather think I do.'

His smile was winning, the expression in his eyes bringing back old memories. 'But you have to understand this paternity thing is important to me. If Katie's mine I have a right to know. And the way things are it might be the only crack I get at fatherhood.'

She nodded, planting a sympathetic look on her face. 'I can understand that Zach – of course I can. But if Katie was yours, I'd have told you. I knew you weren't the sort of man who'd renege on his responsibilities. But she's *not* yours – she's Adam's.'

Her eyes were crystal clear as she told the lie. His were sceptical, a half smile playing around his mouth.

'So why don't I believe you? Perhaps it's because the bottom line is I think she looks like me. Her hair's a similar colour to mine – not black like yours or dark brown like your husband's. And I've checked out her birth date behind the scenes. It all fits.'

She looked shocked. 'What do you mean? How did you do that?'

He shrugged smilingly. 'Friends in high places. There are ways around these things if you know who to ask. Which brings me to the test. I can arrange it on the quiet. I have contacts. Your husband need never know. Unless Katie proves to be mine, of course. Then we'll have to deal with it. What do you say?'

Natasha wrung her hands together. Everything seemed to be snowballing out of control. She mustn't lose it. She reached in her bag for her tablets.

'What are those for?'

'I… I've not been too well. I've had problems with my nerves in the past. All this stuff with the police isn't helping. Nor is you turning up on my doorstep.'

'Are you happy, Tash?'

Confusion flickered over her face. Only Adam called her that and he wasn't here to help her. She felt a burst of anger against him. All this was his fault – him and his bloody barbecue. If he hadn't made that discovery none of this would be happening. She wouldn't have the police traipsing everywhere; wouldn't have given that wretched interview, wouldn't have Zach turning up in her life again – threatening her.

'Happy enough.'

He took her chin gently in his fingers. 'I don't think you are. He seemed a nice guy, your husband, but he's not like us. I don't hold any illusions about myself, or you, but I always felt we understood each other. Why didn't you answer any of my calls after we broke up that summer? I was desperate to carry on seeing you. I was in love with you.'

He smiled, shaking his head reminiscently as if it was a nice memory.

Perhaps it was because they *were* so alike, she realized now. She hadn't liked herself even in those days, so it would have been too much to expect that she'd go for someone with similar traits to her own. But age seemed to have improved him. He wasn't as bullish as he had been, or as arrogant. Just confident, in an attractive way.

'There's hardly anything of you,' he murmured, his hands sliding down her body to span her waist. 'If we were to make love now, would you snap in two, I wonder?'

Excitement lurched in her stomach as she saw a way of possibly delaying the inevitable. It was only digging a deeper hole, she knew that, but she held his gaze provocatively. 'Why don't we try it out and see? For old time's sake?'

The air between them stilled as his eyes locked intently with hers. Then, without saying a word he took her hand and pulled her with him as he rose from the settee.

But as he made love to her in the quiet intimacy of his bedroom, his powerful thrusts driving away the darkness of her anxieties until she was crying out with pleasure, she clung to him with a fierceness that matched the desperation in her heart. It was the beginning of the end, she knew, and there wasn't a thing she could do about it.

'So, next week?' he said as they parted company at the tube. 'I've set the test up for Monday. The address is on the card I gave you. I'll meet you and Katie there.'

'Okay.'

She had no intention of keeping the appointment.

He pulled her to him and gave her one final lingering kiss. 'I've missed you, Natasha. Maybe we were all meant to be together? You, me and Katie?'

As soon as she got home she picked up the phone and dialled the police station.

'Sergeant Briscombe please, it's Natasha Campbell … well can I leave a message for him? I need to talk to him about a case he's working on. I know it's the weekend coming up, but could you ask him to call me? It's urgent. Thank you'.

She poured herself a gin and tonic and downed it in one. If this didn't work, she didn't know what she was going to do.

***

Hannah clicked off her mobile and turned to look at Jess excitedly. 'That was Miss Williams, the head. They had the Governor's meeting last night and they've reinstated me. She told me to take the next week off up to the end of the month and start on 1st March. I can't believe it.'

'Oh Han, that's fantastic. I told you it would all be fine. But I'm going to miss you. It's been such fun working together. Sure you don't want a permanent job?'

Hannah smiled. 'I've enjoyed it too, you know that. But teaching's always been my thing. I've missed my babies.'

'God … there are days *my* baby drives me mad. She's been coming into our bed every night this last couple of weeks. I don't know what's the matter with her and it's making Fraser and me really grumpy with each other.'

Hannah hesitated. 'She did mention in the car the other day that you and Fraser had had an argument that morning. It's not anything to do with me, is it? You've been such a support over all this but I wouldn't want to think …'

She didn't miss the way Jess's body tensed up. Or the awkward expression that crossed her face.

'It *is* because of me, isn't it? And all this business with Sophie? If it's causing problems between you and Fraser …'

'Oh, honey don't be silly, of course it's not.' But she wouldn't meet Hannah's gaze. 'Fraser's been going through a tricky time at work, that's all,' she said lamely.

'Jess, I know you well enough to tell when you're fobbing me off.'

To her consternation her friend looked even more uncomfortable, and she stared at her in alarm.

'What's the matter? There *is* something. Please tell me.'

Were those tears in her eyes?

'I don't think I can,' Jess said miserably. 'I feel so bad about it.'

'What are you talking about? What can you possibly have done to feel bad about? You've been my rock this last couple of weeks.'

'I'm pregnant.'

Hannah stared at her in shock. *'What!* But that's fantastic news. Why would you feel bad about that, when you've been trying for so long? How many weeks?'

'Eleven, but ... it's just such awful timing. You've got all this stuff with Sophie going on and here I am about to have another baby. It's seems so unfair. I didn't know how to tell you, knowing what you're going through at the moment.'

Hannah moved over and gave her friend a hug. 'Oh, Jess, the day I can't be thrilled by news like that from my best friend ... and anyway, life *is* unfair, we know that. I'm only surprised you're surprised.'

'But it shouldn't be. I want you to have some happiness, too. If only things could start looking up for you.'

Hannah smiled. 'I expect they will one day, probably long after I'm dead and gone!'

'Oh, Han.'

'That's enough. Don't start feeling sorry for me, or I'll crack up.'

'I just wish you could meet someone – start over.'

'Jess...'

'I know – I'm not going off on one.'

'Good.'

'But that doesn't mean I won't stop hoping.'

'Get off my back, will you?'

Jess laughed. 'Okay, lecture over. So ... what do you want to do about carrying on working here? I'll feel mean dragging you in when you're meant to be taking a holiday.'

'I like coming in, you know that. But ... maybe I will take a few days off between now and the end of the month? I've been thinking about decorating my bedroom.'

'Hey, get you! That's a terrific idea.' Jess looked at her thoughtfully. 'I know this stuff about Sophie's been awful for you but ... you know what?' She took her friend's hand in her own and squeezed it. 'There's been a change in you this last couple of weeks. I've seen glimpses of the old Hannah and it's good to see.'

'I think you're seeing what you want to see. I've felt like crap most of the time. I've made such a mess of my life.'

'*Hannah*, how can you say that? You've had mega stuff to deal with and despite it all, you went to university, did your teacher training and got *on* with your life. Would you be thinking I was a failure if I'd done all that?' She studied her friend's face. 'You know what I'm saying's right. Don't be so hard on yourself. Be proud of how you've coped. Most people would have had a complete car crash. Now, come on.' She moved over to where the books were laid out on the table. 'Let's have a look through these while it's quiet. I'll help you decide on the wallpaper for your bedroom.'

CHAPTER NINETEEN

'Sorry to drag you out on a Saturday morning,' Natasha said without preamble leading Harry through to the lounge. 'But we need to talk.'

'I know we do. Look ... I'm a shit I know for saying this, but ... what happened the other day was a mistake. I'm not exonerating myself – I sure as hell enjoyed it, but to take things any further would be suicide for me. I can't wreck my career. I'm sorry.'

He tailed off, lamely.

'Okay.'

His eyes fixed on her in astonishment. 'You don't mind?'

'Not at all, if you feel that bad about it. It was only a kiss after all. Having an affair is meant to be fun. If you're going to spend your whole-time agonising about it, what's the point?'

'Thank God you're not offended. It's not that I'm not attracted to you, you know I am, but...'

'No need to explain, Harry. I'm happy to forget all about it, but in return, there's a little something I'd like you to do for me...'

'I can't do that,' Harry said when she'd finished. 'There's no way I can interfere with that stuff. It's done in a totally different department for a start. It would be impossible for me to tamper with the results. And why would you want me to anyway?'

'I can't say, but there are things that have gone on in my past where ... it really wouldn't be good for me to have my DNA on a database.'

'Natasha.' He ran his hand through his hair. 'I don't believe what I'm hearing. What can you possibly have done that would worry you enough to ask me to tamper with police evidence?'

'I haven't *done* anything. But there's certain information I don't want coming out. I need you to do this for me.'

'I'm sorry, but I can't.'

'Oh, I think you can, Harry.'

Her eyes bore into his. 'I don't have to remind you of what we *nearly* did. Some people might see that as taking advantage of someone who's quite vulnerable at the moment. My husband would certainly take a dim view on it – as would that nice boss of yours I'm sure.'

'You're *blackmailing* me?'

'Of course I'm not, but it can't be that difficult for you lose my DNA record … or even swap it for someone else's, surely? No one need ever know.'

'Even if it were possible, *I'd* know.'

'Well …' her expression was pragmatic. 'We all have our little indiscretions to hide – no one knows that more than me. Believe me you learn to live with them.'

He shook his head slowly. 'I can't do it. *Won't* do it,' he corrected. 'I may have been stupid enough to get involved with you when I was working on a case but to do something like that is moving to another level completely – and I'm not *that* stupid. You do what you want, but I can't do what you ask.'

'Don't you realise you could lose your job if I were to report you?'

'Of course I do.' He stood, his face tense. 'I'm sorry it has to end like this. I'm not proud of the way I behaved, but I think you have even less to be proud of. I'll see myself out.'

Natasha held on until she heard the front door shut, then she crumbled, sinking her head into her hands with a sense of despair. She wasn't used to losing, and to fail now over something so crucial…

She reached for her cigarettes and lit one with a shaky hand. Her life was collapsing around her and any day now it would all come out. It would be in the newspapers, on the television. Everyone would be talking about her. She couldn't face it.

***

Adam opened up for the weekend surgery, his mind crammed with the events of the past few days as he prepared automatically for his clinic. He was angry that Natasha had refused to talk about things last night. The trip to London had apparently worn her out. But he couldn't get what the police had told him out of his head. He was beginning to realise he didn't know his wife at all. All those years ago when he *thought* they'd been in love, and she hadn't even been truthful with him then. Their marriage was a sham. An empty shell of nothingness – and it was destroying him to admit it. He'd always been the strong one in the relationship – the one holding their precarious family unit together – but now he didn't feel strong at all. He pressed his fingers to his eyes and drew a breath. He needed to pull himself together.

Six hours later, he washed his hands and turned back to the last client of the day – a little boy, clutching his dog so fiercely that he had to smile. He was a scruffy little urchin and his mother wasn't much better. He knew where they lived, a dilapidated mobile home on the outskirts of Hertford. They didn't have much and certainly couldn't afford to be paying vet fees.

'Bring her back in on Monday and we'll just check the stitches are healing,' he said with a smile.

'We can't afford to come again,' the mother said flatly. 'I only brought her in 'cos Bobby was upset that it weren't healing right.'

'Well, he was right. It could have turned nasty if we hadn't dealt with it. Come at the end of surgery around five thirty. It won't cost you anything. I just need to see that those antibiotics are working. I'm sure she'll be fine now.'

'There y'are Bobs – I told you she'd be okay. All that fuss for nothing.'

But her eyes, as she ruffled her son's hair, were loving. It brought a lump to Adam's throat. He'd never once seen Natasha act like that with Katie.

He tidied his stuff away and looked at his watch. The surgery closed early on a Saturday but the last thing he felt like doing was going home. He shook off his guilt as he finally confronted the urge that had been tugging at him all day. He knew what he was going to do.

Outside her door he hesitated. He knew damn well he shouldn't be here but he wanted to tell her he was glad it hadn't been her daughter. And he needed some breathing space before he went home.

He could probably be done for invasion of privacy, he thought, as he waited for her to answer the door. It had to be an infringement of some sort that he'd checked their computer records to get her address.

'Oh!'

She was wearing a pale pink shirt tucked into tight jeans, her short blond hair tucked casually behind her ears.

'Hi, hope I'm not interrupting anything?'

Through the door he could hear voices. Clearly, he was.

'Uh … no, but what are you doing here?'

Good question. What *was* he doing there? He thrust the chocolates at her. 'I bought you these. Just to say I'm glad it wasn't your daughter. Look, I can see I've called at a bad time–'

'No, you haven't actually. It's my birthday and a couple of my friends dropped by with a bottle of champagne to celebrate. We started early as you can see, but they're just leaving. You can come in if you want?'

The offer was diffidently given, but he found himself following her into the small comfortably furnished flat. He looked around as he entered. It was tastefully decorated but very bare. No photos or knickknacks anywhere. Nothing on the walls. She led him into the lounge where two women were sitting on the sofa.

'Hi … I'm Jess Dean,' one of them proffered, her eyes curious. 'I don't think we've met?'

'Adam.' His hesitation was barely perceptible. 'Campbell.'

'And I'm Lucy,' the other girl said. 'You're a dark horse, Hannah.' Her eyes were mischievous and Hannah felt her cheeks reddening.

'Weren't you just leaving?' she asked pointedly. 'You'll be late for the film if you don't push off. I'm sorry to be a wet blanket. I'm just not in the mood for chic flics at the moment.'

Outside the door, Jess looked at her incredulously. '*Hannah*, what are you doing?'

'What?' Her tone was defensive.

'That's the man, isn't it? The one who found the baby in his garden? I remember the name from the papers.'

'So?'

'So - what's he doing here in your lounge? For a start, he's married!'

'Oh, Jess. It's not like that.'

'Isn't it?'

'No! We've just got things in common over what's going on at the moment.'

'Yes, and let's face it, you don't know *what's* going on. He could be responsible for that baby's death, for all you know.'

'Oh, come off it! Does he look the type to be a child murderer.'

'Did Ben look the type to be a woman-beater?'

She saw her friend's face and reached out to take her hand. 'I'm sorry, that was out of line – I don't want to upset you. But be careful, okay?'

'Of course I will. But I seriously don't think I've got anything to fear from Adam Campbell.'

As she closed the door after them though, she took a shaky breath. Could Jess have a point? Could Adam somehow be implicated in all this? She couldn't really believe it – but then her track record on judgment of character wasn't great.

She walked slowly back into the lounge. He was standing by the window looking out onto the back garden.

'Pretty garden you've got. Someone spends time on it?'

'The Landlord has a guy who comes and cuts the grass, but I get out there when I can.'

She put the chocolates carefully down on the table. 'Thanks for these, it was thoughtful of you.'

He smiled. 'And well timed by the sound of it. Happy Birthday.'

He looked as if he hadn't shaved in a couple of days but it suited him somehow – added to the tough outdoor look of him. She saw him glance at the bottle on the table, and following his gaze she relaxed a little.

'Would you like some? There's still half a bottle left and I'm off to my Mum's this evening. It'll only go to waste.'

He grinned. 'Can't have that. Thanks.'

He took the glass she offered and sat down opposite her. 'You must be relieved – that it wasn't your daughter?'

She shrugged. 'I am of course, but it still means I'm no nearer to knowing what happened to her.'

'So, what happens now? It seems hard on you if it all just gets filed away again.'

Hannah was silent for a long time. She longed to share the latest development with him but caution held her back. What if he said something and word got out about the hair sample? She wouldn't compromise Sophie's safety.

'That may well happen,' she said finally, 'but there is *one* new lead they've got. It might not come to anything, but if it does…'

She couldn't keep the gleam of hope out of her eyes.

'Am I allowed to ask what it is?'

'Probably not. They didn't tell me *not* to say anything, but…'

'No problem. I don't want to pry. Whatever it is, I'll keep my fingers crossed for you.'

She grinned suddenly. 'Detective Chief Inspector Murray's quite scary, isn't he? I don't want to get on the wrong side of him. He makes me feel about five years old.'

'I know what you mean.'

'Have they come up with anything new on the remains they found in your garden?'

She noticed his hesitation. 'God knows,' he said finally. 'They seem to be unearthing all sorts of stuff.'

'What sort of stuff?'

'I'm afraid I *am* banned from discussing it.'

They sat for a moment in silence.

'How did you know where I live?'

He looked embarrassed. 'It wasn't hard. I got your details off the computer. I hope you don't mind?'

She gave it some thought. 'No. It was nice of you to come.' The look she gave him was direct. 'Does your wife know you're here?'

He shook his head. 'No. The way Natasha's feeling at the moment she probably wouldn't have wanted me to come, but I just wanted to say that we were glad it wasn't your daughter. I'm sorry if you feel that puts you in an awkward position.'

Hannah was shocked to realise that she needed to be careful. She didn't know why, but she was drawn to this man, and it had been a long time since she'd felt that way about anyone. She found herself thinking back to the conversation she'd had with Jess - about how nice it might be to have a decent man in her life. But that wasn't *this* man. He was married and off limits. She needed to remember that.

'I don't feel that,' she said. 'Exceptional times make us act in exceptional ways sometimes.'

For a moment, their gazes met. She was shocked by the unhappiness in his eyes.

'Are you okay?'

'Do you ever wonder what life's about?'

'All the time.'

He shook his head and dropped his gaze to the stem of his glass. ''I'm twenty-eight years old and everything feels so screwed up. It's all so different to how I imagined my life would be.'

'Join the club.'

His eyes shot to her face. 'God, I'm sorry. You've had far more to contend with than I'll ever have.'

She shrugged. 'Look, I don't know what's gone on in your life – you have the advantage over me there – but all I can say is that you have to keep telling yourself that soon the good stuff will start to happen. There's an art to it.'

'Is that what you do?'

'I try, but it's not always easy...'

From out of the blue, as if to prove her right, the panic attack whipped through her.

Oh no, not now.

She held herself rigid, gripping her glass tightly as she tried to head off the clammy sensation she'd learned to dread, the suffocating breathlessness.

'Are you all right?' Adam's voice was coming from a distance.

'I'm sorry ...' she sucked in deep gasps of air leaning forward and putting her glass shakily back on the table. 'I feel faint.'

She struggled to draw her breath, the rushing noise in her ears getting louder. Then firm hands were at her head, pushing it down between her knees, holding it there. 'Just close your eyes and breathe in deeply.'

'In that drawer over there,' she gasped, 'a brown paper bag.'

The hands left her, but within a few seconds they were back, one thrusting the bag over her mouth and nose so she could breathe into it, the other back on her head.

'That's it, steady breaths,' he ordered. 'You're doing great.'

She shook her head, her voice panicked. 'I think I'm going to pass out...'

'No, you're not.' His voice was matter of fact. 'You'll only pass out if you hyperventilate. Just keep taking regular breaths and think about something else. We'll talk. What are you doing tonight for your birthday? Have you got plans?'

'Going to my mum's for dinner.' Her voice was muffled by the bag.

She could hear the smile in his voice. 'Sounds like your life's about as exciting as mine. I've got a good one for you now. What are your ambitions for your life?'

It was such a random thing to ask, but it worked, successfully diverting her thoughts as she forced herself to go with the question. His tactics were beginning to calm her she realised, as was the gentle stroking motion of his thumb on her head.

She took a few more breaths then lifted her head tentatively. 'If you'd asked me that two weeks ago I'd have said I wanted to be Headmistress of my own primary school.'

'And now?'

'I just want to find out what happened to my daughter.'

The bleakness in her voice filled the room but he didn't allow her to dwell on it. 'No desire for a partner? More children?'

It was an incredibly personal question, and coming as it did on the back of Jess's comments, it touched on something raw deep inside her. For the first time, she allowed herself to actually consider the possibility. It wasn't really true that she wanted to spend the rest of her life alone, she realised. She'd love to meet the right person. She just wasn't sure he was out there.

172

'I'd like that,' she said in a quiet voice, 'but it's not very likely. I've got a cartload of baggage. Not many men would want to take that on.'

'Don't you think you're being a bit harsh on the male species?'

'Am I?' Her lips twisted wryly as she lifted her head higher to look at him. 'You've just experienced first-hand some of my issues. Would you be rushing to take on someone who's a bundle of nerves like that?'

His gaze as it held hers was steady. 'All I saw was a woman who's going through a rough time having a mild panic attack. It's no big deal.'

'For you maybe...'

But she was grateful to him for making her feel less of a freak. Just like that, she was beginning to feel calmer now, the attack passing over. She took one final breath from the bag then drew back. 'Thank you. I'll be okay now. Stupid ... you must think I'm pathetic.'

He shook his head as he straightened up. What he actually thought was the complete opposite. She had to be a very strong woman to endure all she'd gone through. He tried not to think about the silky softness of her hair as he'd cradled her head. He'd enjoyed touching her he realised, stroking her ... and he shouldn't. He moved carefully away from her and back to his chair.

'You're not pathetic at all. You've been through a lot and it would be abnormal if it hadn't had some sort of an effect on you. Does that happen often?'

'I've not had an attack in months but I've had two this week. I'm sorry you got landed.'

'Glad I was here to help. Can I get you a glass of water – or perhaps some tea – to complete my services?'

Hannah managed a shaky smile. 'A glass of water would be good. Thanks. The kitchen's along the hallway straight ahead of you.'

He walked in the direction she indicated but as he made his way down the hall his eyes were drawn to a colourful name plaque on a door to his left. *SOPHIE,* it said simply. He hesitated. He shouldn't, he knew, but the door was slightly ajar and acting on impulse he moved over and gently eased it open.

The scene before him halted him in his tracks.

Along one wall a beautiful antique cot with patchwork bedding was home to a host of cuddly toys that peeped out at him through wooden bars.

At the windows, brightly coloured curtains, adorned with fairy-tale mermaids, co-ordinated lovingly with the hand painted motifs on the walls. In the corner, a small furry rocking horse sat in lonely vigil, a Harrods 2007 teddy bear propped carefully up in its saddle.

From the rich creamy carpet to the mass of vibrantly coloured toys, it was a room that exuded love and warmth; yet when he gently lifted the baby's hairbrush on the dressing table next to him, the area surrounding it was thick with dust.

Replacing it quietly he backed out of the room.

'Here you go,' he said a couple of minutes later, handing her the water. 'Are you feeling better now?'

'Yes thanks.' She took the water and sipped from it gratefully.

He knocked back the last of his champagne and looked about him.

'How long have you lived here?'

She looked surprised. 'About six and a half years. Why?'

He shook his head and smiled. 'No reason.'

'I know what you're thinking. That it doesn't look very lived in, right?'

'I guess it's the simplicity of it and lack of knick-knacks that makes it look a bit that way. Don't get me wrong though. It's very nice.'

She bristled. She knew the flat was boring but really, she hadn't felt like making it homely. She'd wanted it to reflect the grey existence her life had become.

'It suits me fine,' she said stiffly.

'I'm sure it does. I didn't mean to offend you. I have a habit of putting my foot in it sometimes.'

His smile was easy and she found herself relaxing. She guessed he was the sort of person it would be impossible to stay annoyed with for very long.

'I doubt that somehow. You strike me as being the tactful sort.'

He laughed. 'I'm not sure my wife would agree with you.' He looked suddenly uncomfortable. 'Which is where I should probably take myself off, let you get ready for going out. Thanks for the drink. I've enjoyed our chat.'

He stood up, and Hannah rose too, then wished she hadn't. It had narrowed the gap between them – making her all too conscious of the tug of attraction that seemed to draw her like a magnet. His face was sober as he looked at her.

'I probably shouldn't have come, but I'm glad I did. You're very strong you know. So, don't ever call yourself pathetic. I don't think I could have gone through what you have and stayed sane.'

His eyes seemed to settle on the gentle curve of her mouth and there was a subtle shift in the atmosphere. She was shocked by an urge to close the gap between them and feel that mouth on hers, and even more shocked as the image of it took over and she imagined his surprise turning to passion as their kiss deepened. Shocked, she put a rein on her thoughts. The air between seemed suddenly filled with tension. He was staring at her as if he could read every thought in her head.

Dear God, she hoped not.

For a long moment, their gazes locked and she seemed incapable of breaking that contact. Then Adam turned abruptly away and headed for the hall. She willed her feet to follow him. At the door, he turned one more time to look at her. The heat had gone from his gaze, but his expression was intense.

'Good luck with everything.'

'Thanks. You too.'

And he was gone, striding down the path without a backward glance.

Hannah shut the door and leant heavily back against it, aware that her heart was hammering. *What had that been about?* And for goodness sake - *whatever* it had been about, there was no mileage in it. He was a married man, and she *wasn't* a marriage wrecker. Other people did things like that, but not her.

Taking a deep breath, she walked back into the lounge. Their conversation had struck a chord with her and for the first time since Sophie had been taken, she took a long critical look at the rather depressing picture it must present to the outside world. Not a single photo on the windowsills, bare walls devoid of pictures and paintings. No throws or colourful cushions to brighten the place up. When Ben had lived here, it had been filled with expensive furniture and objects of art, with original paintings from art galleries covering the walls and luxurious rugs in all the rooms. She'd wanted none of it when he'd left. She'd kept the carpet and curtains, and Sophie's room had remained untouched of course, but that had been it. It was no wonder it felt more like a motel than the home it could and should be.

She felt an inexplicable urge to do something about that and without giving herself time to analyse it, went into her bedroom and pulled out a large box file. They were all still there – photos of her childhood, her parents, her school friends. She reached slowly for the large silver-framed photo lying face down on top of the others. She knew what it was. She picked it up and turned it over. It had been taken the day before Sophie had disappeared and Hannah looked so proud, so *happy* as she held her tiny daughter in her arms. She'd had no idea how quickly her life was about to change. She looked at the picture long and hard but no tears came. Instead, baby moments too numerous to log flitted through her mind like the shutters on a camera, vividly evoking the memories of those precious three weeks. Sophie's warm, slippery body in the bath, so fragile as she supported her, her tiny arms and legs shooting out like a startled rabbit when she was laid on the changing table. The sweet scent of baby shampoo when she kissed the top of her head...

And the most precious memory of all – her daughter's peppered murmurings, the only sound to break the silence of the night, as she suckled contentedly at Hannah's breast.

She traced her fingers lovingly over the photo, following the line of the little pink and white bonnet Sophie wore, then looked around for pride of place.

Over there, on the shelf above the television she decided.

Once she'd started she couldn't stop, fixing collages to the walls, pulling out all her old favourites – ransacking the garage for the coloured cushions she knew she'd stacked away in bags. And when finally she'd finished, she looked around pleased with her efforts. It may not be much, but it was a start.

And for the first time ever, it felt like home.

CHAPTER TWENTY

The light was on in Natasha's room when Adam swung into their drive. He'd sat a long time in the car outside Hannah's flat, trying to make some sense of his feelings; but, there was no sense to be made. He shouldn't have called on her, plain and simple. Any idiot could have told him that. And now it had opened up a can of worms. He hadn't expected to be attracted to her like that. And he had no business *being* attracted to her.

He drew a breath as he faced the reality of his feelings. He didn't love Natasha – hadn't done so for a very long time, even though his awareness of her needs had created a different sort of relationship where he felt responsible for her. Had he ever loved her? Their courtship had been so intense and the news about the pregnancy so quick he'd barely had time to think about anything. She'd wanted him, and with her mother dying and a baby on the way, it hadn't even occurred to him not to do the honourable thing. Within nine months of meeting, they were married. And within three months of being married he knew he'd made a terrible mistake.

Striding into the lounge he was almost bowled over by his daughter's exuberant greeting as she threw herself at his legs.

'Daddy, daddy – look what I'm doing. Grandma bought me a sticker book.'

He looked at the stickers painstakingly matched to each individual picture. 'That looks like jolly hard work. Well done.'

'Mummy said I could have two stories tonight if I was good and didn't *intrupt* her. Will you read to me?'

He ruffled her hair as he lifted her back onto her chair. 'We'll see. Maybe mummy and I can do a story each. How about that?'

'Goodee.'

'You carry on with what you're doing while I go upstairs and see mummy. I'll come back down soon.'

He took the stairs two at a time. She was sitting on her bed writing in her journal when he walked in but she put it down carefully when he said they needed to talk.

'Do we? What about? And where have you been anyway? I called you at the office ages ago and you didn't pick up.'

His gaze shifted uncomfortably and she frowned, picking up on it. 'You haven't been talking to the police again?'

'No.'

'Where were you, then?'

He sighed. He wasn't about to start adding lying to the list of problems between them. 'If you must know, I went to see Hannah Walker. To tell her we were happy that it wasn't her baby they found.'

'You did *what*? Why would you do that?'

'Because I thought it was a nice thing to do.'

'Oh *right*. And I'm sure you'd have done the same if she'd been some straggly old bag not worth a second look. How did you know where she lived?'

Her look had become suspicious.

'She brings her cat to the surgery. Her address was on the system.'

'I can't believe you *did* that. Were you planning on telling me if I hadn't asked?'

Adam met her look levelly. 'Probably not. I wouldn't have wanted to upset you.'

'Oh, why on earth would I get upset just because my husband's chasing around after other women?'

'I'm not chasing around after anyone. I just wanted to offer her some sympathy. The poor woman's been through hell and back over all this.'

'*And we haven't?* But of course, I was forgetting ... Adam, the *conscientious* carer, always looking after everyone else's needs. Maybe if you're extra nice to her she'll thank you in an extra nice way.'

'Stop it, Natasha.'

'I notice you don't deny it. And how long can you go without sex Adam? Even you must crack at some point.'

It was so near the truth of where his thought had been only a few minutes ago that he felt the colour rise in his cheeks.

'Oh, just leave me alone,' Natasha said irritably, turning away from him.

'I'm not going anywhere until we've talked.'

She turned back. 'What about?'

'How can you even ask that? Your father living in this house for one thing. The *skeleton* for another. What the hell's going on? Is it all connected? Is it something to do with your past. Or your family?'

'Don't be ridiculous, of course it's not. You're beginning to sound like the bloody police.'

'Well, maybe I am. But I'm trying to understand why it is that your father lived here before us, and is *still alive*, and you never happened to mention those facts to me.'

Her face contorted. 'I told you why that was. And if all this *is* anything to do with him and my stepmother then I certainly didn't know about it, and no doubt the police will uncover that soon enough. What was the point in telling you about him when we knew he was emigrating? He was never a proper father to me and certainly wasn't a decent partner to my mother. He left us for that tart when I was fifteen and after that it was nothing but arguments. We saw as little of him as we could.'

'But I was your *husband*. Why wouldn't you have told me your father was still alive? If you had issues with him I was someone you could have offloaded to. I felt a complete idiot not knowing anything about him.'

She looked over at him, her eyes mocking. 'Oh dear, we can't have that can we? Poor Adam, feeling like an idiot.'

Suddenly he was angry. 'Natasha, that's not what I mean and you know it. Why was it such a big secret?'

'Don't keep putting *pressure* on me,' Natasha shouted, covering her ears with her hands. 'I can't take much more. What do you want to hear? That he *abused* me? That my mother knew about it and still didn't want to split up with him? Because that's how it was, Adam. I tried to tell her but she didn't want to know. What sort of a mother doesn't listen to her child when she tells her something like that? She screamed at me for telling such dreadful lies. I was twelve years old.'

Adam stared at her stunned. He took a step forward but the venomous look in her eye stopped him dead.

'Don't touch me! I'm sick to death of people touching me, prying – thinking they know what's best for me when they don't. Only I know what's gone on in my life and if I choose not to share it then that's my business. Remember how shocked you were that I never cried when my mother died? Well now you know why. She never stopped loving my father, despite what he'd done to me. She'd have gone back to him at the drop of a hat if he'd asked her. How do you think that made *me* feel? And how do you think you'd have reacted if I'd told you all that when we were going out? I'll tell you how; you'd have dumped me at the first opportunity. I wouldn't have seen you for dust.'

She laughed hysterically. 'How silly is that? I'm going to lose you now anyway, aren't I? I've seen it in your eyes. You're fed up with me – fed up with having a lunatic for a wife.'

'Stop it. Stop talking like that. You're not a lunatic and you should know me better than to think I'd have dumped you. I'd have supported you, if you'd let me. But you never did. You shut me out. I've tried over and over to be there for you, but how can I help you if you won't let me?'

'Oh – just get out,' she screamed. 'I don't want your pity.'

'Tash ...'

'Get out! Do you hear me? Leave me alone. I don't need you...'

CHAPTER TWENTY-ONE

Harry sat facing Murray across his desk and waited for the explosion. It didn't come. Instead Murray looked at him with resignation in his eyes.

'What a thing to greet me with first thing on a Monday morning. You're a fucking idiot – but you don't need me to tell you that.'

'No, sir. I've been thinking the same thing myself the whole weekend.'

'What the hell were you thinking of, man?'

'Not much at the time to tell the truth. You can't make me feel any worse than I already do.'

'Do you think she'll report you?'

'I don't know. I can't fathom her out at all.'

'I can't believe you could be so stupid. I should report you myself, or at the very least take you off the case.' Murray was silent for a moment giving it some thought then he sighed.

'Be grateful we're so short-staffed Harry, and that it was a kiss and nothing more. I think for the time being, as far as I'm concerned, we haven't had this conversation. We'll bide our time and see what happens. But Christ Almighty, you don't go near Mrs Campbell on your own again. And if you're lucky enough to get away with it this time, let it be a lesson to you for the future. You might get away with one mistake, but two ...'

'I've been an idiot, I know.'

'Well, I won't argue with that. Let me know as soon as her DNA result comes through. I'm curious to know what Mrs Campbell has to hide from her deep past.'

Harry let out a breath, even if it was only a temporary reprieve, and passed Murray a wad of papers.

'I've got the signed statement from her father here. The Melbourne police said he seems a pretty straightforward sort of guy but quite a cool customer. His wife is Australian, which is apparently why they emigrated. She wanted to go back to where her family were. There's no telling of course if that was the real reason, but they hereby deny all knowledge of any baby being buried on their land.'

Murray sighed and took the statement. 'It may be that someone has to go and interview them out there. But we won't waste the taxpayers' money quite yet.'

Natasha's mobile rang at mid-day exactly. She looked at the caller ID and rejected it. Zach wouldn't be happy that she hadn't turned up with Katie for the DNA test. She hadn't figured out what to say to him yet. But she couldn't think about that at the moment. It was the least of her problems. She lit a cigarette with hands that weren't steady and drew deeply from it.

***

'It's through! Natasha Campbells' DNA. Wait 'til you read this.'

Murray snatched the report from Harry's hands and read it. 'Get your coat,' he said, grabbing his own. 'I'll meet you by the car.'

There was a dark car parked in their drive as Adam pulled in and he frowned, recognising it as DCI Murray's. The phone call from Natasha had been terse and to the point. The police were there and he needed to come home. He hurried into the house and found her sitting on the sofa in the lounge. She looked haunted and recognising that look, he sat down next to her and took her hand in his.

'What's going on?' he asked, pinning his gaze on the two men. 'And where's Katie?'

'She's in the kitchen with one of my officers,' Murray told him. 'We were just asking your wife a few questions, Mr Campbell. I'm afraid we're going to need to take her down to the station to ask her a few more.'

His tone was serious and Adam felt a knot of apprehension.

'We've had the DNA results back now. They show that the remains we found have a genetic link to your wife. In fact, it would appear that the infant was her daughter.'

Adam's expression was one of stunned disbelief as he looked at his wife. 'Tash?'

Her eyes were deceptively calm. She was trying so hard not to think about that other baby. She'd prepared herself for this moment but she still felt sick with apprehension. Her voice was flat as she spoke.

'It was before you and I met, Adam. I had her when I was fifteen. My mother took me to Ireland when we realised I was pregnant – to my aunt's house. The plan had been to have her over there and put her up for adoption but when it came to it, I couldn't do it. I brought her back here and had terrible rows with my mother over it. She wanted me to go back and finish my education. She'd told my school I had depression those last couple of months when the pregnancy was showing. And then ... the day after we got back ... my baby died. I went into her room one morning and she was lying so still and so cold.'

She broke off with a little shudder; then carried on in the same flat tones.

'We hadn't seen anyone since we got back. Hadn't had time to register her even. Mum said that if we involved the emergency services there'd be lots of questions - they'd want to do a post-mortem – cut her up. I couldn't bear the thought of that. We knew my father was away in France, so that night, we took her around to his house and buried her. A week later my mother sent me back to school and told me I needed to put it all behind me and move on with my life. There was plenty more time for me to have babies.'

Her voice was completely devoid of emotion and she was holding herself rigidly, in a way Adam recognised only too well. It wouldn't take much to tip her over the edge.

'Someone must surely have known about your baby, Mrs Campbell?' Murray questioned carefully.

Natasha shook her head. 'Only my mother and my aunt. I didn't realise myself until I was nearly seven months and my mother took me straight over to my aunt in Ireland as soon as we realised. She didn't want anyone knowing. As far as she was concerned, I'd let the side down.'

'What about the father? Can you give us his name?'

If possible, her body went even more rigid. 'No.' Her eyes dipped away from that shrewd stare. 'I was a bit of a rebel in those days. It could have been one of a couple of people. As I hadn't intended keeping the baby it didn't seem relevant.'

There was a desperation about her that had Adam's eyes narrowing. There was something she wasn't saying. But he wasn't about to start questioning her in front of the police. She was walking too tight a line as it was. A horrific thought struck him – almost too awful to contemplate as he remembered their earlier conversation about her father. He couldn't go there. Not yet.

He sat reeling from the enormity of it all. How could he have lived with this woman for the last seven years, yet know so little about her?

Murray was reopening his notebook. 'Could we have your aunt's address? We'll need to check the facts with her.'

'It's in my address book. Adam, can you ...?'

Her hands were trembling he noticed and he jumped up swiftly and moved over to the dresser, pulling open the drawer that housed the address book. She took it from him and painstakingly wrote the details onto a piece of paper, handing it over to the Inspector. 'I'm not in contact with her now, but this is her address.'

'Thank you. I have one more question. Had your baby been dropped or suffered any accident that you were aware of?'

'*No*. At least … she'd had a bit of a cold but that was all. I shook her when I found her – trying to wake her. But she was already dead. I know she was.'

She whirled around to face Adam, clutching at his sleeve. Her expression was fierce and she was trembling from head to toe.

'I didn't kill her, Adam. I swear I didn't – she was already gone.'

Her face crumpled and she started to weep, silently at first, and then small heart wrenching sobs that gathered in strength and tore at Adam's heartstrings. He held onto her tightly.

'It's okay,' he said automatically, stroking her hair.

But it wasn't okay, he knew that. He looked at the down-bent head leaning heavily against his chest, felt the sobs shaking against him, and wondered how someone so fragile could harbour such awful secrets.

He looked at the Inspector.

'You said she needs to go down to the police station. Does it have to be tonight? I can bring her down myself tomorrow after we've dropped Katie at school. I'll take responsibility for getting her to you.'

Murray hesitated, looking at his watch and then at Natasha Campbell. It was five o'clock and she certainly didn't look good. He doubted it would do any harm to wait.

'Okay, Mr. Campbell. We'll leave the formal interview until tomorrow. If you could bring your wife down to the station sometime in the afternoon ... say four o'clock? That'll give us time to check out a few things first. Then I'll need to take a formal statement from you, Mrs Campbell.' He hesitated. 'You have a right to a solicitor if you want to bring one.'

Natasha looked at him fearfully, clutching at Adam's wrist. 'What will happen to me?'

Murray's tone was neutral. 'I can't say yet. We'll need to check out the facts of what you've told us – have a word with this aunt of yours. But I have to warn you, there's a possibility that formal charges may be made. One of the baby's arms was fractured and we need to get to the bottom of that.'

Natasha's grip on Adam tightened.

'I didn't kill her, Adam. They won't put me in prison, will they?'

He didn't know what to say.

'We'll be there Inspector,' he said grimly. 'We'll just need to drop Katie off at my mother's first, after school.'

He got up from the sofa and escorted them to the door. Outside, he was shocked to see that the predicted snow was falling with a vengeance, and already settling in a thick carpet on the ground.

'We'll see you tomorrow then,' Murray said, pulling his collar up as they took their leave, 'assuming we're not all snowed in by then.'

'You mentioned about the solicitor. Do you think we need one?'

He felt disloyal to Natasha even asking the question.

'It's up to you, Mr Campbell. I'd maybe take some advice.'

Back in the house, Adam looked at Natasha. It was another thing she hadn't told him. And it was huge. He was beginning to feel he was walking a tightrope himself.

'Why didn't you tell me, Tash?'

'What would you have done about it?' Her voice was toneless. 'Dug her up? Look at the mess we've got into now that her remains *have* been found. I knew I could never tell anyone.'

She was looking drained, her usual air of defiance gone.

'Is there something you're not telling the police?'

'No. I've told them all they need to know. Why should there be anything else? Isn't that enough for you?'

He returned her look helplessly. He desperately wanted to believe her - believe *in* her. But it was getting harder by the minute. What sort of a mother would bury her baby in a back garden for Christ's sake. Even if she was only fifteen? What else had she done that he knew nothing about? He felt as if his whole world had shifted this last couple of weeks. And though he desperately wanted to, he simply couldn't ask the really big question about the baby's father. Not yet.

'Telling them all they *need* to know isn't the same as telling them everything, and I think I know you well enough to recognise when you're being economical with the truth. Can't you at least tell *me* the rest of it?'

'I don't know, Adam. Can I?' She turned to look at him, her eyes calculating. 'Tell me, would you support me come what may? Whatever I might be hiding?'

He didn't answer straight away and her mouth twisted.

'You see. You're having to think about it. That's why I don't feel I can trust you.'

'*For Christ's sake, Tash.* I want to be able to support you, I really do. But you're not making it easy. I feel I don't know you anymore. I'm beginning to wonder if I ever did.'

Natasha reached jerkily for a cigarette just as the phone rang. She picked it up without thinking. 'Hello?'

'*Where the hell were you today?* Why didn't you turn up?' *Oh God!*

She took a deep breath and turned to Adam, her face set.

'Do you mind? It's private'

He held her look for a long moment. Then with an angry shrug, he stalked out.

Natasha turned back to the phone. 'I'm sorry Zach. The police have been here today about the investigation. It's just impossible for me to get up to London at the moment.'

'*Natasha.*' his voice was determined. 'I'm warning you now. If you don't meet me at that address tomorrow, I'll call your husband and tell him everything. It doesn't need to be like that, it's up to you.'

'*Look* – surely there's some other way of doing this, where I don't need to actually bring Katie with me?'

'Bringing her with you is the only way I can know for sure that the sample's hers. Don't mess with me Natasha. This is important to me.'

'Okay, okay.' She hesitated. What the hell, what was one more lie? She just needed to get him off her back. 'We'll be there,' she said. 'Eleven o'clock.'

Out in the kitchen, Adam pulled out his mobile and in desperation, dialled his mother. The thoughts exploding in his head were threatening to spiral out of control. He needed to talk to someone sane – find out where he was going wrong, so he could start to put things right.

There was no answer.

He sat down on a chair and slumped over the table. He felt completely powerless. He was failing his wife, unable to give her the unquestioning support she had a right to expect, yet he didn't know how to change that. How did he start believing in her again, so that everything was back to the fragile but familiar routine they'd established over the years? He was losing his grip, and he couldn't afford to.

He felt a shudder run through him, and he buried his head in his arms on the table.

It was some minutes later that a gentle hand on his shoulder made him raise it again. It was Natasha.

'It'll be all right Adam,' she said stroking his hair. 'I promise it'll be all right.'

Jesus, one of them was going mad, that was for sure. And he was beginning to think it was him.

'But it's *not* all right Natasha – can't you see that? Tomorrow, I've got to take you down to the police station for formal questioning. They may even *charge* you. And something tells me there's still more to come out.'

For a long moment, they stared at each other and he saw his own despair mirrored in her eyes. Then her brows snapped together. 'Oh, for God's sake pull yourself together.

I'm the one in trouble, not you. You'll be okay whatever the outcome. And by the way, your work mobile was ringing.'

She turned and left him and Adam dragged himself up to find his phone.

'I need to go up to Halls Farm,' he said, walking back into the lounge a few minutes later, hauling his jacket on. 'One of their cows is in labour and having problems and Tim's on another emergency. Will you be all right if I go?'

He felt guilty suggesting it, knowing that he should probably stay with her, be there for her. But what was the point? Nothing he said or did was ever right. And the truth of the matter was he needed some space to clear his head.

She was sitting, legs hunched beneath her, gently rocking in her chair – her vacant expression fixed on the cartoons Katie was watching on the television screen. He frowned.

'Tash? I can ask Jeanette to do the call if you'd rather?'

She flipped out of her trance to look at him. 'No, go. I'm fine. I'll get supper under way.'

'I'll be as quick as I can.'

'Fine.'

Natasha waited until he'd gone, then settled Katie with a drink and biscuits in front of the television before heading upstairs to her bedroom. She really had no choice now. Her past was about to come out and there was nothing she could do to stop it. A feeling of inevitability swept through her. She didn't want to have to face it. That was her choice, wasn't it?

Just briefly, she considered Katie and Adam. Their lives were going to be so messed up when all this came out. But there was nothing she could do to prevent it now. They'd get over it.

Her mind felt a terrible jumble and she could feel herself slipping back into the terrible darkness of a couple of years ago. *Where were her pills? She mustn't let that happen.*

She remembered how yesterday she'd thrown a piece of plastic wrapping onto the fire and watched it shrivel up and disappear into nothing. She'd feared as she'd watched it that the same could happen to her, and nobody would even notice she'd gone.

It was how she felt now.

She reached for her tablets and took two. She couldn't afford to lose the plot. Not now. She needed to plan.

**

DCI Murray slammed the phone down. So that was a complete blind alley. Had Natasha Campbell known the aunt was dead?

He went to the door and called Harry in. 'Mrs Campbell's aunt died last year,' he said tersely, his expression reflecting his frustration. 'Have you checked if there was a birth certificate?'

Harry shook his head. 'The office was closed. I'll do it first thing in the morning.'

'Remember to use her maiden name when they're doing the search. And here, this is the aunt's address in Ireland. Check *her* local GP surgeries while you're at it – see if any of them have any records relating to the pregnancy. One of them should.'

He moved back to his desk and opened an envelope someone had put in his priority tray. He stared at the piece of paper, dumbfounded.

'Well, who'd have thought that?' he said, showing the contents to Harry.

Hannah Walker's flat felt like a haven of normality when Murray dropped by on his way home that evening. There was a welcoming warmth to it that had been lacking before, which he realised was due to a change in décor.

There was another woman sitting tucked snugly into a chair brandishing a glass of wine, and she smiled cautiously at the policeman as he refused Hannah's offer of a seat.

'I won't be stopping, thanks, but I have some news for you, Miss Walker that I'd thought you'd want to know straight away.' He glanced briefly at her companion. 'You might prefer to discuss things more privately?'

Hannah smiled, her expression the most relaxed he'd ever seen it. It seemed a pity that he was about to disturb the nice evening they were obviously having together.

'No - it's all right Inspector. This is my friend Jessica Dean. There's not much she doesn't know about me.'

'Okay.' He paused. 'The fact of the matter is ... that hair sample you gave me ... it's come back as a match to your DNA.'

Hannah froze, her brain seemingly incapable of functioning, as she tried to absorb the significance of his words, not wanting to get the *wrong* end of the stick.

Was he saying what she thought he was? That Sophie might be...?

She hardly dared voice the question. 'What ... what does that mean exactly?'

'It means that your daughter's alive,' he said gently.

He watched as the colour drained completely from her face. *'What!'*

Her friend jumped up. She looked almost as shocked as Hannah did. 'I'll get you a glass of water, Han.'

Hannah was staring at the Inspector as if her life depended on it. *'Alive?'* she whispered, shakily. *'Sophie's alive? Are you sure?'*

'Unless you've had more than one child – then yes, we're sure.'

'Oh my God!' For a moment, she simply stared at him, stunned. Then her face broke into a radiant smile.

'I knew it,' she cried. *'I knew she wasn't dead!* Didn't I always *say* so? But...but what does it mean? Where do we go from here?'

Murray sighed, wishing he could be more positive for her. 'It means your daughter's alive. However, we're still no nearer to knowing what happened to her, or where she's living.'

Her face fell.

'I'm sorry I can't be more encouraging. The truth of the matter is, those results have only just come through and I haven't had a chance to think about what we do next. But now we know she's alive, well, it's a start, and I think there'll be a strong case for getting the investigation reopened. It may not be me who deals with it though, and I have to warn you there's not much to go on.'

Hannah's eyes were swimming. '*Thank you* – thank you so much for coming over to tell me yourself. I don't know what to say, but ... it has to be *good* news, right?'

'Absolutely,' he reassured her gently. 'We'll do our best to find her, I promise you.'

***

After she'd phoned her mother and Jess had gone, Hannah picked up the phone again. It had to be done ... especially after last time when he'd been so angry not to have been kept in the loop.

'I'm coming over,' Ben said straight away, when she told him the news.

'*No.* There's no point.'

But he'd already hung up. She looked at her watch. It was seven o'clock. It would take him about an hour. A knot tightened in her stomach – a long-forgotten sensation that was becoming all too familiar these days.

CHAPTER TWENTY-TWO

Natasha looked one more time around the cosy, familiar bedroom. There was nothing for her here – that's how it felt. She was an alien trapped in a world that was at odds with what was going on in her head.

But then wasn't that how she'd always felt? A misfit, existing in a parallel world – so different to the reality of her own? No-one ever *listened* to her. Never had. They made her feel like an idiot, as if she was of no importance at all. And it was all very well Amanda saying she should trust Adam. She knew she should, but she just couldn't. She didn't trust anyone, and now it was too late to try even if she wanted to.

Straightening her back, she stood up. Everything was in place. She'd left a note for Adam, propped up against her pillow.

Now for the hardest bit. Saying goodbye to Katie. She did love Katie in her own way, she really did. It was just that she'd been second best and always would be.

She exhaled fiercely. She wished she could shake off the terrible lethargy that seemed to have taken hold of her. She knew she was in a bad place mentally and that one call to the doctor was all it would take. But, what was the point? Nobody could help her now.

Downstairs, Katie barely glanced up as her mother walked into the lounge, and that annoyed Natasha. Didn't she realise the significance of what was about to happen?

'Kate?' She tried to make her voice soft, loving; but the little girl took no notice, her eyes remaining glued to the television.

Natasha felt her temper rising. Hadn't she always known that her daughter didn't like her? Didn't love her like she did Adam?

'*Katie.*' This time her voice was sharp, demanding a response and Katie looked up.

'Come here and give Mummy a cuddle.'

'In a minute, Mummy. I'm watching Tom and Jerry.' She turned back to the television screen, then looked up fearfully as Natasha stormed over to her.

'Don't tell me to wait a minute when I'm telling you to do something. I want to say goodbye to you. Mummy's going away for a while.'

She grabbed her daughter by the arm, yanking her to her feet.

'*Mummy ... you're hurting me.*'

Natasha's grip tightened as she shook her. 'Why do you always do this to me? You'd kiss Daddy goodbye if it was him, wouldn't you? You're a bad, wicked, little girl. You wouldn't care if I wasn't here anymore, would you? You'd be *happy*.'

She was shaking her hard and Katie shrank back, struggling to free herself.

'I want Daddy,' she screamed. 'Let me go. I *hate* you.'

Somehow, she managed to break free of Natasha's grip, running out of the door and up the stairs before Natasha even realised what was happening. Natasha went crashing after her, a blinding rage snapping in her head.

'*Come back here. Do you hear me?* How *dare* you run away from me? How *dare* you say you hate me?'

Ten minutes later she was driving recklessly down the drive, heedless of the treacherous snow swirling around the car. Her body was shaking, her eyes a blurry mist as she skidded out onto the road. The rage in her head was beginning to subside, only to be replaced by a huge sense of remorse. It was a nightmare ... a *nightmare*. How could everything have gone so wrong? She hadn't wanted to hurt her daughter. She only wanted to say goodbye – to have a cuddle so Katie would have *nice* memories of her. Katie had pushed her to it. She really had. And now this was something else the police would have against her. There really was no turning back now.

She stopped at the end of her road, looking both ways. The snow was building up on her screen and she increased the wiper speed to clear it. If only it was as easy to clear the jumble that was her mind. Which way should she turn? She looked frantically from side to side. Where *did* you drive to when you were about to take your own life?

The woods, she decided, trying to get a handle on herself. Perhaps near the old woodman's shack where she and Adam used to picnic when they first met. It would be deserted in this weather, so it would be unlikely anyone would disturb her.

But first, there was something she needed to do, and she'd go to Mario's to do it.

The coffee bar was warm and cosy, as always, and she stamped her feet on the mat, dislodging the snow before closing the door behind her.

'Evening, gorgeous, you're looking as lovely as ever.' Mario's warm Italian gaze slid over her appreciatively. 'Do you want your usual?'

For once, Natasha didn't respond in kind to his flirtatious manner. Nodding her head distractedly, she made her way over to a small table in the corner and opened her bag. First, she pulled out the long, detailed, letter she'd written. Then she fished out the small notepad she'd put in and stared at it for a long time before slowly starting to write. It didn't take long. In fact, it was only a couple of lines, but once she'd written them she knew an easing in her mind. Knew also there was no going back. She tried not to think about the bleak, isolated woods, waiting for her. She sipped unhurriedly from the chocolate Mocha that Mario had prepared for her, then rising from her seat, she left some money on the table and stepped out into the night.

Half an hour later, she'd posted her letters and found her spot, a small car park near where she and Adam used to go, that was empty tonight, but would surely have walkers and their dogs frequent it during the day. She didn't want to be missing indefinitely.

She turned off the engine. She didn't feel calm like she had done the last time, when she'd taken the pills. This time she felt agitated. She looked in the rear-view mirror and saw the piece of hosepipe sitting on the back seat. She wasn't even sure how to do it, but she'd read something on the internet and she'd seen enough clips in films to work it out, she was sure.

But, just to be on the safe side, she pulled her pills from her bag. The bottle was almost full – a cocktail of her medications that she'd been saving for weeks.

Without giving herself time to think, she tipped them all into her mouth and reached for the water bottle.

CHAPTER TWENTY-THREE

Adam knew something was wrong the moment he entered the house. It was eerily quiet and now he thought about it, he realised Natasha's car hadn't been parked in the drive.

Still he found himself calling out her name.

'*Tash? Katie?*'

Nothing.

'*Natasha.*'

He walked swiftly through the house checking the ground floor before taking the stairs two at a time. In her bedroom, his heart plummeted when he saw the envelope propped against her pillow.

Snatching it up, he tore it open.

Dear Adam,

I'm sure in the long term this letter can only come as a relief to you. I was never good news as far as you were concerned, or anyone else for that matter. As I'm sure you've realised, my past is about to catch up with me and I choose not to face up to it. This time, I promise, I'll do it properly.

Forgive me for the hurt I know I'm going to cause you.

Natasha

He stared at the letter, a cold fear gripping his heart. He should have stayed with her, got someone else to do his call-out. Why hadn't he realised how bad she was?

Then another fear struck him – so terrifying that it made his blood run cold.

Katie. Where was she? She hadn't taken her with her? *Christ*, she surely wouldn't have done that?

Throwing the note back down on the bed, he rushed out onto the landing to Katie's bedroom. He flung the door open. The room was empty but his eyes widened in horror at the sight of the broken mirror and overturned chair; the little ornaments and knick-knacks usually so carefully arranged on her dressing table, that were now scattered all over the floor.

'*Katie,*' he roared.

No answer.

He tried to keep a handle on his fear as he searched every inch of the house. He couldn't believe Natasha would have taken Katie with her. She wouldn't, surely?

It didn't take him long to establish that neither of them were in the house. Without wasting any more time he grabbed the phone and dialled 999.

'Can you get a message through to DCI Murray from Hertfordshire police?' he asked the girl after she'd taken the details. 'He knows our case and I'm sure he'd want to be informed.'

'I can't guarantee it, sir, but I'll relay that request on. Someone will be around to take details off you soon.'

'I won't be here. I need to go out and look for them. This weather's treacherous.'

'I'm afraid I must ask you to stay put for a while. We'll need more detailed information and it'll make it easier and quicker for us to track them down if you're there to supply it. We'll get someone over to you as quickly as we can.'

Hanging up, Adam quickly dialled his mother's number. He had no intention of sitting around waiting for the police to turn up. His mother could supply any information they needed.

'I'll be over in ten minutes,' she said straight away. 'Why don't you get some soup on and put it in a flask? If you find them they could probably do with it in this weather.'

She was giving him something to do to occupy his mind he realised, but it calmed him going through the mundane task.

***

Natasha worked swiftly and methodically in the freezing night air. It was snowing hard now and her fingers felt stiff and unwieldy as she forced them to do their work. It was a messy job as she tinkered around the exhaust – and she hated dirt, but finally, after what seemed an age, she had to be satisfied. She climbed back into the car and sat for a long moment with her head on the wheel.

Why didn't it feel right? Last time she'd been so high and divorced from reality that it had felt like a blessed escape. But this time she knew exactly what she was doing and it frightened her. Yet so much shit was about to hit the fan. What choice did she have? She'd never been good at facing up to stuff.

She raised her head and pulled the mirror down to take one last look at herself. But all she saw was Katie's terrified eyes staring back at her. She could still hear her daughter's screams in her head from when she'd hit her.

'I'm sorry, sweetheart,' she whispered, then flicked the mirror back up, rejecting the image of that haunted little face; closing her eyes and trying to replace it instead with Adam's craggy, good natured smile – the sort he used to give her when they first got together.

But it didn't work. All she could see was him as he'd been the past few weeks; tense and *resigned* almost, as the final nails in the coffin that was their relationship had been ruthlessly hammered home.

She tried to blame him for the situation she now found herself in. After all, if he hadn't dug up those bones, she wouldn't have got so stressed, wouldn't have started taking more of the drugs that fed her depression, wouldn't have started suffering again with the recurring nightmares that for a while she'd learnt to put behind her.

But she couldn't blame him, not really. It felt as if she'd been waiting for this moment all her life.

She'd always known the truth would come out. And now it had. And in a strange way, she was *glad*. There was no need to live a lie any longer. And it was a blessed relief. Perhaps *that* was why she wasn't so keen on ending everything this time. Because once the truth was out, that was surely the hardest bit?

She snapped her brows together. No point thinking like that. And anyway, who was she kidding? There was no alternative. If they locked her up in prison – or worse, an institution.

No, never. She wasn't putting herself through all that again.

Huge snow-flakes were piling up on her windscreen. The car was already beginning to feel like a tomb. She peered out of her window to the side and clung to the beautiful, silent picture it presented; the large flakes falling thickly from the sky, coating the branches of the trees before settling in swirling layers on the ground.

How insignificant we are in the face of the elements.

She thought of a tiny baby, plucked prematurely from life; imagined herself holding her in her arms in just a little while.

For the first time in her adult life Natasha Campbell said a prayer. Then she reached for the key in the ignition and switched it on.

CHAPTER TWENTY-FOUR

The insistent peal of the doorbell was enough to tell Hannah that Ben wasn't in a good mood.

She moved cautiously to the door then looked in surprise at the sullen faced girl standing on the doorstep at his side.

'This is my fiancée, Rebecca.' Ben said without preamble. 'She insisted on coming with me.'

He didn't look pleased about it.

She stepped aside to let them enter. 'I told you, there was no point you coming.'

'I had to. Have you got a whisky?'

She suspected he'd already consumed some alcohol. She wasn't going down that path.

'I've got tea, coffee or orange juice, she said coolly.

'I'll have an orange juice please,' Rebecca said quickly, looking at Ben. He shrugged. 'I'll have the same then.'

She led them into the lounge and headed for the kitchen to get the drinks.

'There was absolutely no need for you to come all the way over here at this time of night, especially in this weather,' she said a couple of minutes later, placing the tray down on the table. 'I've got nothing to add to what I said on the phone.'

'But she *is* alive? They're sure about that?'

'Apparently.'

'How do they know?'

Briefly she filled him in on the lock of hair.'

'Well at least it proves to those bloody bastards that you and I had nothing to do with her disappearance,' he said bitterly. 'I've a good mind to sue someone over all that. And I'd start with that bloody reporter that seemed to have it in for us.'

'It wouldn't serve any useful purpose, Ben.'

'Says who? We could probably claim a tidy little sum out of it if we got a good lawyer.'

Hannah looked at him in disgust. 'I can't believe I'm hearing this. We've just found out that our daughter's alive and all you can think about is making money out of it?'

His shrug was defensive. 'Some good might as well come out of it. And if we ever found her – think of the interest there'd be in a case like that.'

She stood up, her lips tight. 'Just go, Ben. I can't bear to even look at you when you talk like that. If ever I needed reminding of why you and I split up...'

She turned the full impact of her gaze onto the girl at his side.

'And if I were you, I'd think very carefully about spending the rest of my life with this man. It was the best thing I ever did when I ended our relationship, and I'm sure I don't need to tell you why.'

'*You little...*' Ben's face was ugly as he made a move towards her. 'I came over here to offer you some support.'

'Bullshit. You came over here to see what you could make out of the situation, and to see if I'd play ball. But if you think for one minute I'd try and capitalise on Sophie's circumstances...'

For a long moment, they stared each other out. Ben's face was twisted in anger. Then he raised a supercilious eyebrow, his expression switching in an instant. 'If they find our daughter,' he said calmly, 'I'm warning you now, I'll go for custody of her. It shouldn't be too hard convincing people that you're still barking, after your nervous breakdown.'

Hannah didn't flinch. 'I didn't have a nervous breakdown, as you well know.'

'It was as near as dammit - enough to plant seeds of doubt that you're not a fit mother.'

'Just get out, Ben. And *I'm* warning *you.* If you start causing trouble for me I won't hold back this time.'

'If you're referring to your ridiculous accusations that I'm some sort of wife beater, I don't think you'll get very far. Rebecca here would back me all the way. All it would do is expose your accusations for what they are – the pathetic, desperate ramblings of a pathetic, desperate woman.'

Without another word, he turned and headed for the door. 'Come on, Becky. There's no point staying here. You need a man to give you a good stiff seeing to, Hannah. Only I doubt you'd find anyone prepared to take you on. Have a good life.'

When they'd gone, she closed the door and sank weakly back against it. What a repulsive man he was. How could she ever have thought herself in love with him? But at least she'd managed to salvage her conscience by suggesting to Rebecca that she dump him. And that was about as much responsibility as she was prepared to take for a complete stranger's life.

She moved listlessly back into the kitchen and put the kettle on. She needed some coffee to settle her nerves. His threats had struck home. If they found Sophie, she knew he'd leave no stone unturned to try and discredit her.

She *wouldn't* let that happen.

***

Adam was standing by the patio doors when the sound of the doorbell alerted him to the arrival of his mother. For a moment longer he stared out onto the garden, still visualising the crime scene behind the rhododendrons that had started all this. Then he went to open the door.

He embraced his mother tightly and she hugged him back.

'Where will you go?' she asked, as he pulled back from her and reached for his jacket.

'I haven't a clue. I'll just drive around and see if I can spot them. I have to go and look for them, Mum. This weather's a killer if they get stranded.'

'What if the police want to talk to you?'

'I've got my mobile. I can answer any questions they've got over the phone. Thanks for coming.'

He choked on the words and his mother gripped his arm. 'It'll be all right, you'll find them.'

He covered her hand with his for a moment, drawing from her strength. Then he left. God knew where he was going to start looking, but anything had to be better than sitting around waiting to hear the worst.

It was as he was climbing into his car that he noticed the side door to the garage swinging slightly in the bitterly cold breeze. He stared at it puzzled. They never used that door in the winter.

Following some sixth sense, he got back out of the car. The snow had settled and everything was eerily quiet as he crunched his way to the garage. He didn't know what he feared but his heart was hammering as he opened the door wider and peered in. He breathed a sigh of relief when he saw that the garage was empty. What had he expected? To find Natasha's body swinging from a rafter? He shuddered and was about to leave the garage again when his eyes came to rest on a small tartan quilt lying on the floor. His blood ran cold. It was Katie's *'quiltie'*. The comforter she took to bed with her every night. What the hell was it doing in here?

His eyes darted around the garage again, this time more probingly. He could almost taste his fear as he looked around.

'Katie? *Kate* ... are you in here?'

There was no answer. He found himself walking slowly towards the old wardrobe in the corner. The door was slightly ajar and he could see something protruding very slightly in the gap. Horrified, he realised it was a child's shoe ... a foot. Blood thundered in his head as he covered the remaining ground in three swift strides.

'*Katie?*' He threw open the door.

She was lying crouched in a shivering bundle in the corner. Her hair was a mess, her green eyes huge with fear as she looked up at him, and on one side of her forehead a large lump was an angry red.

For a moment, he was frozen into immobility. *Had Natasha done this?*

Then recovering swiftly he bent down and scooped her gently into his arms. 'It's all right, sweetheart,' he crooned softly, kissing her. 'Daddy's here. What are you doing out here in the cold all by yourself? I've been so worried about you.'

She was whimpering quietly and shivering, and he held onto her tightly as gradually the breath that had been squeezed in his chest began to release. She clung to him, not saying a word and he let her be. Time enough for explanations later.

'It's okay,' he soothed again. 'It's okay... Nana's in the house. Let's get you into the warm, shall we? You're frozen.'

Inside, sitting by the Aga in the kitchen, he checked her over gently, breathing a sigh of relief as he realised there was no serious injury. He settled her onto his lap and rubbed some warmth into her frozen limbs as his mother rushed around making clucking noises.

'Some nice hot chocolate I think, and maybe some pancakes. They used to be Grandpa's favourite when he needed cheering up. You can sit there with daddy and watch me make them.'

Katie's sombre eyes stared back at her from the safety of her father's arms.

Adam didn't press her to talk, just sat there in a daze holding her, waiting for her to speak in her own time, battling with the fact that Natasha could have had anything to do with this.

'Where's Mummy?' she finally whimpered.

'She's not here. She's ... gone out.'

She clutched him tightly. 'She said I was a bad, wicked girl. She frightened me.'

Adam couldn't swallow for the lump in his throat. 'She didn't mean it, sweetheart. Of course you're not bad. Mummy's not very well at the moment. You know sometimes she says things she doesn't really mean. She would never have wanted you to stay locked in the garage like that.'

'She told me we were going out in the car but then she took me in there and told me not to come out else she'd be really angry with me. I was scared, Daddy. And it was cold.'

Her voice broke on the last words and she started to cry quietly.

'Ssh...' He gathered her to him, passing his own body warmth on to her. 'It's all right now. Nana and I are here with you. There's nothing to be frightened of anymore.'

He looked up as his mother brought a plate to the table. He shook his head helplessly.

'Here you go,' she said in a soft voice, putting it down in front of them. 'Pancakes with sugar and lemon and ice cream. That'll make you feel better. And daddy will probably let you eat them on his lap, if you're very lucky.'

It was a long while before Katie would let them settle her down, and the police arrived just as Adam had finished doing it. Swallowing his guilt over exposing Natasha, he told them quietly what had happened.

'Has you wife done anything like this before?' the police sergeant asked.

'Not the Katie thing, no …never. That's why I'm so worried about her. She's not been herself these last few weeks. I'm frightened that she really does mean to harm herself. She's tried once before to commit suicide.'

'Okay … well, we've got an alert out on the car. I'll need to take a quick look at your daughter now, to make sure she's okay, and after that we can leave her with you and your mother for tonight. But I'm afraid I'll need to file a report for the Children's Services. Someone will probably be in touch with you tomorrow about that. If your wife should return tonight you'll need to let us know and we may have to reassess the situation.'

'I understand.'

He couldn't believe what was happening, but he knew there was no covering up what had gone on. Natasha had over stepped the mark this time and the consequences would be serious.

After he'd shown the sergeant out, he turned a determined face to his mother. 'I'm going out to look for her. Will you be all right here on your own? If Katie wakes, call me.'

CHAPTER TWENTY-FIVE

"Wife in Baby Skeleton Case Goes Missing!"

Hannah stared appalled at the headlines in the national newspaper and then flinched as her attention was caught by a photo of Ben smiling out at her from the adjoining column. *"Our Daughter Is Alive. Confirmed."*

'Oh no,' she whispered, horrified.

Glancing at the clock, she moved swiftly over to the television and turned on the morning news. It wasn't long before the cameras flashed to Ben being interviewed by a reporter outside his smart London home.

'As you can imagine, Hannah and I are both ecstatic,' he was saying enthusiastically. *'We can't keep the grins off our faces. Of course, the police still have to find out who's keeping her, but we feel confident that with the improved resources and technology that exist today, it won't be long before we have Sophie back safe and sound where she belongs.'*

"Which is where?" the interviewer asked. *"I understand you and Miss Walker separated a number of years ago. During the first investigation in fact?'*

Ben looked a bit uncomfortable at that. *'Yes, that's true ... but we've remained friendly. Unfortunately, Hannah suffered from severe depression after Sophie went missing and had a nervous breakdown – understandable of course, but all this new stuff hasn't helped her condition. It may be that it would be better for Sophie to live with me and my fiancée – give her the stability of two parents rather than one. But obviously, we'd need to talk it all through with Hannah first.'*

The *bastard*! She knew exactly what he was doing, but how could he put Sophie at risk like that? Didn't he realise what could happen to her if her abductors panicked? *The idiot.*

She didn't know what to do. Should she phone Inspector Murray? He hadn't exactly told her not to tell anyone, but she was damned sure he wasn't expecting to have it blabbed all over the media like that and she didn't want him thinking she'd had anything to do with it.

On second thoughts, she decided to leave it. If he had a problem with her, he'd be in touch soon enough.

Another fear gripped her, even more terrifying as she stared at Ben's flawlessly handsome features. He looked so much the epitome of the moral, upright citizen as he stood there, his handsome face beaming engagingly at the reporter, that she was convinced he'd have no difficulty whatsoever persuading people she was incapable of looking after Sophie. How could she ever hope to beat him?

She straightened her back, snapping the television off. She wouldn't think about it. Not yet. Not until she had to.

Her gaze returned to the newspaper sitting on the table.

And then there was the thing about Adam's wife.

Pouring herself some coffee she settled down to read the article. When she'd finished, she sipped quietly at her drink and pondered the situation. Adam must be going through hell. Should she go and see him – offer him support as he'd done for her? It was surely what anyone would do in the circumstances?

She pondered the situation a bit more. How to go about it? It was unlikely he'd have gone into work with his wife missing, but did she really feel she was justified visiting his home? And why did she feel such a compelling need to do just that?

Perhaps it was because she remembered that look of utter desolation on his face when he'd been talking about how everything seemed to have gone wrong in his life. She sensed he wasn't the sort of man to share that sort of revelation lightly. Knew also what it felt like to feel like that.

She was still no nearer making up her mind that lunchtime in the shop, when she offered to go out and get sandwiches.

'That would be good,' Jess said, 'but just put mine in the fridge when you get back, will you? I've got a one o'clock appointment in Welwyn, so I'll be gone for a while.'

The next thing Hannah knew, she was pulling up outside Adam's house. There were two cars parked in the drive but the house looked deserted. Maybe he'd gone into work after all? As she crunched carefully up the path through the snow, she found herself half hoping that he had.

Adam looked drained when he answered the door. And surprised to see her. She thrust her freezing hands deep into the pockets of her jacket and smiled awkwardly at him 'Hi. I know this isn't a good time, but... I just wanted to say how sorry I was to hear about your wife.'

'Thanks.'

'No news yet?'

'No.'

Coming from inside the house she could hear a childish treble, querulous and close to tears, and an older female voice, calm and soothing.

She hesitated. 'It's not a good time, I can see that, but I appreciated it the other day when you came to see me and I guess I just wanted to let you know I was thinking of you.'

She broke off awkwardly, feeling a bit of an idiot. She didn't know what else to say.

'That was thoughtful of you.'

It was obvious that he had no intention of inviting her in and Hannah's discomfort grew. All she could think now was to make her escape as quickly as she could. *Why had she come?*

'Well ... I won't keep you then. I hope your wife turns up safe and sound soon.'

Just for a moment he dropped his guard and she saw the worry lines around his eyes, the dark circles that told her he hadn't slept.

'So do I.' He ran a hand through his hair. 'I'm worried as hell about her. She's been very low recently. God knows where she is. I spent most of last night driving around looking for her.'

He looked over her shoulder, his expression distant, as if he expected Natasha's car to swing into the drive at any moment. It was obvious his thoughts were a million miles away from her and the conversation they were having.

'I know it's unlikely, but if there's anything I can do?'

'Thanks, but there's nothing. I'm sorry … I'm not good company at the moment.'

'I understand.'

She resisted an urge to probe further. Instead she simply touched his arm gently before turning on her heels and heading back down the path.

Adam watched her go, an unfathomable look on his face; then he closed the front door quietly behind her.

'Who was that?' his mother asked, coming into the hall.

'Just a friend calling to see how we were.'

His mother's eyes were curious but she didn't pursue the subject.

'That was thoughtful of them. How about you sit with Kate for a bit now while I get lunch dished up? She says she's not hungry but I've done toad in the hole. We'll see if that changes her mind.'

'Thanks, Mum. I don't know how I'd cope without you.'

Damn, he was in danger of breaking down completely.

'You'd manage absolutely fine as you always do,' his mother said prosaically, 'but no point struggling along on your own when you don't have to. She'll come back Ad, I'm sure. And when she does …' her usually good-natured face took on a firm expression, 'you've got some sorting out to do. She needs to go back and see the psychiatrist at the hospital. The business with Katie isn't going to go away overnight and if she can do that once …'

'I know.' Adam's voice was terse. He didn't need anyone telling him how serious Natasha's behaviour towards Katie had been. It had been one of the reasons he hadn't slept last night – the fear that Katie would be taken away from them and put into care.

CHAPTER TWENTY-SIX

Adam threw back the bedclothes and headed for the shower. He'd had another crap night driving around in treacherous weather conditions, looking for Natasha and calling on the few friends she had, to see if she'd taken refuge with them. Nothing. He hadn't got to sleep until gone three o'clock and he felt like death. But he needed to get out there again – carry on looking until he found her. She'd been missing for nearly forty hours. Where the hell was she? How could she just disappear off the face of the earth like that?

He stood under the shower, letting the warm water flow soothingly over him. When he was dressed, he poked his head around Katie's bedroom door. 'Ten minutes to breakfast, poppet. Do you want a hand with that?'

She was sitting on her bed struggling with her shoes.

'No.' The little girl's eyes were filled with determination. 'I can do it myself, Daddy. An' if I'm a good girl, Mummy will come back.'

Adam's heart twisted as he moved into the bedroom and sat down next to her. 'It's not because of you that Mummy left,' he said, helping her with her buckle. 'You mustn't think that. Mummy's not been well, poppet, and when people aren't well they sometimes do silly things.'

Katie looked up at him, her eyes filling up. 'But she was cross with me. That's why she left.'

'Oh, Kate …' Adam took his daughter in his arms and sat her on his knee. 'It has nothing to do with you, sweetheart. She was just as cross with me. Do you think she left because of me?'

'N …no.'

'Exactly. She left because she's not well. And when she comes back the doctor will make her better and everything will be fine again. You'll see. Okay?'

The little girl thought about it, then nodded. 'Okay. Is Nanna still here?'

'Yup. She's downstairs in the kitchen getting breakfast ready.'

'Goodee. She said I could have dippy eggs this morning.'

Adam managed a smile as she jumped off the bed and headed for the door, but his expression soon became weary again. Perhaps he shouldn't have done that – filled her with what may well turn out to be false hope. What if Natasha really had...?

He refused to go there. They'd find her – or she'd come back. And when that happened, he'd make sure they tackled this depression thing together. Once and for all. It wouldn't be easy with everything else that was going on, but then, he'd got used to life for him and Natasha not being easy. He'd just be grateful if they could get back to some semblance of normality.

He walked down the stairs, the sound of the morning's post coming through the door momentarily distracting him. He moved over to pick it up and walked into the kitchen where his mother was cooking breakfast.

'What time did you say the police were coming?' he asked, leafing through the mail.

'Nine o'clock the Inspector said. I'll take Katie to school. I can nip home after that and catch up on a few chores.'

'Thanks. I'll head off again after breakfast...'

He broke off abruptly, catching a breath at the sight of the familiar scrawling handwriting on one of the envelopes. 'Excuse me a minute, Mum.'

Without another word, he left the room and went into his study. Tearing the envelope open he started to read.

God Adam, where to start?

It's taken me three days to get this letter right, and I feel so jumbled up in my head it still probably won't make sense. But I don't care anymore. I live in hourly dread of the police knocking on our door to arrest me and I can't face that. So I

216

want to set the record straight – for you mostly, but also for them.

I guess the best thing is to go back to the beginning and there's no easy way of telling you this, but Katie isn't your daughter. I'm sorry – that will hurt you I know.

I had a brief fling that last term of school with Zach Baker (the chap you met the other day). I didn't mean for it to happen but I was lonely stuck away in boarding school. When I realised I was pregnant, I didn't know what to do. I was back home by then and mum was just starting her treatment and was so ill. It just seemed easier to let you think the baby was yours.

I hated being pregnant, and I hated giving birth but I was stunned by the love I felt for Kate – and when she died I was devastated.

She'd been unwell for a couple of days and neither of us had had much sleep. I remember talking to you about it on the phone and you told me to call the doctor if I was worried … but I wasn't. The nurse at the clinic had seen her and said she just had a bit of a cold, it would pass. Only it didn't, and one night she wouldn't stop crying. I was so tired – I hadn't had a good night's sleep in four days. I ended up picking her up and shaking her – not hard, I swear I didn't shake her hard. I was so upset when the police said her arm was fractured. How could I have done that to her?

She still didn't stop screaming and I was in such a state myself that I knew I had to leave the room. I put her back in her cot and left her. Eventually she went quiet and I went to sleep.

But in the morning when I went in she was lying so still. I knew she was dead straight away. I didn't know what to do. I was so shocked. I wrapped her in her swaddle and just sat cuddling her for most of the day, wondering how I was going to explain myself. To you, to the police. I wanted to call you but I didn't dare. I was terrified that if I did, the police would come and arrest me.

I don't remember much about that day but the next day I found myself down at the baby clinic watching the other mothers going in and out with their babies. I couldn't believe what I was thinking. And then Hannah Walker came out. I'd seen her the week before at the clinic and I knew her baby was only a couple of weeks younger than Katie. I found myself following her home, and when she put her baby out in the garden it seemed like a sign. Then her partner came out and drove off and I knew if I was going to do anything I had to act quickly. So, I took the baby, put it in the carrycot in my car and drove home. It was as simple as that. Nobody suspected anything, not even you. I couldn't believe how easily I got away with it.

And that should have been the end of it, except that I couldn't get it out of my head what I'd done to Katie and that she was there, in the garden. It's why I had the affairs. No excuse, but sex and drugs both did it for me – helped me forget for a while.

But then you found the grave and now everything's caving in on me. It's only a matter of time before I get found out and I can't go through all that. I'm sorry. Everything's logged in my Journal. If you show that to the police, it will prove that you knew nothing of what I did.

If they haven't found me by the time you get this letter, get them to look near the woodcutter's hut in the woods. We had some good times there in the early days, and I hope when all the fuss dies down, you'll remember them sometimes.

Tash x

Adam clenched and re-clenched the letter in his hand, reeling from the shock. He could almost feel her presence in the room – this woman he'd spent the last seven years living with, who he didn't know at all. Yet now it all made perfect sense, the pieces of the puzzle slotting finally into place.

He didn't know how long he stood there trying to absorb it all. So many emotions were rampaging through his head he didn't know how to start prioritising them. Disbelief at what she'd revealed. Anger at her duplicity. Guilt that he'd let her down when she most needed him – and, most of all, pity, that she'd been forced to endure things no child should ever have to go through.

The list was endless. But the one over-riding emotion that bypassed them all – slicing straight to his heart – was fear, and the certain, painful knowledge that he was about to lose his daughter. The shock of discovering she wasn't biologically his was nothing compared to that.

It left him facing an impossible dilemma. He knew what he *should* do, but for the first time in his life, duty seemed irrelevant, swept aside by a much stronger, more primal need – to keep what was his, close. How could he even contemplate giving her up?

He barely registered the sound of the doorbell ringing, not until he heard the familiar tones he was beginning to fear would haunt him for the rest of his days.

'Is Mr Campbell in? It's DCI Murray. Sorry I'm a bit early … it's not good news I'm afraid. We've found his wife.'

Without giving himself time to reconsider, he slipped the letter carefully into his pocket and walked out into the hall.

'Who found her?' he asked a few minutes later when they were standing in the lounge.

'A man walking his dog early this morning. Said he'd seen the car in the distance two days running and got curious so he wandered over to take a look.'

'Did you ... see her yourself?'

'Yes. If it's any consolation, she looked very peaceful.' He paused, allowing Adam some time before he said. 'You'll need to formally identify her, and there'll be a post mortem I'm afraid.'

Adam tried not to think about that. He took a deep breath. 'I'll come now, if that's all right? No point putting it off.'

'I'll drive you. You've had a shock. One of my men can drop you back.'

In the car, Murray switched on the radio.

'Yes, well of course typically we don't hear much from the police as to where they are with the investigation,' a man was saying. *'But I'd like to think that after the botched-up way they handled it last time, this time they'll be more on the ball.'*

'And are they any nearer solving the mystery of who's holding your daughter do you think, Mr. Short?'

Murray groaned out loud and went to turn the radio off.

Adam's heart flipped, the letter burning a hole in his pocket making him feel like an accomplice. 'Do you mind leaving it on?' he asked abruptly.

Murray shrugged and left it.

'I doubt it,' Ben Short said. *'But I'm older and wiser this time around and I won't rest until she's found. Unfortunately, Hannah's struggling with it all emotionally. It's rather taken its toll on her I'm afraid. But my future wife and I will do our best by Sophie if she's found. She's going to need a secure stable family life and I'm determined to see that she gets it.'*

CHAPTER TWENTY-SEVEN

Hannah let out a cry, staring at the letter in her hand in total shock. The writing was the same scrawling style as the last letter she'd received, and she read it over and over again, the words leaping out at her.

"I took your baby when ours died. I'm sorry.
Natasha Campbell."

That was all it said. Her hands were trembling so much the letter was visibly shaking. Even her legs were threatening to buckle under her. She collapsed down onto the sofa. Never ... *never,* could she have imagined this scenario.

Her mind worked feverishly. *Could it be true?* Was that why Natasha had run away? Why was she telling her now?

And Adam! Her thoughts switched to him in horror. *Had he known?* Had he got to know her just so they could keep a track of what was going on with the police investigation?

She couldn't believe it, didn't *want* to believe it. Yet ... her expression hardened. How could he *not* have known? It was inconceivable that his wife could have done something like that without his knowledge.

She sat there for an age, the thoughts crashing around in her head in a complete muddle. She could make no sense of any of them.

But none of them were important, she realised, galvanised into action as she jumped up from her seat. What was *important* was that she could be about to find her daughter.

Inspector Murray. She needed to talk to him straight away ... tell him. She picked up the handset then slammed it down again, grabbing her coat instead. This was too important to do over the phone. A sensation lurched in her stomach – an indefinable cross between exhilaration and dread. Was she really about to find Sophie after all these years? She couldn't believe it could be true.

In the car, she heard Ben's interview and her heart plummeted. She could see what he was doing and it terrified her. It shouldn't be possible that he'd get custody of Sophie. Not with his history. Yet when it came to it, what did she have on him that she could uphold in a court? He'd hit her once according to official records and no doubt he'd argue that they'd both been under extreme stress over Sophie at the time. He was clever. He'd do whatever was needed to get custody of their daughter.

And she was about to drop that opportunity right into his lap.

***

'You bastard!'

Before she could stop herself, Hannah launched herself at Adam in the police reception area, fists flying as she punched at him. She was shocked by her own rage. To think she'd *trusted* him. Even, she acknowledged, had *feelings* for him.

'What the ...!' Appalled Adam fended her off.

'How could you do it? How could you take my baby?'

'Miss Walker ... *Miss Walker!'* Murray's expression was stunned as he dived in to break them up. 'What are you doing? What are you talking about?'

'*He stole my baby.* It was *him.* I've got the proof here.'

She thrust the letter in her hand at him, her anger dissipating as quickly as it had arisen.

'He stole my baby ...' she uttered brokenly, her face crumbling. 'All these years...'

Murray looked at the envelope she gave him in bemusement, then pulled out the letter and scanned its contents.

His gaze swung to where Adam was still recovering from the shock of her attack, but now there was another expression in his eyes too, one Murray had seen often enough before.

Guilt.

'Harry, escort Mr Campbell to interview room one, will you? I'll be with you in a minute.'

He turned back to Hannah, but before he could say anything, she cried defiantly. 'I'm not leaving until I know the truth.'

His hesitation was barely perceptible.

'Susie,' he called out over his shoulder.

'Sir?'

'Take Miss Walker to my office, will you? Get her a drink of something if she wants it.' He turned back to Hannah. 'I'll come back to you as soon as I can.'

Adam found himself being escorted to a room on the next floor up. A single table with two chairs set either side of it identified it clearly as an official interview room. He looked around uneasily

'Sit down there please, Mr Campbell. The Inspector won't be long.'

He'd never have imagined the sergeant could sound so stern.

'Look, I can explain …'

'Not until Inspector Murray's here please.'

They sat in silence, during which time Adam tried to calm himself. He'd done nothing wrong, they had nothing on him. Only the fact that he'd concealed Natasha's letter, and thank God, he had that.

The door opened with a flourish and Inspector Murray walked in. He sat down next to his sergeant and faced Adam across the table.

'I need to ask you some questions, Mr Campbell. You have a right to a solicitor if you want one?'

Adam shook his head.

Without preamble, Murray thrust the note Hannah had given him down on the table in front of Adam. 'Is this your wife's handwriting?'

'Yes.'

'Perhaps you'd like to explain it?'

It took Adam no time at all to read the few simple words. 'I know what it must look like, Inspector.'

'Do you now? Well just for the sake of clarity I'll tell you what it looks like. It looks like you and your wife have been stringing us along all this time, and I don't like being strung along, Mr Campbell.'

'I've done nothing of the sort. I knew nothing about any of this until this morning, just before you came to my house.'

'This morning? It seems unlikely if you don't mind me saying so. I find it hard to believe that your child could have died and your wife taken someone else's baby without you being at the very least, a little suspicious?'

'It happened while I was away at University. I was only coming back every couple of weeks. I swear to you I had no idea.'

He rummaged around in his pocket and pulled out Natasha's letter. It wouldn't go down well that he'd concealed it but there wasn't much he could do about that now.

'This came this morning, just before you arrived. It's a letter from my wife. I know I should have shown it to you straight away, but ... I was so shocked I needed time to get my head around it.'

Murray took the letter from him and scanned its contents in silence. When he'd finished reading, his eyes met Adam's across the table. Suspicion was still evident, but when he spoke, his voice had lost some of its heat.

'And you say you had no knowledge of any of this?'

'None.'

'It seems hard to believe.'

'Do you think I don't know that? How stupid can a man be? I was shocked when Natasha told me she was pregnant, but I just assumed we hadn't been careful enough. It never occurred to me that Katie wasn't mine. And I certainly never noticed she'd changed babies on my visits home.'

What sort of a father did that make him?

He dropped his head in his hands and Murray looked at him for a long moment before switching his gaze back to the letter. 'Well, this would seem to put you in the clear, Mr Campbell, but we'll need to take a look at the journal she mentions?'

'It must still be in her wardrobe. I didn't get time to look at it before you came.'

'Someone will drop around to pick it up then. Harry here will take a formal statement from you now while I go and talk to Miss Walker.'

'Will I have any rights over Katie, do you think?' Adam's face was expressionless and Murray hesitated.

'It's a complicated one. I'd get some advice if I were you. We're going to need to take a DNA sample from your daughter to confirm everything.'

'What happens in the meantime? Katie's just lost her mother – she needs to be in familiar surroundings with her family. If there are issues around her staying with me, I'm sure her grandmother – my mother – would be happy to look after her. I don't want her going into care.'

'I don't think there's any need to do anything differently right now. Not until the results come through. After that, if your wife's story is confirmed, social services will be actively involved and it will be out of my hands. I'm afraid there's no way we can avoid that.' His manner eased off as he looked at the other man. 'I'm sorry. I realise it's a very difficult situation for you to be in.'

'Yes.'

'When you've finished making your statement, Harry will take you down to the morgue and then he'll drive you home. Please accept my condolences.'

Adam watched the older man rise from his chair, saw him hand Natasha's letter to his sergeant as he left, who took some time to read it. Maybe he was being kind, giving him some space. – and God knew, he needed it. None of this seemed real.

'Right sir, if you're ready?' Harry finally said.

***

Hannah jumped up the minute the inspector walked in, her eyes fixing desperately on his face.

'I think you'd be better off sitting down, Miss Walker.'

'Please, just tell me. What did he say? Was it them who took her?'

Murray hesitated. 'It's a bit more complicated than that, but the fact of the matter is, I think it's possible you may have found your daughter.'

'Oh!' Her hand flew to her mouth. 'Are you sure?' she gasped.

'We can't be a hundred per cent sure without a DNA test on the little girl. One of my officers will go over to the Campbells' house later today to do that. I'm afraid you'll have to be patient just a little longer before we know for absolute certain.'

Hannah shook her head, a look of utter bewilderment on her face. 'I can't believe it. Why did they do it?'

'It's a long story, but I think the main thing you need to know is that Mr Campbell had no knowledge of his wife's actions until this morning, when he also got a letter from her, admitting that she'd taken Sophie when their baby died. It was as big a shock to him as it was to you.'

'But how could she do that? How could he not have known?'

'He was away at University when it happened and their baby was a similar age to yours. He had no reason to be suspicious when he got back.'

'That's unbelievable...'

'When you've been around as long as I have and seen the things I've seen, believe me, nothing is unbelievable.'

He closed the file on his desk and looked at her. 'There'll be a lot of hoops to go through but the good news has to be that your daughter's alive, doesn't it? And not only that, she's healthy and happy and has been well cared for. You can never make up for the lost years, I know, but I'm sure with time and help you can start to rebuild your lives together.'

She shook her head, the smile on her face almost pitying. 'You make it sound so easy. But I've done nothing but think about it all since I got that letter. My daughter has spent the last six years of her life being someone else's child. How does she adapt to suddenly being told she has a new mother and being taken away from the only parents she's known? And Ben will fight for custody when he hears she's been found. He's already making noises about me being an unfit mother.'

Murray's look was dismissive. 'I heard him on the car radio earlier. It's all talk. Anyone can see that you're perfectly capable of being a mother to your little girl.'

Hannah shook her head, the enormity of his words sinking in. *A mother to her little girl.* How she'd longed to hear those words. Yet now it was a real possibility. The thought terrified her. What did she know about being a mother to her little girl?

She looked at him through worried eyes. 'I wish I could be as sure. It's all such a mess. And it's going to be dreadful for ... *him*, isn't it?'

'Mr. Campbell you mean?'

She nodded.

'I'm afraid it is. I'll tell you in confidence that we discovered his wife's body this morning. It looks like she committed suicide.'

'Oh, God, that's awful.'

And complicated things even more.

Murray rose from his chair, signalling that the interview was over.

'I'm afraid I must ask you not to go anywhere near the Campbells' house for the time being. Not until we get the results through and know for sure. I appreciate how hard that might be, but I'll see if I can speed things up and get them done as quickly as possible.'

Hannah nodded, not knowing how she'd get through the next couple of days. 'And after that? If it's true? What happens then?'

'That'll be for the Children's Services to sort out with you and Mr Campbell.'

'I don't want her going into care. They wouldn't do that, would they?'

He hesitated. 'I can't say for sure. You'd need to liaise with them directly on that one.'

'It would be much better for her to stay where she is until...'

She realised she couldn't bring herself to say the words *until she comes to me*. She still couldn't believe that possibly, perhaps, in as little as even a week or so, she might have her daughter back.

Another thought suddenly struck her. 'What about Ben ... her father? Will you tell him?'

There was no way she was doing it.

Murray's eyes met hers calmly. 'I don't think Mr Short needs to know anything for the time being, do you? Far better we make sure we have all our facts right before we involve him in this.'

Hannah's eyes were grateful. 'Thank you. I'd like to tell my Mum if that's all right? She'd be very discreet.'

'I'd rather you didn't, Miss Walker. If you can possibly keep quiet for just a little longer? I realise it's a lot to ask but it's going to be big news with the media when it comes out. And Mrs Campbell has been somewhat economical with the truth on previous occasions. If by any chance it's not true...'

Not true? How could she even contemplate that possibility now?

She shook her head. 'I'll try, Inspector, but it's not going to be easy. You will let me know?'

'As soon as we know, you will.' he assured her.

After she'd gone he looked up as Harry walked in. 'Got Mr Campbell's statement okay?'

Harry nodded. 'Yup, just waiting while he visits the gents then I'll get him over to the morgue. We've also heard back from the police over in Ireland. No record can be found of Natasha Campbell having any baby over there. And no record over here of any pregnancy when she was fifteen.'

Murray's eyes were thoughtful. 'Looks like her latest confession could be the truth then. Who'd have thought it? See if you can get them to process the little girl's DNA a bit quicker than the last lot, will you? The sooner we get this sorted the better. It's going to be one hell of a mess to sort out. What's happening about getting the sample?'

'Someone's going over this afternoon when she gets back from school.'

'Good. Looks like we can start winding down the investigation, Harry.'

CHAPTER TWENTY-EIGHT

She just couldn't do it. How could they expect her to?

Twenty-four hours had gone by since Hannah had received Natasha's letter and she hadn't got a wink of sleep in all that time. She'd waited so long for this moment, and now the waiting was killing her. She wanted to see what her daughter looked like, hear what she sounded like. It could be several more days before the results came through.

If she were to sneak over there and just take a peek from a distance?

Throwing the paper she'd been trying to read down onto the table, she grabbed her coat and a warm scarf and headed for the door. There'd been more snow overnight and the frost bit at her hands as she tackled the white flakes and hard lumps of ice on the windscreen. She stamped her feet and climbed into the car shivering. It was seven forty-five in the morning and she was undoubtedly a little mad. But if she was patient, maybe she'd catch a glimpse of her daughter when she left for school? That was all she wanted.

The closer she got the more difficult it was to contain herself. What would she look like? She had blond hair – she knew that from the sample that had come through the post. But would she look anything like Hannah?

She drew up a little way from Adam's house and tried not to look conspicuous as she sat and waited in her car. Half an hour went by and she was just beginning to wonder if the snow meant the school had been closed, when the front door opened and a middle-aged woman came out of the house, followed excitedly by a little girl wrapped so efficiently in her hat and scarf that it was absolutely impossible to get even a hint of what she looked like. Without even realising she was doing it, Hannah got out of the car and started to walk.

'Katie!'

Hannah stopped abruptly as Adam suddenly came into view behind them and bending down on his knees, he opened his arms to the little girl. 'You forgot my kiss.'

Immediately she was running back up the path and flinging herself into his arms. 'Look at the snow!' she shrieked. 'Can we build a snowman later, daddy? Can we? And use coal for his eyes and a carrot for his nose?'

He hugged her tight and Hannah couldn't hear his answer. But his expression as he stood up said it all. He looked like a man who'd lost everything, his shoulders hunched, his eyes haunted as they followed her right up until she disappeared around the corner out of sight. He turned slowly to go back into the house, but then he halted and she realised with a shock that his gaze had settled on her, recognition dawning slowly on his face as she found herself unable to look away from those tortured eyes.

For a long moment, they simply stared at each other. Then Hannah found herself moving slowly towards him, her gaze locked with his, looking for any sign of rejection that would halt her in her tracks. But it didn't come.

When she stood in front of him her eyes were swimming. 'I'm so sorry.' she whispered.

'You shouldn't be here.'

'I know. I just had to see her ... I'm sorry.'

She turned away and heard his frustrated sigh as he said abruptly. 'Oh, what does it matter? What does any of it matter? You can come in if you want to?'

She hesitated, knowing that DCI Murray would have her guts for garters, but she followed him quietly into the house.

He led her through into the kitchen. It was warm and smelt of toast reminding her that she hadn't had any breakfast.

'There's a radiator there if you want to take your coat off and warm yourself,' he said, putting the kettle on.

'Thanks.' She draped her coat on the back of a chair and went and stood by the window. She shouldn't be here. If the police found out...

She watched as he pulled a couple of mugs from the cupboard.

'I'm sorry about yesterday,' she said, '– going for you like that.'

He shrugged, setting the mugs down on the counter. 'You've nothing to be sorry about. It's me that should be apologising to you for what my wife has put you through these last few years.'

'The police told me you didn't know?'

'No. It doesn't seem possible, I know. But I didn't.'

He poured two coffees, then moved slowly over to the table and sat down. The only sound to be heard for several moments was the scraping noise of his teaspoon as he stirred his drink carefully.

'I got a letter from Natasha too yesterday. It told me everything.'

'Is that why you were down at the police station?'

'No. I was down there to identify my wife's body.'

'Oh … I'm sorry.' But Hannah was looking confused. 'I don't understand though. Why did the Inspector look so shocked when I showed him the note Natasha sent me? Hadn't you already shown him your letter?'

'No.' Adam's tone was abrupt. 'It was such a shock to realise that Katie wasn't mine, I couldn't bring myself to tell him straight away. I needed time to adjust.'

Hannah's voice cooled as the implications of that sank in.

'So, you knew but didn't say anything?'

'Yes.' He sighed. 'I know how it sounds…'

'Do you?' She was shocked by the sense of betrayal she felt. 'And do you have any idea how it *feels*? That knowing what I'm going through, you chose to say nothing? Maybe you'd *never* have said anything if I hadn't got a note too?'

'Christ, Hannah, of course I would. But try and see it from my point of view, will you? I love Katie. I've spent the last six years bringing her up as my daughter. All that doesn't just blow away because I find out she's not genetically mine. Can you begin to imagine how I feel, knowing she's probably going to be taken away from me?'

'I think I have a fair idea.'

'Shit. That was a stupid thing to say. Of course you do.'

He buried his head in his hands for a brief moment before looking up again, his eyes mirroring his frustration. The look he gave her, though, was conciliatory, rubbing the edge off some of her anger. 'I'm sorry. I really am. I was always going to tell; I just needed some time to adapt. And some time with Kate.'

Her anger seemed to dissipate as quickly as it had arisen. How could she blame him? He'd only done what any parent probably would have done, given the same circumstances.

'It's a mess, isn't it?'

'Yes, it is.' He looked her straight in the eye across the table. 'I love Katie. I don't want for us to fall out, but you might as well know; I'll be asking for some sort of access to her.'

His words hung between them. A comfort or a threat?

A comfort, she realised. For both Katie and her.

'I wouldn't want it any other way,' she said quietly. 'However things get worked out, as far as I'm concerned, you're Katie's father and she'll need you more than ever now. I won't come between you.'

She saw relief flicker briefly in his eyes, some of the anxiety dispelling. 'Thank you.'

He hesitated. 'I heard your ex on the radio yesterday, and he was on television last night. You know he's going to fight for custody when he finds out?'

Hannah nodded.

'Is it true what he said about you having a breakdown?' He paused sensitively, but she knew what he was really asking and he'd tapped into her deepest fear.

'No. I didn't have a breakdown, but I was on tranquilisers for a while,' she answered. She found she couldn't meet his eyes. 'But who wouldn't be in the circumstances? He's trying to build it into something more than it was. He scares me though. He sounds so plausible when you hear him.'

Adam's eyes darkened. 'The thought of someone like that bringing up my daugh ... Katie,' he amended stiffly. '

'I won't let it happen,' she said. She clasped the hot mug tightly, wishing she could sound more convincing. Her eyes followed Adam's gaze to the special Barbie placemat at the end of the table. Katie's mat.

'I can't imagine life without her,' he said, staring at it. 'How's she going to cope with losing both of us?'

He buried his head in his hands again; his elbows on the table, and acting on impulse, Hannah scraped back her chair and moved over to comfort him.

'It'll be okay. We'll work things out,' she said, patting his shoulder awkwardly.

He looked up at her, his eyes bleak. 'Will we?'

'Yes,' she said firmly. 'Because we both want what's best for our daughter.'

It felt strange saying that, creating a bond between them that didn't really exist. Yet, how else could she describe it? Adam had been far more of a father to Katie than she'd been a mother all these years – and a better father than Ben could ever be.

'We'll work it out,' she said again. 'You'll see.'

She became conscious of the hard, rippling muscle beneath her hand, the waft of aftershave that drifted lightly in the air between them. It made her aware of him in a way she shouldn't be, and she made to release her grasp, feeling suddenly awkward. But his hand, coming up to cover hers, stopped her.

'Thanks,' he said, squeezing her fingers. 'You're right. If we have the will to work it out, we can.'

His grasp was warm and strong, and she was aware of an inappropriate desire to hold onto it.

'I should go...'

'Of course...'

He scraped his chair back and stood up, the action bringing him so close to her that she could have reached up to touch the lines of stress on his face. His deep brown eyes were looking at her in a way that made her realise he wasn't immune to her either, and it shifted her universe, the breath catching in her throat as she stared back at him.

She needed to put some distance between them.

But she didn't.

She stood mesmerised as his hands reached out and drew her towards him. Then somehow, they were kissing. Passion flared, silent and fierce. His kiss was consuming, as if by sapping her strength he could drive the demons from his mind. His hand found its way beneath her jumper and she gasped at the contact.

'*Adam!*'

She wasn't sure if she was speaking his name in protest or pleasure, but either way it didn't stop him, and she couldn't prevent her arms from sliding tighter around his neck.

It felt so good – but it was wrong. So wrong.

'Adam ...' she breathed against his lips, '*we shouldn't.*'

This time she felt him tense. The pressure from his mouth stopped. He shuddered against her and buried his head deep in the hollow of her shoulder, his arms tightly encircling her.

'I'm sorry,' he muttered into her neck. 'God, I'm sorry.'

For a long moment they clung to each other, not moving. She could feel his heart pounding in his chest – feel her own frantic heartbeat mixing with it. As sanity slowly reared its head, there was no getting away from the mortification she felt. She made an effort to pull away from him, but he didn't release her.

'Are you okay?' he whispered.

She didn't answer. *Couldn't* answer.

He drew back to look down at her. His face was etched with shock, as if he couldn't believe himself what had just happened. 'God, what must you think of me, with Natasha only just …'

'*Don't*. It's not your fault,' Hannah said agitatedly, 'It was the heat of the moment and we're both overwrought.' She slipped swiftly from his hold. 'But I must go.'

'No, wait.' Adam drew a deep breath and ran his hand raggedly through his hair. 'Look … give me time to think things through, okay? I don't know what the hell I'm doing at the moment, but I don't want you thinking I'd have done that to anyone. There's been something there between us. You must have felt it too?'

She looked at him bewildered. 'But it's not right,' she whispered.

His face closed over. 'I know it isn't.'

For a moment neither of them spoke and she could see the effort he was making to re-gather his wits. 'We have to stay focused,' he said finally. 'What you said was true, we *can* work this out … but we need a strategy if we're going to take your ex on.'

She nodded, feeling huge relief at the thought that she wouldn't be dealing with Ben alone. 'Let me think on it,' he continued. 'I've got a friend who's a solicitor. I'll take some advice.'

With a supreme effort, she turned away from him and moved over to where her coat was hanging on the back of the chair.

'I must go,' she said again. She was already heading for the door, and this time he didn't stop her.

As she hurried down the path, back to the sanctity of her car, her mind was in turmoil. She should never have come. What if she bumped into DCI Murray now? He'd be furious.

But somehow that ranked unimportantly against the other thoughts spinning in her head. A line had been crossed today, a line that shouldn't have been crossed. She'd known from the start that she was attracted to Adam Campbell – ever since she'd heard his voice that night in the garden if she was honest with herself. But entering into a relationship with him was something entirely different. What had she been *thinking*, letting that happen? It could only end in disaster.

Fifteen minutes later she found herself walking up the path to her mother's front door, not entirely sure what she was doing there.

As she rang the bell and waited on the doorstep, she observed that the path had been cleared of snow and gritted. She was impressed. Her mother had obviously been hard at work.

The door opened and she took a startled step back at the sight of the man standing on the threshold.

He looked as surprised as she did, then he smiled ruefully.

'I'm guessing you must be Hannah? I'm David Wakefield, a … friend of your mother's.'

'Oh.' At this time of the morning? Hannah was floored and hoped she didn't look as stupid as she felt.

'Uh, right. It doesn't matter. It's nothing urgent. I can come back later.'

She started to back up but already he was turning into the hall and calling out.

'Helen, Hannah's here. I'm off now. I'll call you later.'

He gave Hannah another brief smile. 'Nice to meet you. Sorry to rush off but I'll be late for work if I don't get going.'

She watched him go in a daze.

'Hannah?'

She turned back to find her mother in her dressing gown on the doorstep; her expression one of embarrassment mixed with surprise as she looked at her daughter. 'Are you all right, love? Is something wrong?'

'I, no. At least … who was that, Mum?'

She watched in disbelief as the colour crept into her mother's cheeks.

'I'm sorry. I've been meaning to tell you for a while now, but somehow the timing never seemed right. Come on in.'

'But who is he?' Hannah asked, following her mother into the kitchen. 'How long have you been seeing him?'

Her mother smiled as she went to put the kettle on. 'Isn't it meant to be *me* asking *you* those sorts of questions? Just let me get the coffee under way, then I'll tell you everything.'

Once the coffee was made and they were sitting together in the kitchen Helen looked at her daughter. 'David's one of the doctors at my local surgery. He's divorced too and was very supportive of me when I was having a difficult time after your dad. But it was all completely platonic back in those days.' She grinned sheepishly. 'You could have knocked me over with a feather when he suddenly asked me out for a meal a few months back. And it's just sort of grown from there. I'd really like you to meet him properly – if you feel you'd like to?'

It was all too much. Hannah felt the tears blurring her eyes.

'Oh darling, don't cry … you don't have to if you don't want to. I know it must come as a shock.'

Hannah shook her head and pulled out a tissue. 'It's not that. I'm happy for you, really, I am. There's just so much going on at the moment … so many changes. I can't seem to get a handle on anything. Stupid.'

Her mother reached a tentative hand across the table and covered Hannah's with it. 'It's not stupid, it's perfectly natural. I can't begin to imagine what it must be like. I know how I'd have felt if someone had taken you from me. It was bad enough when you went of your own free choice as an adult.'

'Biggest mistake of my life,' Hannah said, sombrely.

'You were feeling abandoned. I can just as easily blame myself for all that went wrong,' her mother said quietly. 'And I do.'

They sat for a while in silence.

'I'm sorry I didn't come to Dad's funeral.' The words tumbled out before she'd even realised she was going to say them.

Her mother looked surprised, taking a moment to respond. 'I don't hold that against you Hannah. Not anymore. I was hurt at the time but the main reason I tried to persuade you to come was because I didn't want you to regret not coming ...'

'And you were right. I *do* regret it. Back then I hated him, but sometimes now I remember the good times. Like when he got all emotional when I did that solo of Silent Night, or how he'd usually be the one to patch up my wounds when I hurt myself, and turn it into a game of doctors and nurses.'

'I was never good at that sort of stuff. Too squeamish.'

'I was so angry that he'd destroyed our perfect family.'

'So was I.'

'But you *forgave* him. If you could do that, what was wrong with me that I couldn't?'

'I never really forgave him,' her mother said. 'And he knew that. But who else was going to look after him? When he told me he was ill, I felt trapped. I'd just started to pick up the pieces of my life again. As you yourself said at the time, why should I take him back and look after him just because *she* wouldn't? But I couldn't turn my back on him. There was a part of me that still loved him for all the good times we'd had together. And we were actually quite happy those last few months, although he regretted the distance between you and him.'

Hannah's eyes were solemn as she returned her mother's gaze. 'I hated that he left me that money in his Will, even though I used it to go to Uni. It felt hypocritical touching it after the way we'd fallen out. My feelings about him are so mixed, Mum.'

'Let them rest, love. Dad wasn't perfect and he hurt us both. But he never stopped loving you, you know.'

Hannah looked down at the table, at the hand still lying beneath her mother's and turned hers over so that she could grip it tightly. It felt good. So many times her mother's love had been there for her, she realised. A familiar and solid thing that had nourished and nurtured her when she was growing up, comforted her when it seemed the world was against her. Those strands of love had never really been broken, just stretched a little, and now they'd reach out to embrace her grand-daughter as well – a rock-solid bond that would add to the tiers of support Katie could rely on in the future.

'They think they've found Sophie,' she said quietly. 'Only her name's Katie now.'

She didn't care about Inspector Murray any more, or what might happen if he found out she'd broken her word. What could they do about it anyway?

Helen's clasp tightened spasmodically. *'What?'* She looked totally bemused. *'Where? When?* I don't understand …'

'I'm not meant to say anything until it's confirmed, and if it comes out I've told you …'

In a low voice, she explained. She didn't mention the very last bit of course – what had happened between her and Adam.

'That's where I've been this morning,' she finished up. 'I wanted to park outside her house and see if I could get a glimpse of her.'

'And?'

'She was so tightly wrapped up in her scarf and hat that I could hardly see anything.' Hannah laughed, a light of excitement in her eye. 'But I know it's her, Mum … I just know.'

'Oh my God. I'm shaking. When will you find out for sure?'

'Any time now. The police said they'd try and rush it through.'

She hesitated, her expression darkening as her real worry – the one she'd been doing her best to suppress since leaving Adam – the one that had brought her here to her mother, she realised now, burst to the fore.

'But it's all going to be such a mess, isn't it? Adam Campbell invited me in for a cup of tea today. I shouldn't have accepted. It was awful seeing what it's doing to him knowing he's going to lose her. And it made me start thinking about Sophie .... Katie, and how it's going to affect her if she gets taken away from him. Especially when she's just lost her mother. If I really love her, shouldn't I leave her where she is? She's my daughter and I want her ... of course I do. But is that what's best for *her.*'

She felt her mother's clasp tighten. '*Of course it is.* You're her mother and you're the best person to be bringing her up. I know you can't just uproot her from the only life she's ever known, but you'll work through that, I don't doubt it. And Sophie will be where she belongs – with you.'

She looked at Hannah, a slow smile stretching the corners of her mouth. 'Well, your news knocks the socks off mine any day. I can't *believe* it.'

'You *will* keep it to yourself for the time being? I'm not meant to tell anyone, and I'm dreading Ben's reaction. He'll go out of his way to make my life hell once he finds out. I know he will.'

Her eyes welled up and she brushed at them angrily.

'Oh God, I'd forgotten about him.' Helen scraped back her chair and got up from the table. In an instant, she was at Hannah's side, pulling her out of the chair and into her arms. 'Don't you worry about Ben,' she said grimly, hugging her hard. 'Over my dead body will I stand by and let that man have care and custody of my grand-daughter – and you'd better believe it.'

The tone of her voice left Hannah in no doubt that she meant business. A tigress fighting for her cub, she realised. And as Hannah's arms, frozen for so long, slipped tentatively around her mother's waist, she realised it made no difference that it was *her* cub they were fighting for. To her mother it was one and the same thing. Her love encompassed them both. How could she ever have thought she could survive without that love?

'Can we make a new start? Helen murmured into her hair, 'try and put what's past behind us? When Sophie comes back into the fold, she'll need a good solid family to come into and we can give her that.

'I'd like that.'

And with those few muffled words, she realised she'd done what she'd always been destined to do. Turn circle and come home.

'But her name's Katie now. We'll need to remember that.'

CHAPTER TWENTY-NINE

'Ben's a bloody nightmare, isn't he?' Jess said, handing Hannah a mug of coffee the next morning. 'Did you see him on the telly again last night saying how he'll go for custody of Sophie if they find her? For God's sake what's the matter with the man? How do you put up with him?'

Hannah sighed. She didn't want to think about it.

'I don't. And yes, I did see him. He phoned me last night to tell me to watch the interview. He's doing his best to stitch me up and unless I'm prepared to go into the limelight like he's doing, there isn't a thing I can do about it.'

She broke off as the phone rang. Jess picked it up.

'Yes, she's here...'

She held the phone out to Hannah. 'It's for you. The police.'

Hannah's heart jolted. She grabbed the phone.

'Hello?'

'Ah, Miss Walker, Sergeant Briscombe here. Inspector Murray was wondering if you could come down to the station this afternoon?'

'Yes, of course. Have you ... have you got some news?'

'We will have by this afternoon. Shall we say around two thirty?'

'That'll be fine.' She put the phone down and tried not to give too much away in her expression to Jess. 'They want to see me this afternoon ... two thirty ... is that okay?'

'Of course. Did they say what it was about?'

'No.'

She felt bad fibbing about it, but she couldn't face going into the details. What if it all turned out to be wrong?

She jumped up from her chair and started busying herself rolling up some material. 'God, I hate all this waiting around.'

'Look, why don't you head off at lunchtime? Relax a bit at home before you go to the police? I haven't got any more visits to do. I can deal with everything here.'

'I don't like letting you down.'

'Hannah.' Jess gave her a firm, no nonsense look. 'Go. I mean it. You've been brilliant coming in, but I'm going to have to get used to being on my own again sometime, you know.'

Hannah had barely been in the flat two minutes before the phone rang. She picked it up, frowning.

'Hannah?'

She recognised the voice straight away. 'Yes?'

'It's Adam.'

He sounded competent and business-like. Nothing like the walking bag of nerves she seemed to have become since their last meeting.

'I need to speak to you and I wondered if we could meet up. Have the police been in touch?'

'Yes.'

'Me too. Any chance you could meet me for lunch today?'

'I'm not sure.'

'Please!' His voice was persuasive. 'Look. If what my wife claimed about Katie is true, we both know you're going to have a problem with your ex-partner when it all comes out. I've been giving it a lot of thought. I think I may have a solution.'

He'd lost weight from that first time she'd met him she realised, and supposed she shouldn't be surprised by that. She'd worried that the incident yesterday might have made things awkward between them but he didn't look at all discomforted as he stood to greet her. In fact, he looked reassuringly confident, making her feel that if anyone could work a way through all this, he could.

244

'It's only pub-grub I'm afraid,' he said, handing her the menu. 'Nothing fancy. What would you like to drink?'

'I'm not hungry. Perhaps a glass of white wine and some crisps?'

He reappeared a few minutes later and sat down opposite her.

'How have you been?'

'Fine,' she lied. 'And you?'

He nodded. 'Not too bad.'

His eyes dropped and he twirled his glass thoughtfully as if pondering his next words. She waited patiently.

Finally, he lifted his gaze to look at her again. 'I've been thinking about our situation. It seems to me that we both have a lot to lose if things turn out as the police seem to think they will. If Katie really is your child then I lose my daughter and you're probably going to have a big custody fight on your hands. I'm not saying you'll lose it necessarily, you may well win, but only after a long and harrowing court case by the sound of it.'

He took a deep breath. 'I know this is going to sound bizarre, but what if we say we'll bring her up together?'

Her eyebrows flew up in shock. 'What do you mean? How?'

He pushed his hands through his hair but his face was wearily determined. 'I haven't worked all the details through yet. But you have to understand that the only thing that kept me in my marriage almost from the word go was Kate. The thought of losing her now – and having that man bring her up ... can you really stand the thought of him getting custody?'

Her response was unequivocal. 'No.'

It took no effort whatsoever to remember Ben as he'd been with her when they were together, or on the phone the other morning yelling at his girlfriend. She shuddered. There was no way she wanted Katie living in a home like that.

His eyes didn't flinch as they met hers. 'Neither can I. I'm not sure exactly how we'd go about it. It might mean going for shared custody of her, or at least giving me a legal right to have continued involvement in her upbringing. We'd need to speak to a solicitor about it and I've made an appointment with my friend for tomorrow, if you want to come along. It wouldn't cut your ex out of the picture completely as obviously he's still her father and would have his own legal rights, but if we both said that was what we wanted – what we felt was in Kate's best interests – the court might just agree to keep me in the legal loop. We'd need to put up a solid front though and you'd need to be adamant that you wanted me to play an active part in Kate's life.'

'I'd want that anyway, Adam. I told you that.'

'I know, but … you letting me see her isn't the same as getting a legal Agreement giving me the right to be involved. Ben Short will put up a good fight for getting custody, and he can afford the best lawyers. But if you and I show a united front in our argument – that it's what's best for *Katie*, maybe the authorities will agree with us. I also happen to believe very strongly that that *is* the case. It would be terrible for her to lose Natasha, me, and her home all in one go.'

He broke off abruptly. His face reflected no emotion, but it was there, she could see, held in check beneath the surface. A father's love for his child, even if she wasn't his blood child. It left her awed that he should love Katie so much.

When she said nothing, he looked at her impatiently. 'What do you think? For God's sake say something.'

'I think it's a good plan,' she said slowly. 'I don't know if it'll work, but I'm willing to give anything a shot that will help me stop Ben from getting custody.'

As if by magic his face cleared. His eyes met hers and he reached for her hand where it lay on the table. 'We're going to win this Hannah. And whatever happens in our lives in the future, I promise you I'll always be there for you and Kate.'

She believed him. Integrity shone from the depths of those warm, brown eyes. She wanted to tell him that there was no need for promises – she already trusted him.

'I'd better be going,' was all she said, carefully withdrawing her hand. 'My appointment with the police is at two thirty.'

'Mine's at three.'

He smiled. 'How about we start our united front approach by seeing them together? Sow a few seeds while we can.'

CHAPTER THIRTY

Murray looked surprised when he saw them sitting in the waiting room.

'Hannah and I wondered if we could see you together, Inspector?' Adam asked. 'Seeing as the information you have affects us both?'

Murray's eyes flicked from one to the other, his gaze narrowing. 'I wasn't aware that you two knew each other?'

'Neither were we until we bumped into each other down here at the station the other day,' Adam embellished smoothly.

'I see.' He turned to look questioningly at Hannah. 'Are you sure you want this, Miss Walker? There may be some personal stuff that comes out that you don't necessarily want to share.'

She raised an eyebrow. 'I can't think what. I'm fine with it.'

'Okay, if you're sure. Come through then.'

His face was serious as he sat facing them. Between his fingers he held two pieces of paper. Hannah twisted her hands nervously, glancing at Adam. Her insides felt so tight she was glad she hadn't eaten lunch. It would have taken very little to bring it all back up again.

'I have here the results of the DNA test on Katrina Campbell.' Murray said fixing his gaze first on Adam and then on Hannah.

'They confirm that you *are* her mother, Miss Walker.'

Hannah gasped, her hand flying to her mouth. Then she burst into tears. Murray offered her a box of tissues in the manner of a man well used to doing such things, before switching his gaze to Adam. He was sitting frozen in his chair, the twitching of a small muscle at the corner of his mouth the only tell-tale sign of the tension he was feeling.

Murray waited while Hannah wiped her eyes and blew her nose fiercely. 'I'm sorry...' she whispered shakily. 'I just can't believe it.'

'Take your time.'

When she'd calmed herself, he faced them both again.

'Now ... as I was saying ... Katie is your daughter. However ...' he held up the other piece of paper in his hand, his eyes penetrating as they bore into Hannah's. 'According to these results, it would appear that Ben Short is *not* her father.'

A pin could have been heard to drop in the shocked silence that followed his words. Hannah sat looking at him, stunned.

'What ... what do you mean he's not her father? Of course he is.'

'Not according to our results. And we've run a check. There's no match to anyone on our database.'

'But who else could it be?'

But she knew the answer to that even as she uttered the words – her brain spinning down a path she hadn't let herself revisit in seven years.

'I think you're the only one who can tell us that.'

Her face suffused with colour as the memories rushed in. She couldn't bring herself to look at Adam.

'Oh God. I had no idea. I never thought for one moment...'

She broke off as the implications behind his revelation suddenly hit her. Ben *wasn't* Katie's father. That meant he had no claim on her at all.

Elation swept through her.

But it was short lived as she realised the Inspector was still waiting to hear what she had to say on the matter. Too late, she remembered his words. *Information may come out that you don't necessarily want to share.*

'It's possible it's true,' she conceded in a low voice, keeping her gaze fixed firmly on Murray's face. Anywhere other than on Adam. 'Ben and I split up for a short while when we were going out and I ... I met someone else extremely briefly.'

She dropped her eyes. She didn't want to go back to that time. Although the memory was hazy and she'd been drunk, she remembered enough of the details to know it hadn't been her finest hour.

It had been one of the parties she'd gone to after she and Ben had split up over the handcuff episode. The same night she'd argued with her mother about her father coming home. She and Jess had gate crashed some girl's eighteenth birthday party, already merry from an evening in the pub.

But then the extra booze had made Hannah morose and she'd taken herself off to the large barn with a bottle of wine, climbed up into the hayloft and tried to drink herself into oblivion so that she no longer had to think about Ben, or what he'd done to her and the fact that she couldn't get him out of her system despite it all.

But one of the guys she'd been dancing with had seen her go and followed her. He'd asked her if he could join her, said it wasn't good to be alone when you were fed up, and she'd ended up confiding in him about Ben and their row. Not about the sex thing though – that was way too personal.

They'd carried on talking until the bottle was finished. He was easy and uncomplicated and he made her laugh a lot. And when suddenly he'd said he'd quite like to kiss her, she'd said straight out that she'd like that too. And she had liked it. He smelt of aftershave and tasted of wine and she'd enjoyed the feel of his hands roaming sensitively over her body. And when a little while later he'd said that he should probably take himself off for a walk, she'd whispered to him not to, kissing him back shyly, giggling when he appeared to be having trouble with her shirt buttons, gasping when she felt his hands on her breasts teasing her nipples into life.

After that, the memory was hazy, but she remembered his voice urgent in the dark asking her if she was sure. Her own voice, softly urging him on. And then the intense waves of pleasure as he took her, pulling out at the last minute.

Which was why she'd never considered the baby might not be Ben's.

They'd fallen asleep where they lay, and when Hannah woke-up a couple of hours later, stiff and cramped in the hayloft, she was alone. Embarrassment had swamped through her, mortifying her. She'd never done anything like that in her life.

It was two o'clock in the morning and she'd ended up walking the two miles to the cab service at the station, berating herself the whole way. How could she have done that? She didn't even know who he was. She'd acted like a *tart.*

Yet through her undoubted mortification, a little bubble of satisfaction had dared to raise its head. Ben was wrong. She wasn't some sort of sex freak after all. She'd just had bog standard normal sex and she'd loved it!

'I'm sorry?'

She came back to the present with a start as she realised DCI Murray had just asked her a question. She still couldn't bring herself to look at Adam but she could feel his eyes boring into her.

'I asked if you'd like a glass of water? It's obviously come as a shock to you.'

'Yes, thank you.'

Murray nodded at Harry and he disappeared off to get one. Then his eyes returned to Hannah and he hesitated, his gaze switching briefly to Adam and back again. 'Would you prefer to conduct the remainder of this interview in private?'

Yes, she would. But Hannah shook her head. Adam was no doubt shocked enough by these revelations and it didn't take much working out to guess what she was probably about to say. He might as well hear the facts and know the truth.

'No, it's fine. There's not much to say really. I'm afraid I can't tell you who Katie's real father is because the truth of the matter is I don't know myself.'

She cleared her throat. 'Ben and I had a brief period in the early days when we split up. I'm not proud of it but I ended up getting very drunk at a party and having a one-night stand with some boy I'd never met before. I never saw him again after that night. A couple of weeks later Ben and I got back together again, and a short while after that I suspected I was pregnant. It might have been naïve of me but... I thought we'd been careful. It never occurred to me that Ben might not be the father.'

'So, your boyfriend never suspected he wasn't Katie's father?'

'No. He'd have killed me if he'd known.'

Inspector Murray leaned back in his chair and smiled. 'It's going to come as a bit of a shock to him then, isn't it? Do you want to tell him, or shall I?'

Hannah suppressed a shudder. 'Definitely you, if you don't mind?'

'It will be my absolute pleasure.'

He scribbled something on his pad, then put his pen to one side and looked at them both for a long moment.

'Well, I think that probably draws things to a conclusion as far as I'm concerned,'

He looked from one to the other of them. 'There will still be arrangements to sort out over your little girl, but hopefully they'll be simpler now. I'd suggest you sit down together and do some thinking about what you'd like to see happen, before the Children's Services get involved. I don't know much about the way they handle things, but at this stage, they'd probably take any mutually agreed suggestions on board if they feel they're in your daughter's best interests.'

He turned to Adam. 'I'm sorry about your wife, Mr Campbell. It's a difficult time for you I know, but her letter is self-explanatory and so is her diary. The post mortem's confirmed death by suicide with no suggestion of suspicious circumstances. So, from our point of view, nothing more needs investigating.' He reached down and pulled out a carrier bag. 'These are her belongings. Everything's there. Please accept my condolences. We'll be releasing her body tomorrow if you want to go ahead and make funeral arrangements?'

Adam took the bag. 'Thank you.'

Murray stood up and shook hands with them both. 'Well, I'll get straight onto telling Mr Short the good news,' he said with a grim smile. 'I don't think we'll be hearing too much from that quarter in the future, do you? Good luck with it all.'

Outside, Adam's face was drawn as he looked at Hannah. 'I know he's right and we need to talk, but…' he looked down at the bag of possessions in his hands. 'I don't think I'm up to it today, if you don't mind?'

'Of course not.'

She'd found her daughter.

'Is it all right if I call you tomorrow?'

She nodded and taking out her pen, she scribbled her mobile number on the back of an old receipt. 'In case I'm out and about.'

'Thanks. I'll call you.'

And he was gone, striding away from her with purposeful strides that somehow seemed at odds with the bleak expression on his face. She turned away with a sigh and headed back to her car. So much to think about. It was almost inconceivable that the episode she'd felt so much shame about all those years ago should turn out to be such a lifesaver now. She'd never have thought she'd be glad of that moment's indiscretion.

That brought to mind her more recent act of indiscretion in Adam's kitchen. The heat crept into her skin at the memory of it. She just hoped that after today's revelations, he didn't think she went around making a habit of doing that sort of thing.

But she couldn't worry about that now. She had far more important things on her mind. She climbed into her car and headed for her mother's. The nearer she got, the more her excitement grew. *She'd found her daughter.* What better news than that could she be sharing with her mum?

CHAPTER THIRTY-ONE

Hannah looked at the clock.

Eight o'clock Adam had said – after he'd settled Katie down. It was nearly nine now. It looked like he wasn't coming.

She'd been on tenterhooks all day thinking about this meeting. He might at least have phoned.

The doorbell rang just as she was about giving up and pouring herself a glass of wine. She took a quick nervous sip before moving to let him in.

'*Ben!*' She reeled back in shock.

'Hello, Hannah.'

She could smell the drink on him as he shoved her aside and walked into her flat. She made no move to follow him but stood where she was by the open door.

'What are you doing here? I told you I didn't want to see you again.'

'Why do you think I'm here? I've come to talk about our daughter. Only she's not *our* daughter, is she?'

She eyed him warily. But she wasn't a timid teenager any longer. Forcing her limbs into action she followed him into the living room making sure to leave the front door ajar behind her. An escape route should she need it.

'You've spoken to Inspector Murray?'

'Is that his name? The bastard. It was obvious he took great delight in telling me the news.'

Hannah hesitated. 'I'm sorry, Ben. I didn't know that Sophie wasn't yours.'

'*Didn't know?*' He swung around to face her viciously. 'How can you *not know* you screwed another man when you were supposedly going out with me?'

Hannah took a deep breath and forced herself to stay calm. 'It was when we had that break. I only did it the one time. I never thought for one minute…'

'And is that supposed to make me feel better? That you only did it the *one* time? Look at the mess that *one* time's got me into! I look a complete idiot now making all those broadcasts about how I was going to look after Sophie.'

Hannah's expression hardened. 'Well, I'm sorry but you've only got yourself to blame for that. If you hadn't been so quick off the mark trying to discredit me...'

'Don't push me, Hannah.' He took a menacing step towards her. 'You always did know which buttons to press to trigger my temper.'

Hannah held her ground. 'Your buttons press themselves, Ben. Please go. I've got nothing more to say to you.'

'You bitch. You think you've got the better of me now, don't you? You think you're so fucking clever.'

Before she even realised his intention, he'd closed the distance between them and had grabbed hold of her. 'I'm not going until you tell me who the bastard is that screwed you when you were supposed to be going out with me. *Who the father of your baby is?'*

'*I am,'* a loud voice said from behind them and the next thing she knew, Ben's grip on her arms had slackened as Ben was hauled off her and thrown unceremoniously across the room. He landed with a crash over the coffee table and sprawled onto the floor.

'What's it got to do with you?' Adam said. His face was white with fury.

Ben stared up at him in shock. 'Wait a minute. I know who you are,' he said, scrabbling quickly to his feet. 'I've seen your picture in the papers.'

'Good. Then there's no need for introductions before I throw you out. Hannah and I have nothing to say to you, Mr Short. You're irrelevant now, so you might as well get used to the idea. And if I catch you anywhere near Hannah again, I'll beat you to a pulp. You'd better believe that. Now you heard Hannah, get out.'

He stood aside, leaving Ben a wide berth to pass. For a moment, Ben's expression was so ugly that Hannah thought he was going to fly at Adam but he knew he was no match for the tough, broad shouldered man standing in front of him. His look hovered venomously from one to the other before he said, with a final mutter, 'You haven't heard the last of this,' and stormed past them out of the flat.

Adam shut the door firmly behind him and for a long moment there was silence.

'Charming chap,' he remarked, watching her carefully. 'He's no more appealing in real life than he was on the television.'

He moved slowly into the room, noting the pallor of her cheeks. 'Are you okay?'

She nodded shakily. 'I'm sorry you had to witness that. Thanks for intervening. I didn't think you were coming.'

'Kate was playing up. It's affecting her, Natasha's death. I didn't want to leave her with my mother until I knew she was asleep.'

Hannah nodded again. It should be *her* comforting her little girl. But it wasn't her place to do that. Not yet.

She turned away, hiding her emotion. 'Do you want a drink?' she asked, moving over to the bottle of wine on the sideboard.

'I think we could probably both do with one.'

She took her time, collecting herself, as she poured a glass and handed it to him.

'Cheers, and good riddance to bad rubbish,' he said, raising his glass and flashing her a sudden grin.

She found herself smiling back, the tension easing just like that.

'You must be wondering what I ever saw in him,' she said, sighing.

'Love's a strange thing.' His eyes were unreadable as he said it. 'And I'm certainly not one to preach.'

She moved over to the window and gazed out into the dark. 'It was never love. Not really.' She found it easier to talk staring out of the window rather than looking at him. 'When I met Ben, things were difficult at home. My parents had separated because my father had had an affair. Ben was different to anyone else I'd met, so grown up and flash. He took me away from it all, brought some fun into my life; put *me* first. I lapped it up. It was pathetic really. When I told him I was pregnant, he was over the moon. It was the excuse he'd been waiting for to get me to move in with him. I had a terrible row with my mother over it. She wanted me to wait, have the baby at home. She felt it had all happened too quickly. She was right of course, but by then it was too late.'

'We all make mistakes,' Adam said, 'especially when we're young and hot-headed. Don't think you're the only one. I sensed there was something out of kilter with Natasha almost from the word go, but she had such incredible energy. I couldn't help being swept along with it. She used to tell me I was her anchor, and I think it was true. She flew so high she needed to know someone was there to stop her from blowing away. But I knew early on that we'd made a mistake. Now's not the time to go into why she had the affairs, but they put a big strain on our marriage. And I hate to think I've got anything in common with Ben Short, but we do share one thing. I found out from Natasha's letter that I wasn't Katie's real father. That was some boy she'd been seeing at school.'

Hannah turned to look at him, knowing how much that must have hurt.

'I should feel livid with her about that, and I do, but in some ways, it helps lessen some of my guilt.'

He sighed. 'It's been hard coming to terms with how unhappy we'd both become. This wasn't the first attempt she'd made on her life and I'm realising now that I wasn't as understanding as I could have been. A couple of years ago her mood swings were so bad that she was sectioned for a while. I couldn't relate to it at all. I blamed it on the fact she

258

took recreational drugs ... but she told me some stuff about her past before she died. I had no idea what she'd been through.'

She resisted an urge to comfort him, remembering what had happened the last time she'd done that.

Her tone when she spoke was matter of fact. 'You're not a mind reader. If she didn't tell you stuff then you can't blame yourself for not knowing. I've tried to find it in me to forgive her for what she did but I don't think I ever can. I've missed so much of Katie's life and I'll never get that back. What she did was wrong. There's no excusing it.'

'I know.' His eyes met hers. 'I'm not excusing her. It's just hard when you've always considered yourself the stronger one in the relationship, to realise you got it so wrong.'

He looked around the room. 'I like what you've done with this room. You've transformed it.'

She took his change of subject without comment, her eyes following his to the photos on the ledges, the cushions and the throw on the settee.

'You can take some of the credit for that. It was after your visit that I had something of an epiphany. I knew I wasn't happy as I was, and I realised that unless I changed things for myself, that's how I'd stay for the rest of my life. It was a depressing enough thought to make me decide to do something about it. It was fun getting my old bits and pieces out.'

'And what about *Sophie's Room?*'

Silence. Her eyes darted to his.

'I couldn't help noticing it last time I was here, when I went to get you the glass of water. The door was ajar. I'm sorry. I shouldn't have looked.'

'Nobody else has seen that room.' Her voice was low. 'Sometimes I'd just sit in there for hours, remembering. It was such a short time that I had her, yet she was such a huge part of me. I couldn't bring myself to clear her things away. I felt like that would be admitting she'd be gone forever. I just couldn't do it.'

'And now you don't have to.' Adam said with his quick smile. 'You'll be seeing her soon enough and maybe I can give you a hand redecorating it for when she's here?'

'I can't wait.' Hannah's eyes lit up but there was also anxiety in the gaze she turned on him. 'How are we going to handle this, Adam? I so want to see her and get to know her, but I know I can't just rush in and expect her to start loving me.'

'Look, it won't happen overnight, but it'll happen. I've already made a start. I explained that there was a mix up when she was a baby and that she was taken by the wrong mother. She's too young to understand it properly but I've told her that you want to meet her and that we'd explain it all properly when she's older. She seemed to accept it without too much of a problem, but understandably she's nervous about meeting you, and worried about being taken away from me.'

His eyes, as they looked into hers, were steady. 'The thing to remember is that we're both on the same side. We want what's best for Kate. I'm sure the Children's' Services people will have good advice on how to handle things, but that's the thing we mustn't lose sight of. The rest will work itself out.'

Hannah nodded, wishing she shared his confidence.

'I know. I had a visit from the Children's Services today. I told them I was happy for her to stay with you for the time being and that I'd rather that was the case than she goes into any sort of foster care.'

'They told me. Thanks. They said as long as you're happy with the arrangement there's no reason why she can't, especially in view of the fact she's lost her ... Natasha, so recently.'

'I also told them that I'll wait until after the funeral before I meet her. I really want to see her – and I don't know how

I'll survive that – but it doesn't feel right somehow, doing it before. I don't want to make a difficult time worse for her.'

Adam reached for her hand and squeezed it. 'You're going to be a great mother you know that? This must be so hard for you, but it's only a few more days. We'll get something set up for as soon as possible afterwards. I thought you might like these in the meantime.'

He let go of her hand and pulled an envelope from his jacket pocket. She knew what was in it without him saying anything.

'Thanks,' she said, taking it from him and putting it down on the coffee table without opening it. Looking at photos of her daughter was something she'd do in private.

Later, when she was alone, she picked it up again and opened it. Twelve pictures – two for each year of her life. And a note. *You've got a bit of catching up to do, but the rest of your life to do it in. Adam.*

And it was true, she thought, as she lovingly absorbed each photo. The next few days would be difficult, but she could get through them knowing that.

***

She tried to stay away, but she found she couldn't. It was difficult to, when it seemed the whole world was turning out to get a last glimpse of the family caught up in what was now generally termed; "The Walker Affair".

She stood well back from the crowd gathered outside the crematorium, a hooded jacket concealing her face, watching quietly as first Adam and then Katie climbed out of the leading black car in the procession. The little girl looked bemused as cameras clicked and reporters called out to her to look in their direction.

With typical resolve, Adam scooped her up in his arms and strode inside the modern building. Hannah sighed with relief and looked back at the hearse. No one could fail to be moved by the sight of the two coffins, one so much tinier than the other, lying side by side in the back.

She turned away. She didn't want to see them being lifted out. She hadn't known Natasha Campbell when she was alive. She certainly didn't want to feel sympathy for her now she was dead.

CHAPTER THIRTY-TWO

Hannah made her way up the snowy path and smiled at the huge snowman, semi-melted now and in a sorry state as it sat in the centre of the front garden. So Katie had got her way.

She took a nervous breath and ran her hand through her hair. Did she look all right? Did she look like Katie would *want* her to look? What should she say? What *did* you say to the daughter you hadn't seen since she was three weeks old – the daughter who hadn't even known you existed until a few days ago? She stood on the doorstep gathering her courage, then lifted her hand and knocked on the door.

The door opened and a middle-aged woman was standing on the threshold smiling at her. Adam's mother, she realised, noting the same brown eyes; slightly more faded, but just as warm. Next to her, the more familiar features of Ellie Hanson, the woman she'd already met from Children's Services.

'How are you doing?' Ellie asked her gently. 'Are you ready for this?'

'As ready as I'll ever be,' Hannah responded, feeling slightly sick.

'Hello, Hannah,' the other woman said impulsively, taking her hand. 'I'm Anne Campbell, Adam's mother. They're in the lounge through there. We thought it might be better for it to be just the three of you to start with. Ellie and I will be in the kitchen if you need us. We'll bring you a cup of tea through in a little while.'

'Just remember what we talked about yesterday and you'll be fine,' Ellie said in encouraging tones.

'Thank you.'

Hannah was already making her way in the direction they'd indicated, her heart banging so hard in her chest she

263

thought it might burst, as she slowly pushed open the solid oak door.

She was sitting on Adam's knee by the large open fire, reading out loud to him from one of her schoolbooks. Hannah's breath contracted in her throat as for the first time ever, she drank in the sight of her daughter's furrowed little face, deep in concentration as she stumbled over one or two of the more difficult words. She was wearing a bright pink Gap tracksuit with a navy-blue tee-shirt poking out from beneath the jacket. Against the golden blond of her hair, the pink was vibrant. Hannah's face softened as she slowly released her breath. She was perfect.

Katie had no idea that her mother was there and Hannah made no movement to distract her, drinking in every precious moment of that first sighting, savouring it, knowing that every nuance of that soft childish treble would be locked in her memory and heart forever more. She felt her eyes blur. To think she'd even *considered* terminating her pregnancy.

Adam looked up and sensing the change in the atmosphere, Katie's voice petered out as she too looked across the room. Her eyes were green, Hannah noticed with a shock – like *hers*. And they were looking at her with a mixture of curiosity and apprehension.

'Well look who's here …' Adam said. 'Come in, Hannah, and meet Katie. She's been wanting to meet you, haven't you Kate?'

Hannah forced her legs to move forward, a smile pinned to her face. 'Hello Katie,' she said softly. 'I'm very pleased to meet you at last. I've been looking forward to it.'

Katie's eyes were enormous in her face and Hannah didn't miss the way her hand clung tightly to her father's arm. In that instant, she realised it didn't matter that she'd waited six years for this moment, it wasn't important that her mouth was so dry she feared she might choke on the breath caught in her throat. What mattered was that Katie should be reassured that though change was about to happen, it wasn't going to tear her already fragile life apart. She'd just lost the woman she'd thought was her mother. She needed to know that she wasn't about to lose her father as well.

'Are you my new mummy?' Katie's eyes were mystified, and Hannah smiled.

'Yes, I am, but that doesn't mean you have to forget about your other mummy ... because I know she loved you very much.'

'My other mummy died. That means she's not coming home anymore. Will you die too?'

'I'm not planning on it,' Hannah said cheerfully. 'I hope to be around for a long time yet. Long enough to see you all grown up into a big girl, with children of your own. I live quite close to here and maybe one day you can come and visit me?

Katie's look was wary. 'Can daddy come too?'

'Oh, yes. We wouldn't want him to feel left out, would we? Was that Snow White you were just reading? That was one of my favourite stories when I was a little girl.'

'Daddy and I take it in turns to read,' Katie said importantly. 'You can have a turn too if you like?'

Hannah sat down on the floor and crossed her legs in front of her. 'I'd like that, but I think Daddy should go first don't you? Then you and I can catch him out when he makes a mistake.'

Katie giggled. 'Daddies don't make mistakes. They know *everything*.'

'See?' Adam chuckled, taking charge of the book. 'I've been teaching her well. You never realised I was so perfect, did you?'

Over Katie's head his twinkling eyes met hers. And it was one of those rare moments when time seemed suddenly to stand still – the everyday ordinariness receding into the background as their gazes locked. She thought he was going to say something, but the moment passed as Katie tapped his knee impatiently and looked up at him. 'Come on, daddy, it's your turn now.'

His eyes held hers for a moment longer before he bent his head to drop a kiss on his daughter's head.

'Okay poppet. Now, where were we?'

Hannah watched him as he read, absorbing the strong, clear-cut features, the deep resonant voice that held not only Katie enthralled. She smiled at the way he altered his tone for the different characters, noting how totally at ease Katie was with him as she looked at the pictures and asked questions. He was more relaxed than she'd ever seen him, and she wanted to capture that scene. Treasure it.

When the time finally came for her to leave, the light was fading. Nothing could have prepared her for the rollercoaster of emotions she'd experienced this last couple of hours. They left her feeling exhausted. And different, she realised. She'd always been a mother – losing her daughter hadn't changed that. And the love had always been there, locked tight in her heart. But all it had taken was one sighting of Katie to heal the agony that had pinched at her daily like an open sore. Was this incredible swell of emotion what her own mother felt for her? Did it ever fade? She doubted it somehow. She could only imagine that it grew. No wonder it was so painful when your children spread their wings to fly.

'I'll see you out,' Adam said, as she wrapped herself warmly in her padded jacket and scarf and prepared to take her leave. His hand beneath her elbow was firm as they walked carefully down the slippery path to the car. Once there, he looked down at her and smiled.

'That went well.'

'It was nerve-wracking. Was I ... did I ...?'

'You were great. Kate was charmed by you. She doesn't take everyone up to her room to see her shell collection.'

Hannah shook her head. 'She's perfect,' she said softly. 'I can't wait to get to know her properly.'

'We should probably talk about that – get some sort of a plan mapped out before we meet with the Children's Services again. Are you around tomorrow evening after work?'

'Yes.'

She tried not to let her anxiety show. They needed to do this. To work out exactly how they were going to handle things. But she felt so inadequate. What did she know about what would work best for Katie – for all of them?

She flicked the remote and opened her car, preparing to climb in. The unexpected warmth of Adam's hand, covering hers where it rested on top of the car door, halted her. She turned to look at him.

'We'll work this out, Hannah. We've got a way to go, but life's suddenly looking much brighter, don't you think? We'll get there.'

And as she looked into his dependable face and felt the warm reassuring squeeze of his fingers on hers, it took only the most fleeting of moments before her own hand curled in his palm and returned the pressure, her fears dispelling.

He was right. Between them – the three of them – they *would* get there.

THE END

I do hope you've enjoyed reading this novel as much as I've enjoyed writing it. Reviews are so helpful to authors and if you could take the time to leave a short one on Amazon here: http://amzn.to/1eNtrLb that would be much appreciated.

My next novel, THE JAGGED LINE, has just been released and you can take a look at it here: http://amzn.to/2uU2Ddq or Here for Amazon.com: http://amzn.to/2w4Jh3Z

My 3rd novel, Shadow Watcher will be coming soon. Do visit my website at www.carolynmahony.com where you can sign up to my Mailing List for early notification.

Also, if you'd like to contact me about my book, come and say 'Hello' on Facebook or Twitter, or you can email me direct. All details given below.

http://www.twitter.com/carolynmahony

http: www.facebook.com/carolyn.mahony.3

Email: carolyn@carolynmahony.com

Website: www.carolynmahony.com

CPSIA information can be obtained
at www.ICGtesting.com
Printed in the USA
LVOW03s0004211217
560416LV00031B/2647/P